Cole's voic̲_____sque
than he'd i̲_____re spot.

"I don't und_____. A tiny vertical frown line
formed between Sadie's delicately arched brows.
"It's only fair. I'm certain Poppa would insist."

He shook his head. "My compensation is in
making up for the pain my brother caused. I wish
I could change what he did, Sadie, but I cannot.
This is all I can do." He took hold of the ledgers,
careful not to touch her hands, and turned to
leave before he said more than he ought.

"Cole…"

"Yes?" He looked back at her. There were tears
in her eyes. They might as well have been knives
the way they pierced his heart.

"It's not your fault." She blinked her eyes and
smiled, but her lips trembled. "Thank you for
your kindness."

Her throat worked, her hand rubbed her arm, and
everything in him wanted to hold her, to comfort
her.…

Books by Dorothy Clark

Love Inspired Historical

Family of the Heart
The Law and Miss Mary
Prairie Courtship
Gold Rush Baby
Frontier Father
*Wooing the Schoolmarm
*Courting Miss Callie
*Falling for the Teacher

Love Inspired

Hosea's Bride
Lessons from the Heart

Steeple Hill Single Title

Beauty for Ashes
Joy for Mourning

*Pinewood Weddings

DOROTHY CLARK

Critically acclaimed, award-winning author Dorothy Clark lives in rural New York, in a home she designed and helped her husband build (she swings a mean hammer!) with the able assistance of their three children. When she is not writing, she and her husband enjoy traveling throughout the United States, doing research and gaining inspiration for future books. Dorothy believes in God, love, family and happy endings, which explains why she feels so at home writing stories for Love Inspired Books. Dorothy enjoys hearing from her readers and may be contacted at dorothyjclark@hotmail.com.

Falling for the Teacher

DOROTHY CLARK

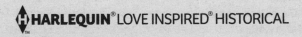

HARLEQUIN® LOVE INSPIRED® HISTORICAL

Recycling programs
for this product may
not exist in your area.

™ LOVE INSPIRED BOOKS

ISBN-13: 978-0-373-82979-8

FALLING FOR THE TEACHER

www.LoveInspiredBooks.com

Printed in U.S.A.

The fear of man bringeth a snare:
but whoso putteth his trust in the Lord shall be safe.
—*Proverbs* 29:25

This book is dedicated with admiration and appreciation to the assistant editors, the art department and all the others at Love Inspired Historical who diligently work to make my books the best they can be. Thank you, all.

A special thank-you to Sam. I've run out of words, but not out of gratitude for your faithfulness, humor and friendship.

"Commit thy works unto the Lord, and thy thoughts shall be established."

Your Word is truth. Thank You, Jesus.

To You be the glory.

Chapter One

June 1841
Pinewood Village, New York

Pinewood. Sadie crowded back into the corner and tugged her bonnet forward as her hired carriage rolled through the village. The news of her return would spread like a brush fire if she was recognized. *Sadie Spencer is back. Sadie Spencer is home.*

Her stomach quivered. In two weeks it would be four years since the incident. Memories surged. She closed her mind to the bad ones—or tried to. Perhaps returning to Pinewood would exorcise them—and the fear. How she wished she could live without that fear! *Please, Almighty God, grant that it might be so.* She took a breath to calm her stomach and pulled the small purse dangling from her wrist into her trembling hands.

The driver's polite touch of his hat brim sent her pushing deeper into the corner where she would not be seen by two women standing at the edge of the road waiting to cross. A wagon passed by loaded with baled shingles and traveling in the other direction. She released her pent-up breath and lifted her head.

The horse's hoofs clattered against planks and the carriage lurched as the wheels climbed onto the wood. Stony Creek Bridge. A smile trembled on her lips. How many hours had she, Callie, Willa and Ellen spent in the cool shadow beneath its span trying to best Daniel at skipping stones on the water?

The carriage rocked off the bridge, swaying left onto Brook Street. A snap of the reins urged the horse to greater speed and her smile died. It wouldn't be long now.

Her chest tightened with longing to be back behind the brick walls of the young ladies' seminary in Rochester. She'd not been outside those walls since she'd fled there four years before, and if not for her grandparents' need, she would be in that safe haven still. She would never have willingly returned to Pinewood. *Never.*

The carriage tilted, slowed as the horse started up the incline outside of the village. She slipped back to the center of the seat and caught her breath at the sight of the forested hills on either side of the dirt road. Only one more turn to make when they reached the top of the hill.

She dug her fingernails into her palms, struggling against a surge of dread. When she'd received Callie's letter, she'd told herself it would be all right, that she would care for Nanna and Poppa in the safety of the Sheffield House, but that was not to be. Her grandparents had left Sophia's hotel and returned home to Butternut Hill.

She had to go back there.

Oh, Lord, give me strength.

* * *

"Your grandfolks are in the garden. I'll take these up to your room." The housekeeper picked up her bags and looked at her. "It's good you're home, Miss Sadie."

The underlying sadness in Gertrude's voice constricted her throat, making speech impossible. She nodded, removed her bonnet and walked down the entrance hall and into the dining room. The window framed her grandparents seated on the wooden garden bench, the stockade fence and the wooded path beyond. Love swelled her heart, blocking out the fear. She pushed open the door, ran across the porch and rushed down the steps. "Nanna! Poppa!" Their gray heads turned her direction. They stared. Her feet took wings.

"Sadie!"

She leaned down and hugged her grandmother, reveling in the feel of the soft arms holding her close, the small pudgy hands patting her, offering comfort as she sobbed out the long years of loneliness against the shoulder that had so often been washed by her tears as a child.

"Oh, Sadie…Sadie…Sadie…" Her grandmother patted her back, her shoulder, touched her cheek, smoothed her hair. "Hush, sweeting, hush. It's all right. Everything is all right."

Tears and laughter bubbled into her throat at the old-fashioned, familiar endearment. It *was* all right. Her grandmother knew her. After reading Callie's and Willa's letters, she'd been so afraid…. She straightened and wiped the tears from her face. "Oh, Nanna, I have missed you so."

She kissed her grandmother's soft, moist cheek and turned toward the silent man staring at her from the bench. "And you, Poppa." She kissed his cheek at the edge of his gray beard, felt his arm slip around her in a hard hug. One arm.

"Wel…come…home, Sa…die."

The words were hesitant, slightly slurred. Tears clogged her throat again. She sank to her knees in front of her grandfather and took hold of his hands. His left hand gripped back; the right moved slightly, stilled. Her chest tightened. "I made arrangements to come home as soon as I heard of your illness, Poppa." Remorse flowed on a torrent of tears. She laid her cheek against their clasped hands. "I'm so sorry I was not with you when you needed me."

"Daniel should have brought you home."

Daniel? She jerked up her head.

Her grandmother huffed and patted her shoulder. "What's more, he shouldn't have taken you off prowling through the woods in the first place. I worry when you go off with your friends, Sadie."

Her heart twisted at the absent look in her grandmother's eyes. Her grandfather's hand squeezed hers. She glanced at him, read the message of protective concern in his eyes and gave a slight nod. "I'm sorry, Nanna." She rose and brushed the dust from her skirt to gain a moment to control the sorrow flooding her heart. Callie and Willa were right—her grandmother was ill in her mind. "I won't go off again."

Boots thudded on the hard-beaten path behind her— the path that trailed through the woods to her grandfather's sawmill. Her heart stopped, her lungs seized at the remembered sound. She whirled, stared at the tall, broad-shouldered man dressed in logger garb who stepped from the shadows under the trees and strode toward her, just like before. The early evening light receded, the earth swayed.

The man rushed forward, reached for her.

"Put her there on the settee! I'll fetch water."

Cole frowned and watched Rachel Townsend hurrying toward the kitchen. Would she return, or forget what she was doing? He looked down at the slender young woman draped across his arms, and his breath shortened. He had no doubt things would change now that she'd returned. And not for the better. Not for him.

He leaned down, laid Sadie Spencer on the settee, lifted her limp arm and placed it across her body.

A small, breathy moan escaped her. Her eyelids fluttered then stilled, the long lashes forming dark smudges against her pale skin. He glanced at the small pearl buttons fastening the high collar of her brown dress and his fingers twitched to undo them to make it easier for her to breathe, but given the past, that action could be misconstrued. He stood frozen, staring at the fine-boned, patrician features of the woman his brother had attacked. She looked so…fragile. And the terror in her eyes when she'd turned and seen him…

The brutal savagery of Payne's deed struck him anew. He sucked in air, clenched his hands at his sides. He'd spent the past four years working to live down the shame of Payne's act, to prove that he himself was decent and honorable, and the people of Pinewood were finally beginning to trust and befriend him. And now Sadie Spencer had come home.

He gazed down at Manning Townsend's granddaughter lying so still and pale against the blue silk of the settee. Odd that such a beautiful young woman would be dangerous for him, but Sadie Spencer could undo all of his hard work simply by her return. Her presence in Pinewood was bound to stir people's memories, to bring back the anger and distrust that had faced him when he'd come to Pinewood to find Payne and tell him of their parents' deaths.

He stiffened, breathed hard against the pressure in his chest and rubbed the tense muscles in the back of his neck. He hadn't suspected the violence and depravity that ran in his brother's veins until that day—had been sickened when he'd learned what Payne had done. Now, his brother's actions seemed more real. And if seeing Sadie Spencer made *him* feel that way…

He huffed out a breath and pushed away the memory of the terror in her eyes when she saw him. Sorry as he was for her, he couldn't let her destroy all the goodwill he had so painstakingly cultivated and ruin the new life and business he'd built here. He'd have to convince her—

"What are you doing? Get away from my granddaughter!"

He jerked his head around. Rachel Townsend stood in the doorway, a scowl in the place of her normal pleasant expression, her hands gripping a wet cloth.

"I said get away from my granddaughter!" She rushed toward him, her lips pressed into a tight line, her small, free hand waving through the air.

Was her anger because of the confusion that was occurring more often? Or was her reaction to his being there beside her granddaughter nothing to do with her slipping grasp on the present? Was the condemnation toward him for Payne's heinous act already returning?

He clenched his jaw, stepped away from the settee and headed outside to get Manning.

The trembling woke her. Bile pushed at her throat. She'd had the nightmare again. Sadie drew in a slow, deep breath to control the nausea and opened her eyes.

"Feeling better, sweeting?" Her grandmother frowned down at her. "What happened, Sadie? Why did you swoon like that? Are you ill?"

She blinked, took another breath. Her head cleared. She was home. "No, Nanna, I'm not ill. It must have been the…excitement of coming home." Something cold slid across her temple. She lifted her hand, removed the wet cloth and pushed to a sitting position, still quivering. The nightmare had never before come while she was awake. It must have been returning to Butternut Hill that—

The sound of boot heels thudding against the wood floor jolted her upright. She turned toward the doorway, stared at her nightmare in the flesh.

"It's…all right, Sa…die."

She glanced at her grandfather being carried in the man's arms, looked back up at that bearded face, shuddered.

"I'm *Cole* Aylward, not…my brother." He strode across the room toward them.

Payne Aylward's brother? She backed up, bumped against the settee and grasped the high, curved arm.

"Give me the cloth, Sadie. You're getting everything wet."

She looked down at the dripping cloth, eased her grip on it and handed it to her grandmother—bit down on her lower lip to keep from calling her back as she started from the room.

"Thank…you."

She darted her gaze back to the man lowering her grandfather into his favored chair, brushed a wet tendril of hair back off her forehead and tried to make some sort of sense of everything. "May I ask what you are doing here, Mr. Aylward?" *I should think this home is the last place you would want to be.* She pressed her lips together to keep from turning the thought into speech.

"Manning's not yet able to get around by himself. I drop by throughout the day to see if he needs anything."

She stared at his broad shoulders, his powerful arms and hands. "You come every day?" Her voice quavered and she took a breath to steady it, squared her shoulders at his answering nod.

"Then I'm certain you'll be pleased that will no longer be necessary. As I'm here to care for my grandfather now, there'll be no need for us to impinge on your… kindness…further."

Her courage failed when he straightened and turned to face her. She hid her shaking hands in the folds of her long skirt and stiffened her spine.

"And are you going to carry Manning to his bed when it's time for him to retire? And carry him to the table in the morning when he rises? Or out to the garden so he can enjoy the sun and fresh air?"

His tone was conversational, but there was an underlying steeliness in Cole Aylward's voice that caught at her throat and stole her breath. She stared at him, stunned by the questions he so calmly presented—questions that emphasized how ill-prepared she was for the changed situation in her home. She clenched her hidden hands and lifted her chin. "I shall hire someone."

"No! Want…Cole…"

"Thank you, Manning." Cole Aylward rested his large hand on her grandfather's shoulder, then fixed his gaze on her. "I appreciate your thoughtfulness of my time, Miss Spencer, but there's no need for you to go to that trouble or expense. Neighbors look out for one another, and—"

"Neighbors?"

"Yes." A frown creased his forehead. "I thought your grandmother or…someone…would have written to tell you I took over Pay—my brother's cabin and have built a shingle mill on the property."

He lived in Payne's cabin? So near… A chill skittered down her spine. Her pulse fluttered. She slipped her hand up to cover the base of her throat.

"Are you all right?" He started toward her.

She jerked back and he froze.

Her grandmother bustled into the room, her long skirts swishing back and forth with the sway of her ample hips, and beamed a smile at them. "Gertrude is ready to serve supper. Please bring Manning to the table, Cole." Her smile widened, deepening the wrinkles in her aged face. "You'll be joining us, of course. I had Gertrude set a place for you. We're having roasted beef and potatoes."

No! Don't invite him! She stared at her grandmother in stunned silence. Had she forgotten what had happened? Her stomach roiled. She pressed her hand against it, drew air into her lungs to protest.

"Not tonight, Mrs. Townsend. Thank you kindly for

the invitation, but I don't wish to intrude upon your granddaughter's homecoming. Next time, perhaps."

Next time? So he was going to ignore her wishes.

"I'll just carry Manning in and then come back a bit later to take him in to his bed."

At least he was leaving for now. Good. She would have time to convince her grandfather it would be better to hire someone to help him. Her pulse steadied.

"Nonsense! I'll not hear of it." Her grandmother gave a small, dismissive wave with her pudgy hand. "You're so kind to Father, the least we can do is offer our hospitality in return."

Oh, Nanna, don't—Father? Tears stung her eyes. She bowed her head and stared down at the leaf pattern woven into the blue silk of the settee as her grandmother chatted on about their daughter and her husband also joining them for supper. The tears overflowed. She drew a slow breath and exhaled softly. Her mother and father had died when she was three years old, and her mother had been her grandparents' only child.

"Are you coming, Sadie?"

She lifted her head and curved her lips in the best smile she could summon. "Yes, Nanna, I'm coming. It's been a long time since I've had any of Gertrude's roast beef." She released her grip on the settee and started for the dining room, trying to ignore the despair that gripped her at her grandmother's illness and to smother the unease that filled her at the thought of Cole Aylward sitting at their table sharing their meal.

Chapter Two

Sadie cut a bite off her piece of roast beef and pushed it around her plate in a pretense of eating. She couldn't swallow food. Her stomach was knotted and her throat so constricted it ached.

"Good…trip, Sa…die?"

She looked to the end of the table, smiled even as her heart broke yet again at the sight of her grandfather's right arm hanging useless at his side. "It was long and wearying, but uneventful, Poppa." She looked into his brown eyes, warm with love and concern, and forced a touch of humor into her voice. "None of the stages overturned—though it often seemed as though they might."

"Careless dri…vers?"

Oh, how it hurt to watch him struggle to talk. She shook her head and cleared her throat, widened her smile. "I think it was that they were more concerned with keeping to their schedules than with their passengers' comfort."

"Thankfully Philby is never careless."

She glanced at her grandmother. "Who is—" Her grandfather's fork clanged against his plate. She looked back, saw the warning in his eyes, the quick shake of his head and swallowed the rest of the question.

"This beef is excellent, Mrs. Townsend." Cole Aylward's deep voice filled the uncomfortable silence. "And these honeyed carrots are delicious. You certainly know how to set a good table."

"Thank you, Cole. You're very kind." Her grandmother smiled, then looked her way and frowned. "You're not eating, Sadie. Is the beef not to your liking?"

"It's very good, Nanna. It's only that I'm...weary from my journey."

"Rochester is a long distance." She watched Cole's knife slice through the meat on his plate as casually as his voice cleaved the air over the table between them. "I understand you are a teacher in a seminary there, Miss Spencer. Do you enjoy your position?"

"I did."

His hands stilled. He looked up, focused his attention on her. So did her grandfather and grandmother. Her heart sank. She'd hoped to wait until she was alone with her grandparents to announce her news, but that wasn't possible now. She folded her hands in her lap and took a breath. "I've resigned my position."

"Oh, Sadie, I'm so glad!" Her grandmother clasped her hands, beamed a smile at her.

"Sa...die..."

There was sadness in her grandfather's voice. She looked into his eyes and knew he'd guessed she'd left the seminary because of his illness. She shook her head and smiled. "I know what you're thinking, Poppa—but you're wrong. I wanted to come home. I've missed Pinewood, my friends and both of you most of all. Your illness merely gave me the impetus to leave now."

"So you are staying, not merely visiting?"

Cole Aylward sounded…what? Concerned? Why should that be? She wished she had the courage to look into his eyes and read what was written there. She drew her shoulders back, lifted her chin and fastened her gaze on his black beard. "Yes. I'm staying."

He looked so frail, her strong Poppa being carried off to bed like a child. Sadie gripped the hooped rail of the chair she stood behind and fought to hold on to control. The unexpected encounter with Cole Aylward and the hard truths that had confronted her one after another since her arrival had brought her close to breaking down. Reading about her grandparents' infirmities in a letter was one thing—witnessing them herself was another.

Her grandfather was helpless, his right leg and arm useless, his speech impaired. And her grandmother, her dear, sweet Nanna—

No! She yanked her mind from that path, her emotions too battered to manage it. She clenched her hands tighter, pressed the chair rail into her palms and soft finger pads to curb the need to throw herself into her grandmother's arms and cry away all the hurt and fear threatening to overwhelm her. She had to be the strong one now. *Dear God, please help me to be what they need me to be.*

She dragged her gaze from her grandmother, who was hurrying out the parlor door to turn back the bed brought down from upstairs to what was the morning room. "Sleep well, Poppa. I'll see you in the morning." The quiver in her voice didn't match the smile she forced to her lips.

"Good…night, Sa…die." His stammering response almost undid her. She looked at Cole Aylward and took refuge in her confusion. Why was he spending his time helping her grandfather? Given what had happened, it made no sense—even if he was their closest neighbor. Was he cruel like his brother? She'd seen no sign of it tonight, but that meant nothing. Payne Aylward had hidden his cruelty from everyone—until it was too late.

A shudder shook her. She released her hold on the back of the chair, followed Cole from the parlor and stood in the entrance hall until he had entered the morning room, then lifted her hems and hurried up the stairs to the landing. She didn't want to be down there when he came out of that room alone. She could reach her bedroom and lock him out from here should he come after her.

Such strength in his arms. Like his brother.

Shivers coursed through her, stole her strength. She leaned against the wall, stared at the candle sconce across from her and waited for the memory to pass. She'd given up hoping it would go away.

"…in the morning."

Cole. She held her breath and listened to the sound of his footfalls in the downstairs hallway. The door to the morning room closed. She gathered her courage and moved to grasp the top of the banister to lend strength to her shaking knees. "May I have a word with you, Mr. Aylward?"

He paused, turned and looked up at her. "In the sitting room?"

"This is fine."

The dim light outlined his tall form at the bottom of the stairs. "I am not my brother, Miss Spencer. You've nothing to fear from me."

How easily he discerned her thoughts. She tightened her grip on the banister and braced herself against the memories, the quivering that took her. "We will not speak of that, Mr. Aylward. I only wanted to express my appreciation for the care you have given my grandfather. And to tell you, again, that I intend to free you from that…service, as soon as possible."

"You are going to hire someone to care for Manning?"

"I am going to hire someone to help with the physical labor involved. *I* will care for Poppa."

"I see." Lamplight flickered over the knit hat he pulled from his pocket. "I misjudged you, Miss Spencer. I didn't think you were the sort of woman who would condemn a man who has done no wrong, nor go against her grandfather's wishes." His head dipped in a small bow and he stepped back from the stairs. "I will be here in the morning…and for as long as Manning wishes my help. Good evening." He tugged his hat on his head and strode down the hall toward the dining room. The back door opened and closed.

How *dare* he make her the guilty one! She caught up her hems and ran to her bedroom, crossed to the window and watched Cole Aylward striding down the garden path toward the woods, the rising moon casting silver epaulets on his broad shoulders. Memories drove her from the window before he neared the trees and the entrance to the wooded path that led to her grandfather's sawmill.

* * *

Cole glanced right and left, aware as never before of how the trees encroached upon the path, of their thick trunks and looming branches. He slowed his steps at the curve where it had happened, took a breath against the sudden clench of his stomach. He'd walked this path at least a hundred times, but now he'd seen her. That made it all different.

The sylvan depths drew his gaze, halted his steps. How easy it would be to steal silent and unseen from trunk to trunk in order to overtake someone walking along the path. Is that how Payne had done it?

He raised his arm and scrubbed his hand across his eyes, trying to rid himself of the image of the fear on Sadie's face as she'd stood on the stairs looking down at him. Payne had caused that fear. Payne, who had been so pleasant and funny and kind. What had changed in his brother that he could do that to someone?

His gut churned. Bile surged into his throat. He fisted his hands and continued down the path toward Manning Townsend's sawmill. If only he'd been here when the attack took place. Perhaps he could have prevented it somehow or at least found out what had caused Payne to do such a thing. He knew his brother's habits, had hunted and fished with him. He could have tracked him down, talked him into staying and facing justice, helped him atone somehow. But Payne had already disappeared when he'd come to Pinewood to tell him their mother and father were dead, and Payne's trail had been obliterated by the angry men of Pinewood who were searching the hills for him.

Cole climbed the steps to the sawmill deck and stepped under the shingled roof, walked by the silent saws and entered the attached office. He stepped behind the partition he'd built, jammed his hat onto one of the pegs he'd driven into the wall, shucked his shirt and hung it on another peg, then sat on the wood edge of his cot and tugged off his boots.

The horror and disgust, regret and guilt that had weighed so heavily on him when he'd learned of Payne's actions had returned full force when he'd looked into Sadie Spencer's eyes and now sat like a rock in his stomach—though why it should he didn't understand. He'd stayed in Pinewood and tried to find Payne to bring him back to face justice in spite of the disgust and distrust of the irate villagers who'd watched his every move with suspicion. He'd trudged countless times to the outcropping of rock where the men said they'd lost all trace of Payne's trail to see if he could find something they had missed. It wasn't for lack of trying that he'd failed. He had no reason to feel guilty. But the way she'd looked at him…

He yanked off his socks, flung them over his boot tops, rose and snatched the soap and a towel from the make-do washstand. The rough puncheons scraped against his bare feet as he marched to the end of the sawmill deck, dropped the towel and dove into the deep pool formed by the stone dam. The shock of the icy mountain-stream water drove all thought from his mind.

He soaped his hair, threw the soap up onto the deck, did a surface dive and swam upstream underwater to let the current from the overflow carry the soap film away.

If only it could carry away his troubled thoughts that had resurfaced. He kicked his trouser-clad legs, dug hard and deep with his arms and circled around the pond until his shoulders and arms screamed for mercy and his lungs burned for air. What sort of depravity coursed through his brother's veins that he could look at a woman as delicately beautiful, as quiet and refined as Sadie Spencer and then—

He arched and dove deep, swam to the center of the gently rippling water, flipped over onto his back and stared up at the stars, bright against the dark sky. Peaceful evening sounds filled the night as the water lapped over his chest, but the fear he'd been carrying around for four years wouldn't leave. *Wash me clean, Lord, wash me clean. Don't let that violence and depravity be in me.*

Bats darted and swooped overhead in erratic patterns as they snatched insects from the air. An owl hooted. Another answered. Something rustled through the brush and grasses on the bank. Something big.

A she-bear and her two cubs ambled toward the water. Last year's cubs, by the size of them. He moved his arms beneath the surface to stay afloat but stationary without causing a ripple and hoped the cubs weren't in the mood for a swim. Mama Bear reared up on her hind legs and stared out over the pond, snuffled.

His moonlight swim was over.

He drew in air, sank out of sight beneath the water and stroked hard for the deck ladder, leaving the bears behind. If only he could outdistance the fears that plagued him.

She strolled along the path, humming softly, the basket of berries she'd picked swinging at her side.

Payne Aylward stepped out of the woods onto the path ahead, his tall, broad-shouldered frame large in the sunlight filtering through the leafy treetops. The glitter in his dark gray eyes frightened her. She stopped.

He smiled, his teeth white against his black beard. "I been watching you, Sadie." He stepped forward, reached for her.

Sadie bolted upright gasping for air, her heart pounding, her body quaking. Moonlight flowed in the windows, bathed the objects in the dark room in silvery radiance. She stared at the blanket chest at the foot of her bed, the dark blue-and-white cross and crown woven coverlet that had warmed her every night of her childhood. "It's all right. It was the nightmare. You're safe."

Her whisper trembled on the warm night air. She clutched the fallen sheet, slipped beneath it and curled into a tight ball. She wanted so desperately to believe that was true, but how could she? Cole Aylward was here. Cole Aylward. Payne's brother.

A shudder shook her. She tugged the sheet tighter around her neck and roamed her gaze over the familiar objects in the room to hold at bay the face that hovered at the edge of her fear.

Chapter Three

Sadie left her grandmother in the kitchen discussing the day's meals with Gertrude, carried the stack of washed dishes to the butler's pantry, put them in their proper place on the shelves and continued through to the dining room. Her stomach was settling—not that she'd been able to do more than choke down a few bites of breakfast. But the knots from having Cole Aylward seated at the table were slowly coming undone.

To come downstairs after the sleepless hours haunted by the nightmare made more powerful by her return and to see him there…she paused and pressed her hands to her stomach as the knots twisted tight again. Cole's likeness to his brother unnerved her. And try as she would, she could not ignore his presence—the man dominated a room. She would be thankful when he was gone, though it was clear after last night that he would defy her request. It had to be her grandfather who told him to leave. She would have to find a reason.

She lifted the lamps off the mantel in the dining room and carried them back to the table beneath the window in the butler's pantry. She'd learned long ago that plunging into work the morning after having the nightmare was the best way to bury her fears. Being in control of something drove away the feeling of helplessness—and this morning that helpless feeling was overwhelming. And not only from the nightmare.

It pained her to see her grandfather's efforts to cope with his infirmities and know there was nothing she could do to make him better. She removed the lamps' glass chimneys, wiped them with a soft cloth, then turned up the wicks and picked up the silver trimmers. And Nanna…

"I've been studying on—" The scrape of a chair against the porch floor drowned out the rest of the words.

Cole. She'd thought he'd gone. She leaned toward the window and peered to her left. Her grandfather sat in a rocker on the porch and Cole Aylward stood leaning against the railing. She drew back lest he see her and took a breath to calm the pounding of her heart the mere sight of the man provoked.

"…best sit here on the porch. That sky doesn't look too promising, and it smells like rain."

Her pulse skipped. If they talked on the porch, perhaps she could discover why Cole was being so helpful and—

"What are you doing, sweeting?"

She started, jerked the trimmer handles together and snipped off too much of the wick on the first lamp. "I'm cleaning the lamps from the dining room mantel, Nanna." She tossed the charred piece of wick into the small trash bucket on the table, adjusted the wick and replaced the cleaned globe, straining to hear the conversation taking place outside. Her grandfather's halting words were difficult to understand, and Cole Aylward's deep voice was hard to hear, but she dared not open the window lest they become aware that she was eavesdropping.

"What holds your interest?" Her grandmother frowned and moved into the pantry.

"Nothing, Nanna." She quickly cleaned and trimmed the second lamp and stepped away from the table. "I'm finished."

"What cost…buy…one?"

Buy what? She tilted her head toward the window.

"I'll help you carry the lamps, Sadie." Her grandmother bustled to her side, lifted one of the lamps in her small, pudgy hands and moved toward the doorway to the dining room. "Come along."

She snatched up the other lamp and followed, wishing she could have waited to hear what her grandfather was considering buying. What had Cole Aylward suggested? What was he after?

Her grandmother set the lamp on the fireplace, turned it just so, stepped back and looked up at her. "I'm so glad you've returned."

The smile brightening her nanna's dear face brought a surge of guilt. She should have come home years ago. Willa and Callie had both written of how much her grandmother missed her, of the sadness in her eyes when she spoke of her. Yet she had let her cowardice keep her away. How selfish she was. Well, no more. She was home now and she would make it up to her grandmother. She set the lamp she held on the other end of the mantel, then tugged the bodice of her gown down into place at her waist.

"Turn it so that the knob is on the right, Ivy."

Ivy? She caught her breath and turned.

Her grandmother looked up at her, a mild rebuke in her eyes. "I'm not scolding, Ivy. But I should think that after all these years in our service you could remember that little detail."

Nanna didn't know her. Something awful took her by the throat, squeezed life from her heart.

"Well, gracious! There's no reason for tears, Ivy. I *said* I wasn't cross with you." Her grandmother reached out and patted her hand. "Now wipe the tears from your eyes and come along. We've the lamps in Mama and Papa's room to tend to."

"It's something to think about, Manning." Cole yanked his gaze from the dining room window—for the third time. Or, to be more accurate, from the slender, shapely young woman he could see through the glass. "Cost…ly."

He frowned, braced himself with his extended left leg, shifted his weight onto his right hip and rested his thigh along the railing. "Yes. But no one else in the area has a clapboard machine. I think it will pay for itself with the first few loads we ship downriver."

The fading brown eyes took on a speculative gleam. Manning swept his hand through the air. "Big mar… ket."

The show of enthusiasm brought a smile to his lips. It seemed he might have found a way to get the afflicted man excited and involved in his businesses again. "Very big. I've been doing some letter writing. There's no other supplier of machine-milled clapboard from Olville to Buffalo. And none I could find a trace of from here to Pittsburgh."

He twisted front and leaned forward. "You'd be the first, Manning. The other timber companies will still be riving clapboard by hand, and you know shaving them clean is a slow process. They wouldn't be able to compete with your time or price."

He stared down at his hands dangling in the open space between his legs. Big hands. Strong and powerful from felling trees and making shakes and clapboard. Payne had big, powerful hands, too. He glanced back up at the window and watched Sadie turn from placing a lamp on the fireplace mantel. So lithe and graceful. So unable to defend herself.

Stop it! He clenched his jaw so hard the muscle along the bone twitched. He couldn't throw away four years of effort and hard work because he felt guilty for something that was not his doing.

Lightning flashed white brilliance through the air. Thunder rumbled a warning of things to come. The approaching storm seemed an ominous omen. He pushed off the railing, looked up at the darkened sky and turned to Manning. "I'd best take you inside before the storm hits."

"No." Manning's face worked; his eyes flashed as brilliant as had the lightning. His good hand fisted on his knee. "Stay here. Like…storms."

"All right. If it gets too bad, I'll come back and take you in." He turned toward the steps at another flash of lightning. "You think about the clapboard machine, and we'll discuss it more tonight."

Raindrops angled down from the black clouds rolling in, splatted in a halfhearted warning on the wooden steps, made dark wet splotches on the slate stones of the garden path. "Looks like this is going to be a soaker."

He stole another look at the window. Sadie was not in sight. Disappointment pricked him. He frowned, tugged the collar of his shirt up to cover the back of his neck, trotted down the steps and set off down the path.

Lightning flashed through the room. Thunder rumbled. Sadie replaced the glass chimney on the lamp she'd lit, glanced at her grandmother serenely dusting the serving table for the third time and started for the door. "I'll see if Mr. Aylward is still here to bring—"

"Sadie." She halted, startled by the ring of authority in her grandmother's voice. "Cole Aylward is our good friend. You are to call him by his given name, as you do Daniel. Do you understand?"

Did she mean it? Or was she lost in her own world? She searched her grandmother's eyes for that opaque look she was beginning to recognize and nodded. "Yes, of course, Nanna, if that is what you wish."

"It is. Cole doesn't take you off on dangerous adventures the way Daniel does. Now, you'd best hold the door for Cole. He'll be bringing Manning inside."

She nodded, swallowed back tears at the way her grandmother slipped in and out of the present, wished with her whole heart she could help her. Lightning flashed again. She opened the porch door, then stared agape. "He's gone."

Irritation flared. She stepped out onto the porch, heard the soft splat of raindrops, felt the freshness of a quickening breeze on her face and hands. How would she get her grandfather inside? She cast a sidelong glance at him, worrying over the problem. Perhaps the rockers would slide…

Her grandfather chuckled. His eyes twinkled with

humor, crinkled at the corners. Her own mouth pulled up into a grin, tugged there by the chortling sound that accompanied so many of her happy childhood memories.

"Can't…do it. Too…heavy…for you."

Her amusement fled. "Don't worry, Poppa. I'll get you inside someway." She cast an angry glance toward the garden path and stepped toward him. "Mr. Ayl—" she glanced at her grandmother standing in the doorway "—*Cole* never should have left you out—"

"Stay here!"

She stopped and stared at her grandfather, taken aback by his sharp tone. He reached out his good hand and took hold of hers.

"Not…child." His face worked; his hand squeezed hers. "Told Cole…leave me. Like…storms."

Not child. How humiliating for a proud, independent man like her grandfather to have to accept the care, the control of others. She swallowed hard and pushed back a tendril of hair the wind had plucked free of the thick coil of hair at her crown. "I'm sorry, Poppa. I should have asked your wishes."

"You keep Poppa company, Sadie. I've work to do. Don't go off the porch now." Her grandmother smiled and stepped back into the dining room.

She stared at the closed door, aching with the need to have her grandmother and grandfather well, to have everything the way it was. "I remember, now that you've mentioned it, how much you like storms, Poppa. It used to frighten me when you would stand out here on the porch with the lightning flashing and the thunder crashing." She turned from the door and forced a smile onto her face. "I was usually huddled up on the settee with Nanna."

He tugged her closer, laid his cheek against her hand. "I...miss her...too."

"Oh, Poppa..." She sank to her knees, placed her head against his knee and snagged her lip with her teeth to keep from crying. "Is there nothing Dr. Palmer can do to help Nanna get better? Can't he give her some sort of medicine, or—" Her throat constricted, closed off the flow of words.

Her grandfather shook his head, his mouth working. "Some...thing in her...mind shuts...off...now and then. Doc can't...stop it. Sorry, Sa...die." He rested his big, work-worn hand on her hair, and she closed her eyes and imaged him whole and well and for a moment her world righted itself.

The wind gusted, snatching at her skirts. A door banged. Banged again. Her grandfather tensed. She looked up.

"Stable...door." A frown knit his gray brows together. "Wind break...it."

"I'll go close it, Poppa." She rose and shook out her long skirts.

"Lightning..."

She pushed out a small laugh and shook her head. "I'm not afraid of thunderstorms anymore." *It isn't nature that hurts you, it's men.* "I'll be right back." She lifted her hems and ran down the steps, veered left onto the path that led to the stable. The wind blew her skirts against her legs. Raindrops spattered on her hair and shoulders, chilled her bowed neck.

She grabbed hold of the stable door with both hands and tugged with all of her strength to pull it closed against the rising force of the wind. It moved after a momentary lull, and she planted her feet and backed toward the gaping stable doorway, hauling the big, heavy door with her.

Lightning snapped, sizzling to the earth in a yellow streak. Sulfur stung her nose. Thunder clapped and the rain came—a wild, stinging deluge driven by the wind that snatched the door from her grasp. "Oh!" She ducked her head and jumped inside.

Raindrops drummed on the shakes overhead. The wind whistled across the open doorway and banged the door back against the building again. She stared in dismay at the heavy fall of water pouring off the roof to splash against the ground and tried to work up enough courage to go out and try again to drag that heavy door closed. And then it didn't matter.

A large figure loomed in the opening, then pulled the door closed, shutting out the splashing curtain of water. Lightning flashed through the windows in a watery shimmer, shone on the rain-slick rubber jacket and glittered on the wet, black beard and dark gray eyes of Cole Aylward.

Chapter Four

Ice spilled down her spine, flowed into her arms and legs and froze her in place. Sadie stared at Cole Aylward, saw the image that haunted her nights. His black beard bobbed and his lips moved, but no words penetrated the glacial wall of fear.

"Did you hear me, Miss Spencer? Your poppa sent me to bring you to the house."

His raised voice crumbled the ice, broke through her numbed senses. *Poppa?* How dare he use her pet name for her grandfather! A quaking took her, so strong, so furious in intensity her long skirts shook. "Don't you call him that!"

"Look, Miss Spencer—" He took a step toward her. A towering shadow in the dim light.

She gasped and jerked back, her spurt of defiance dead.

He jolted to a halt and a heavy breath escaped him.

Light flashed on something in his hand. She caught a glimpse of a knob on the object he held before he turned and leaned it against the wall, shrugged out of his rubber jacket and tossed it on top of a nearby feed chest.

No, Almighty God, no! Not again. Her heart thudded. She stared at his hands, raised hers to cover her arms where his brother's hard fingers had dug into her flesh as he threw her to the ground. Memory froze her lungs. A prickly warmth flooded her body, and the room swam in a slow, sickening circle, the edges turning dark, closing in.

Lightning snapped, startled her from the encroaching darkness. Thunder shook the building and rattled the windowpanes. She shook her head to clear away the fuzziness, forced strength into her quivering legs and edged backward, not daring to take her gaze off Cole.

"I came back because the storm worsened and I wanted to get Manning inside before he got soaked by the driving rain. He sent me after you—told me to tell you your poppa had sent me so you wouldn't be frightened. That was his word, not mine."

Did he think her a fool? If that were true, why would he remove his rain jacket? She needed a weapon. Something. Anything! She stretched her right hand backward, groped through the space behind her.

"Obviously, that didn't work." He turned toward her, lifted his hands.

She whirled to run, spotted a hay fork and snatched it from its place in the corner then spun back, the wooden tines extended toward him. Rain beat on the roof. Lightning flickered, and thunder rumbled. The horse in the stall behind her snorted and pawed at the floor.

Tension quivered on the air. Cole stared at her, silent and still, slowly tugged his shirt collar up around his neck and lowered his hands. "I've told you, I am not my brother, Miss Spencer. I abhor what he did to you. But I am at a loss as to how to convince you of that.

Perhaps time is the only answer." His voice, deep and quiet, blended with the drumming overhead. He turned, gestured toward his rain jacket. "That should keep you dry. Please hurry back to the house. Your grandmother is worried about you."

She watched, wary and disbelieving, as he shoved open the door, ducked his head and stepped out into the gray deluge. What was he doing? She stared at the door, waited. It remained closed. The heavy thudding of her heart eased. Her racing pulse slowed. She dropped the hay rake, moved forward on shaky legs and stared down at the object he'd left behind. A furled umbrella with a brass knob in the form of a drake's head.

Your grandfather sent me after you.

Was it true? She picked up her grandfather's umbrella, held it against her chest and sagged back against the wall. Why would her grandfather do such a thing when he knew what had happened to her? Why would he send Cole Aylward, of all people, to come after her when she was alone and defenseless? Had her grandfather's reason, also, been affected by his seizure? Or was Cole lying?

She closed her eyes, fought the clinging fog of weariness and fear. What could she do? She was helpless against Cole Aylward's strength and unequal to an Aylward's cunning ways. She tightened her grip on the umbrella and wrapped her arms around herself in a futile effort to stop the inward quivering, the outward shivering. "Heavenly Father, You know I'm not strong enough or brave enough to fight him. I can't do this. Give me strength and courage and wisdom, I pray."

Her choked, whispered plea was swallowed by the sound of the rain that pounded on the shakes overhead and slapped against the outside of the wall behind her. She opened her eyes and stared down at the rainwater that seeped under the door and trickled across the thick puncheons into the dark interior, trying to understand, to grasp what Cole was after. He had to have a reason for the care he was giving her grandfather. Was it money? Payne had stolen the money from her grandfather's desk at the mill before he had—

A shudder passed through her. She shoved the memory away and thought about the conversation she'd overheard. Cole wanted her grandfather to buy something. It *had* to be Poppa's money he wanted. That would explain why he was working to gain her grandfather's trust— or knowledge of where he kept his money.

Her face tightened. The thought of her grandfather being duped because of his weakened state brought strength. She shoved away from the wall, partially opened the umbrella and waited for another lull in the wind, then slipped outside and slammed the door closed again, leaving Cole's raincoat lying on the chest. She would rather be soaked to the bone than touch a garment that belonged to him.

The stable door banged.

At last. Cole pressed back into the darkness against the wall and watched Sadie run for the house, the umbrella she held bucking and flapping in the buffeting wind, the pouring rain soaking into her dress, turning the fabric black in the dim, stormy light.

No rain jacket. He needn't have bothered leaving it for her. He should have simply left her the umbrella and gone home. He scowled and drew back as she gained the porch. There was no need; she didn't even glance toward the end where he stood, merely hurried inside.

He pulled his wet collar tight against the back of his neck, crossed the porch and trotted down the steps. The wind plastered his wet pants to his legs, blew his shirt flat against his chest and fluttered and slapped the sides of it against his ribs. Rain soaked through the fabric and chilled his skin. He shivered and sprinted to the stable, water splashing from beneath his boots.

The wind wrestled him for the door. He forced it open, stepped through and eased it closed, then stood just inside to catch his breath. The smells of grain, hay and dust mingled on the moist air he drew in. A cold drop of water slid down his neck. He snatched his hat from his head, twisted the knit fabric and watched the water flow off his knuckles and splash on the floor.

The horse sniffed, extended its neck over the stall door and whickered.

"Later, girl. It's not time for your feed." White light flickered through the windows, gleaming on the garment draped across the feed chest. His jaw clenched. For a frightened, fragile-appearing woman, Sadie Spencer had a strong defiant streak.

He looked down at his hands twisting the knitted cap, eased their grip, tugged the hat back on his head and lifted his raincoat off the chest, his fingers digging into the rubber cloth. His mother had also been defiant and strong—in her own way. And that defiance had cost her her life at his father's hands. Would Sadie have died by Payne's hands if that logger hadn't heard her scream and come running to her aid?

His stomach clenched at a sudden roll of nausea. The look of stark terror on Sadie's face when he'd stepped through the door and turned toward her was chilling. And the anger of injured innocence, of a person who has had her sense of peace and security torn from her, lurked in the depths of her brown eyes. It was heart-rending. How could he ever hope to make that up to her?

A lightning bolt crackled through the rain. Thunder clapped. He stared down at the rubber fabric dangling from his clenched hands and wished it were Payne in his grip.

They should be asleep by now. Sadie took a firm hold on the oil lamp and walked to the top of the stairs, listened but heard no sound. She thrust the lamp behind her, leaned around the corner and peeked over the railing. The trimmed lamp on the center table spread dim light through the empty entrance hall. The way was clear.

She gripped the railing and eased down the four steps to the landing, turned and started down the longer flight, glanced to her left. The morning-room door was closed, her grandfather's snoring coming muted through its wood panels. Good. She could check the money box without interruption or explanation.

The soft tap of her slippers blended with the whispered brush of her dressing-gown hem against the polished oak steps as she descended. A loud snort from the morning room froze her at the bottom of the staircase. She held her breath, waited until the snoring resumed, then hurried across the hall into the library. The light from the lamp fell in a golden circle onto the braided rag rug her grandmother had made as a bride. A lump formed in her throat, swelled as she lifted her gaze. This was her favorite room. Poppa's room.

She sniffed the air, smiled at the remembered blend of candle wax, wood smoke and leather, with a hint of bayberry cologne. Her gaze went to the window where she and Willa and Callie and Daniel had crouched beside the lilac bush and watched her grandfather take the flat box from the desk drawer, count money he pulled from his pocket, write something on a small piece of paper, put it all in the box and then return the box to the drawer. She had made the others promise, then and there, that they would never tell anyone about Poppa's money box, especially Ellen, who could never keep a secret.

The light flickered over the settle where she'd curled up on the cushion and looked at books while Poppa worked, then settled to a steady burn as she placed the lamp on the game table where she'd learned to play checkers.

She thrust her childhood memories away and crossed to the tall bookshelf desk that sat between the two windows on the front wall and opened the drawer that held the flat wooden box. She brushed her fingers over the smooth, waxed top, then flipped it open. *Empty.*

Her breath caught. Her grandfather always kept his money in the box. Did he know it was gone? Or had Cole found the box and taken the money on the sly?

She put the box back in the drawer and looked up at the bookshelves behind the glass-fronted doors, stared at a gaping space. Her grandfather's green leather bookkeeping ledgers were gone as well. They were always— *Nanna.* Had her grandmother misplaced them while cleaning? Nanna would never take the ledgers from

Poppa's desk if she were thinking straight, but in her confused moments...

That horrible feeling of loss struck her anew. Heartsick, she looked behind the desk's drop-down slant front and in the drawer again. No ledgers. A quick scan of the books on the shelves in the alcoves on either side of the stone fireplace showed no green leather bindings among them.

Where else could the books be? She lifted the hinged seat on the settle and searched through the box it covered. Two old pillows, a quilt, a dented flask, a pair of worn boots and her torn rag doll. She lowered the lid, straightened, wrapped her arms about herself and slowly rubbed her upper left arm as she gazed about. There was no place left to search. Suspicion wormed its way into her thoughts and took root. Her hand stilled. *He* had them. Cole must have slipped into the room and taken the ledgers along with the money. There was no one to prevent him from doing what he would.

Until now.

She whirled and strode to the table, picked up the lamp and carried it across the entrance hall into the sitting room. She would tell her grandfather what she had discovered and her suspicions, but first she must be certain that what she suspected was true. Her grandmother *could* have misplaced the books and even the money.

Her grandfather's occasional snore was the only sound that disturbed the silence as she searched every cupboard and drawer for the books then moved on to the dining room and butler's pantry. The lamp chased away the darkness, lit every nook and cranny she hunted through. The ledgers were nowhere to be found. Her suspicion solidified into certainty. Cole had the books—but why? She could not go to her grandfather until she knew the answer to that question. Cole had so ingratiated himself into her grandparents' affections, she wasn't sure her grandfather would believe her without proof.

Fatigue dragged at her. She climbed the stairs, her steps firmed by determination. She might have been helpless to stop his brother's attack on her—and she did not come close to matching Cole's physical strength—but God had given her a good mind, and she had taken her turn at tending the books at the ladies' seminary. She would be her grandfather's eyes, and she would find out what scheme Cole was about. But first she had to find those business ledgers.

She entered her bedroom, set the oil lamp in its place and untied the fastening on her dressing gown. She would watch Cole's every move, and when she had discovered what he was about and why, she would tell her grandfather, and he would order Cole from his home. They would be safe then. *She* would be safe then.

Memories pressed upon her. She glanced at her bed and gave up the idea of retiring. Her agitated state would surely bring the nightmare.

The dimmed lamplight reflected off the raindrops falling against the window. She opened the sash and stood listening to the now-gentle rain pattering on the porch roof and on the plants in her grandmother's garden below. Where would Cole have taken the ledgers? The most likely place was his shingle mill at Payne's cabin.

A chill coursed through her that had nothing to do with the cool breeze riffling the curtains and fluttering the edges of her dressing gown. She looked through the darkness toward the trees that sheltered the path leading to the sawmill and wrapped her arms about herself. Payne's cabin was a short distance beyond the sawmill. How would she ever find the courage to walk that path?

So many questions with no answers. She left the window, too exhausted by her confrontation with Cole in the stable and her worries over her grandparents to resist the lure of her bed any longer. The soft sound of the rain dancing on the porch roof calmed her nerves and lulled her to a place of peace. Her eyelids slid closed. She struggled to open them, then sighed and yielded to her weariness. It would be all right. It wasn't Payne Aylward's face she saw against the darkness. It was Cole's raincoat on top of the grain chest in the stable.

It had been a…thoughtful…gesture…. All that… rain…

Chapter Five

A horse's hoofs thumped on the carriage way, and buggy wheels crunched over the gravel. Her stomach flopped. Sadie frowned and covered the teapot with a towel to keep it hot. She wasn't ready to face callers. Perhaps Nanna would go to the door.

She stepped to the window, open in the hope of catching a breeze, pushed aside the curtain and looked toward the stable. A tall, handsomely dressed man was lifting a woman down from a black phaeton. She skimmed her gaze over the woman's attractive green gown and caught her breath at the sight of a thick roll of chestnut hair gleaming red in the sunlight beneath a green hat. *Willa.*

Joy swelled. She whirled away from the window, rushed out the kitchen door. "Willa!" Tears clogged her throat, spilled from her eyes as she raced down the length of the porch.

"Sadie?" Willa stopped dead in her tracks, then lifted her hems and clattered up the steps like they had as children.

She stretched out her arms and was enveloped in a

mutual hug, danced around in circles with Willa, laughing and crying, their voices blending as they choked out words. "It's so good to see you!"

"I've missed you so!"

"It's been so long!"

"So terribly long!"

A throat cleared. "Excuse me, ladies. But if you will let me pass, I will attend to my business inside while you continue your reunion." There was amused patience in the deep, resonant male voice.

She blinked away her tears and looked over Willa's shoulder straight into a pair of smiling brown eyes.

"Welcome home, Miss Spencer. I'm the forgotten man—Matthew Calvert, Willa's husband, at your service." A lopsided grin slanted across his lips. "At least I will be if I can come up on the porch."

"Oh, I'm sorry, I—"

"He's only teasing, Sadie." Willa's hand gripped her arm and tugged her aside. "I keep telling him it's very unprofessional behavior for a pastor."

"And I keep explaining that we all have our little foibles."

She listened to Matthew Calvert's laughter, watched the warm, loving look Willa and her husband exchanged and something stirred deep inside. Envy? Ridiculous. She wanted no part of any man, let alone marriage. The very thought of it made her ill. She stepped toward the dining-room door. "Forgive my lapse of manners, Reverend Calvert. Please come in."

He moved to her side and smiled down at her. "There's no need for the formal address, Miss Spencer. I am Matthew to Willa's friends."

She caught the hopeful look in Willa's eyes and

smiled but couldn't bring herself to offer him her hand. She grabbed the doorknob as an excuse to withhold it. "I'm Sadie—to Willa's husband."

She tried to make it amusing, but acknowledgment of her limited acceptance flickered in his brown eyes, followed by a look of compassion that made her throat constrict. He knew. Willa had told him. A flush of shame prickled her skin.

"Sadie it is. Now, if you will excuse me, I shall go pay my call on your grandparents while you ladies visit."

"They're in the sitting room. I'll show you—"

"No need, Sadie. I know the way. And Willa will never forgive me if I steal one minute of your time." He grinned and walked into the house.

She closed the door on his retreating figure. If only it were as easy to shut out the past.

"I'm sorry, Sadie. I know I promised to never speak of what happened, but I had to tell Matthew." Willa placed a hand on her arm, held her gaze. "He wondered why you didn't come home to visit with your grandmother being ill. And when your grandfather had his seizure…well…I didn't know if you would come. And I couldn't let Matthew think it was because you were uncaring."

But now he would always look at her with the knowledge of Payne Aylward's attack in his mind—the same as everyone else in Pinewood. She pushed aside the shame, smiled and squeezed Willa's hand. "You always were protective of me."

Relief flashed in her friend's blue-green eyes. "Well, I am older than you." A smile curved her lips at their old childhood contention.

"By three months." She gave Willa another quick hug. "It isn't age, my friend, it's a matter of courage. I was woefully lacking in that attribute as a child, and I still am. Now—" She linked their arms and started for the kitchen door. "I've just made tea, in spite of the heat. Let's bring it out here on the porch and visit. You can tell me all about becoming a wife and the mother of two young children at the same time. I can see now how Matthew won your heart. What you wrote me about his grin is true—it really is disarming."

The cravat at his throat was a misery in the heat, and his Sunday suit wasn't much better. Cole shifted in the saddle and shot a quick glance up at the sun. He'd rip the cravat off right now if—

Was that a scream?

He frowned and urged Cloud into a trot around the bend. Dust swirled in the air, gritty against his perspiring face. He squinted his eyes and spotted a buggy jouncing and jolting side to side on the road ahead, dirt spewing from beneath its wobbling wheels. The Conklins?

Women's shouts and screams mingled with the thunder of the horse's hoofs.

A runaway.

He started forward, then stopped. He'd never overtake them on the straight road. He eyed the distance to the incline where the road made a sharp bend at the top, judged the angle required to get in front of the careening buggy, and reined Cloud into the field. "Let's go, boy!" He kicked him into a run, watching the buggy. If they entered that curve before he reached them…

The gelding raced through the tall grasses, gathered itself and jumped a small creek, pounded along the beaten path that led from the water to a copse of trees that bordered the low hill and the Gardner farm. A quick glance at the dangerously swaying buggy showed they'd gained ground and would beat the buggy to the hill.

Trees broke across his vision. He jerked his gaze to the narrow path ahead, leaned low to avoid overhanging branches and urged Cloud on, picturing the area in his head. The stock path trailed left away from the road, but there was a break in the trees... There! He reined Cloud right, heard pounding hoofs and glanced over his shoulder. Frothy sweat covered the heaving chest of the panicked horse running toward them, flew from its driving haunches. *Close.*

"Come on boy!" He kicked his heels, and Cloud leaped forward, thundering onto the road a short distance in front of the wild-eyed runaway, his muscles bunching and stretching to maintain his small lead. "Steady, boy, steady."

He risked another glance over his shoulder and glimpsed the two Conklin women in a tumbled heap in the driver's corner of the seat, no reins in sight. *"Put on the brake!"* One of the women lunged for the brake lever. He turned back, leaned forward as they started up the grade. *Please, Lord, let this work!*

Cloud raced on beneath his urging. He tilted his head toward his shoulder, listened to the thundering hoofs behind him and risked turning for another look when their pounding rhythm slowed. Their lead had increased. It was working! The applied brake and the slope of the hill were proving too much for the tiring horse.

"Ease up, boy." He slowed Cloud and reined him to

the left. The runaway caught up and ran with them neck and neck. He leaned down, grabbed for the cheek strap of the horse's bridle, missed and tried again. The leather strap tugged against his fingers. He tightened his grip, the muscles of his arm and shoulder fighting the force of the horse's thrusting head. "Easy, girl. Easy…"

He settled deeper in the saddle, tugged harder— the mare's head turned, its gait faltered. He held the straining head facing him and reined in Cloud, forcing the mare to slow her wild run. They entered the sharp bend at a trot, the buggy swaying wildly but remaining upright. "Whoa, girl. It's all right. Everything is all right." He kept his voice low, talked the horse calm as he slowed Cloud to a walk, then stopped.

"Good girl." Cole tightened his grip on the cheek strap and slipped from the saddle, willing his hands and voice to stay steady as he reached to where the reins passed through the terrets on the harness saddle and grabbed hold. That had been close! Too close. He loosed his grip on the cheek strap and stroked the mare's quivering, sweat-covered neck. The bay dropped its head and barreled air into its heaving chest.

He turned, playing the dangling reins through his firm grip as he stepped to the buggy. Enid and Chloe Conklin were untangling themselves from the corner of the seat. "Are you ladies all right?"

"Seems so." Enid's voice shook. She tugged her hat to rights and looked down at him, her face pale, her eyes wide with shock. "Thank you, Mr. Aylward. You saved us from a sure accident." She grabbed the dashboard and scooted over on the seat, giving Chloe room. "Fool mare! I don't know what spooked her like that."

"It was a fox, Mother. I saw it run across the road."

Chloe pushed herself to a sitting position, twisted her bodice into place and gave him a shaky smile. "I'm so thankful you happened along, Mr. Aylward. I lost the reins when I grabbed hold of the dashboard to keep from being thrown out of the buggy."

"I'm glad to have been able to help." He glanced at her trembling hands, turned and fastened the reins to a sturdy branch. "I'll look the buggy over, make sure nothing's broken." He tugged his handkerchief from his pocket, wiped the sweat and grit from his face, then stepped to the driver's side and checked the wheels and hubs. The undercarriage looked fine. A rustle of fabric drew his attention. He glanced over his shoulder and watched Chloe climb from the buggy and turn toward the horses.

"You'd best move slow and speak quiet, Miss Conklin. That mare could be spooked easy right now."

She turned and smiled. "It's your horse I'm going to pet, Mr. Aylward. He has a brave, staunch heart— like his owner. He deserves our thanks. As do you." Pink flowed into her cheeks. Her smile warmed. "I'll be careful."

He nodded and turned back to finish his inspection, man enough to dwell on the meaning of that blush and feel a little set up by it. His ego had taken quite a beating since Sadie Spencer had returned.

"Of all the days for Henry to have to stay home from church! I hope that foal he was waiting to help birth proves out steadier than this new mare." Enid Conklin peered out of the buggy toward him. "Everything all right?"

"So far." He walked to the back of the buggy, peered beneath, then moved on to check the other wheels and finally the traces. "I don't see any sign of damage, Mrs. Conklin, but you'd best have Henry give things a closer look when you get home."

"I'll do that. And he can get rid of this fidgety mare, too." A scowl pulled Enid Conklin's brows together. "I don't aim to have another ride like this one again."

"Can't say I blame you." He loosed the reins from the branch and handed them up to the older woman, who had taken the driver's seat.

"I thank you for reminding us to pull on the brake, young man. I forgot all about it in the struggle to keep from being thrown out, but I should have remembered. Henry won't be pleased about that. I'm not."

"I'm sure Henry will be so pleased you and Miss Conklin are safe, he won't give it a thought."

"Perhaps." She smiled down at him. "I'd like to thank you proper, Mr. Aylward, and I'm sure Henry will, too. Would you come for dinner?"

"What a lovely idea, Mother."

Chloe stepped up beside him, leading Cloud. The warmth, the interest in her eyes was balm for the fear in Sadie Spencer's eyes whenever he came near her, but Sadie might be the wiser of the two. She was certainly the one that drew him. He held back a frown.

"I hope you are able to join us, Mr. Aylward. It would give you and your horse a chance to cool off before you ride on home. Our house stays fairly cool, even during a day as hot as this one." Chloe smiled and held out her hand toward him.

He took Cloud's reins, careful not to let his hand touch hers. He'd been very cautious about even a casual, accidental touch of a young woman these past four years. "I'm afraid not. I have to get to the Townsends' place. Manning is waiting for me." He shifted his gaze to Enid. "I thank you for the kind invitation, Mrs. Conklin." He mounted, feeling boorish for not helping Chloe into the buggy, but she was too friendly to encourage. "I'll ride along with you until the turnoff to make sure everything is all right. Let's go, boy."

Cloud moved out in front of the buggy, and he held him at a walk, giving the Conklins' new mare no chance to break into a run. He was already late and wanted no more trouble. Manning would be wondering where he was. Manning. He huffed out a breath. It wasn't the image of the elderly man's gray-bearded face that had been filling his head all during church.

He looked down and brushed at the dust on his suit, scowled at the small, jagged tear in the right sleeve. He'd hoped when Sadie saw him in his Sunday clothes it would help set him apart from Payne in her eyes. That she'd at least entertain consideration of him as an upstanding, churchgoing man and look at him with respect instead of disgust and fear. There was little hope of that now.

He lifted a hand in farewell as he passed the turnoff to the Conklin farm and urged Cloud into an easy lope.

"Joshua and Sally sound absolutely delightful, Willa. How fortunate they are to have you for their mother." Sadie rose and reached for the teapot to hide the sorrow and regret that surely showed on her face. She would never be a mother. Payne Aylward had destroyed that dream.

"And Matthew for their father." Willa smiled and held out her empty cup. "It took a while before they stopped calling him Uncle and me Miss Wright, but we are Mama and Papa to them now. God has made us into a true family. I never knew such love was possible."

There was a warm contentment in Willa's voice. A yearning to know such happiness swept through Sadie. She frowned at the foolish hope, poured Willa more tea, then refilled her own cup. She would gladly settle for freedom from fear, and peace of mind. "I'm truly happy for you, Willa." Honey dribbled from the spoon she held over the top of her tea. "And for Callie as well. Is she as happy as she writes in her letters?"

"Oh my, yes." Willa lifted one of Gertrude's ginger cookies onto her plate. "Ezra adores her. But then, with her beauty and sweetness, what man wouldn't? Except for my Matthew."

There was that sound of contentment again. Sadie lowered her spoon and made figure eights, swirling the honey through the dark liquid in her cup, acutely aware of how much her cowardice had cost her. There were so many things she could never get back. "Has she truly grown that beautiful?"

"Gracious, yes! Wait until you see her. She and Ezra are in New York City at present. There was some sort of business deal that required his presence." Willa laughed and gave a small shake of her head. "God's ways never cease to amaze me, Sadie. Callie fled here from Buffalo to escape the rich men vying for her hand and wound up married to a man wealthier than all of them."

"Yes, she wrote me of that. And Ellen wrote that she is enjoying her position as the beauty of the social set in Buffalo, now that Callie has married." She held back a frown and took a sip of her hot, sweetened tea. Such pleasure was beyond her imagining. She'd spent the past four years *hiding* from men behind the seminary's brick walls.

"I've tried to explain to Ellen that mutual love and trust are important in a marriage, but she brushes such things aside. She cares only that the man she marries can provide the fancy lifestyle she craves."

Time to change the subject. She had no desire to talk about the various aspects of marriage. "How is Daniel?"

Willa set down her cup and looked at her. "Daniel is fine…as I wrote you in my last letter. My mother and her husband are fine. Ellen's parents are fine. Sophia is fine. Her new restaurant in the hotel is doing very well and she is prospering. The new bank Ezra built and the freight-hauling business he started have brought new prosperity to Pinewood. There have been no major accidents or illnesses and no deaths since my last letter. I believe that covers the town and its residents. There's no one else for you to hide behind, Sadie."

She stiffened and brushed back a lock of hair sticking to her moist forehead. "I'm not—"

"Yes, you are. But it won't work. We're going to talk about *you*." Willa's voice was soft but firm. "If Matthew hadn't come to call on your grandparents today, I wouldn't even have known you were here. Why didn't you write me you were coming home? Or send word that you'd arrived?"

"There wasn't time to write." She put down her cup and met Willa's questioning gaze. "When I read Callie's letter telling me about Poppa's seizure, I went straight to the headmistress and resigned my position, then I packed my bags and hired a cabriolet to take me to the station so I could catch the next stage to Buffalo."

"You're not returning to the seminary?" There was a hesitant joy in Willa's voice.

"No. My place is here, caring for Nanna and Poppa." She rose, stepped to the railing and looked out at her grandmother's garden. "I confess I'd hoped I could stay and care for them in the safety of Sophia's hotel. When I learned they'd come home, I—It was…difficult…to come back here." She leaned over the railing and plucked a rose from the climbing bush, sniffed its sweet fragrance. "Nonetheless, I should have done so when you first wrote me of your concerns over Nanna's confusion. Instead, I told myself her lapses of memory were nothing serious because I was too much of a coward to come home and face…everything."

The legs of Willa's chair scraped the floor and her footsteps neared. "You are *not* a coward, Sadie. Any woman would flee after—"

"Not you, Willa. You stayed and faced the humiliation when Thomas left town. And Callie stood against her parents and those men who thought they could buy her for a wife."

"Oh, Sadie, you ascribe me virtue and courage I do not possess. I thought of leaving Pinewood when Thomas deserted me, but I couldn't leave Mama, so I hid behind a lie. And Callie fled from her unpleasant situation at home. We're no different than you." Willa grasped her arm and tugged her around to face her. "God delivered us from our troubles and fears and blessed us with love and happiness. And though our problems did not compare to yours—to what happened to you—He is able to do the same for you, Sadie. And I *know* He will. Trust Him."

She drew her arm away so Willa would not feel the

shudder passing through her at the thought of married life. "I'm happy for you and Callie, Willa, but I do not want a husband. I do not want any man but Poppa to even touch me, now or ever! All I ask of God is the wisdom and strength to stay and care for Nanna and Poppa in spite of my fear."

Chapter Six

"I'm sorry I'm late, Manning. I hope you weren't uncomfortable." Cole held his gaze steady on the elderly man, resisting the urge to look to where Sadie sat reading. There was no need. He could well imagine what she thought of him standing there all sweaty in his dusty, torn suit—not that her opinion of him could get any lower. Still, he'd hoped to improve that situation today. "I came straight here from church—despite my appearance." He almost snorted at the feeble attempt to justify himself to her. He was giving far too much weight to Sadie's power to—

"Reverend Calvert came to call. He helped Grandfather."

Sadie's cool, polite tone, the inference in her words, sent a rod of steel down his spine. She might as well have called him a liar. He drew a breath, then let it go when Manning tugged at his torn sleeve.

"What...hap...pened?"

"Why do you bother to ask, Manning? Daniel is an adventurer. He's always unkempt."

Daniel. He looked to where Rachel Townsend sat

working her needlepoint, noted her opaque, unfocused expression, and his chest tightened in a way that was becoming all too familiar. He'd begun helping the Townsends as a way of atoning in a small measure for the hurt Payne had caused them, but the elderly couple had taken up residence in his heart—they'd become the grandparents he'd never had. He made her a small bow. "Please forgive my appearance, Mrs. Townsend. I did not mean to call in this disheveled state. It was unavoidable."

She stared at him a moment, then bowed her head to her work. "At least you've manners enough to apologize."

"Cole…" Manning gave another tug on his sleeve, pointed to the rip. "Tell…me."

From the corner of his eye, he saw Sadie's head lift and turn slightly their way. The better to hear and sort through his words for another reason to distrust him, no doubt. The day wasn't going at all as he'd hoped. He held back a scowl and focused his attention on Manning.

"Henry Conklin bought a new mare. Turns out she's a nervous one. On the way home from church, a fox ran in front of her and she spooked. Unfortunately, Henry had stayed home and Chloe and Enid were alone in the buggy. In all the jolting, Chloe lost the reins."

"Runa…way?"

"Yes."

"Oh my! Are they all right?" Rachel lowered her work and stared at him, her eyes now clear and focused. Sadie's were narrowed and suspicious. He supposed he should be grateful she hadn't fled the room at his appearing, as was her wont.

"They were a little shaken, but they're fine. I spotted their careening buggy and was able to cut through the field and that copse of trees that borders the Gardner place to get ahead of them."

"Bottom of…hill?"

He looked back at Manning and nodded. "You figured it right."

Manning chuckled, his face creased into a smile. "Smart. Hill would…slow…horse."

The approval felt good. He'd never managed to gain that from his father. "That and the brake. The women had forgotten it in the excitement, but Enid managed to pull it on when I yelled to them. It worked. I was able to drop back and get hold of the bridle."

Manning's smile turned to a frown. "Danger…ous."

He couldn't deny the charge. He glanced down at the angry red streaks crossing his fingers and palm, felt again the power of the mare's thrusting head straining his arm and shoulder. "But necessary. If they'd gone into that sharp bend at the top of the hill at a run, they'd have overturned."

"Still risky…hero…ic."

He glanced toward Sadie, sure she would be irritated by that description. She was looking at his bruised hand. He folded his swollen fingers against his palm and moved his hand back out of her sight. "Hardly. I simply happened along at the right time and the right place. I never could have caught them if it weren't for the hill."

"Nonetheless, you saved them, Cole. And, from the looks of you, it was quite a task." Rachel set her needlepoint aside, rose from the settee and bustled over to him. "Give me your coat. I'll give it a good brushing and mend that tear for you."

He glanced down at the three-cornered rip in his sleeve. "A branch must have caught it when I rode through the trees, but you don't have to—"

"Do not argue with me, young man." A mock scowl knit Rachel's fine gray brows together. She held out her hand.

Warmth filled his chest. It had been four years since anyone had fussed over him. He slipped his arm out of a sleeve and wished he had the right to lean down and kiss her soft, wrinkled cheek.

"You're busy with your needlepoint, Nanna, and I'm only entertaining myself reading. Why don't I brush and mend the coat?"

His mouth didn't exactly gape, but only because he caught himself in time. He froze with his coat half-off and shot a look at Sadie. She'd moved to the settee and was staring at Rachel's needlepoint. He glanced down. There was a hodgepodge of large, red stitches scattered over the beautifully worked, unfinished piece. So that was it. She was protecting her grandmother. From what? His disapproval? Anger? She thought him so cruel that he would berate an ill woman?

He jerked his gaze up to Sadie's face and his spurt of anger died. The sadness in her brown eyes tugged at his heart harder than Rachel was tugging on his arm. He looked down.

"Your coat." She raised her arms, grasped the collar and slid it off his shoulder.

He couldn't refuse her. He pulled his arm out of the sleeve. "You're most kind, Mrs. Townsend. Thank you."

"I'll mend the coat, Nanna." Sadie hurried over. He

glanced at her taut face, wished she would look at him so he could let her know that it was all right, that he understood.

"Nonsense." Rachel draped the coat over her arm and took hold of his hand, turned it palm up. "Come with me to the kitchen, Cole, your hand needs tending." She glanced over her shoulder. "You come, too, Sadie. You can see to Cole's hand while I brush his coat."

Sadie's face drained of color and panic flashed in her eyes. Did the thought of touching him do that to her? He clenched his jaw and gently withdrew his hand from Rachel's grasp. "I'm afraid that's impossible, Mrs. Townsend. I need to go home and get cleaned up. And Cloud had a hard run in this heat—I want to get him fed and turned out to pasture. I'll get my coat when I return this evening." He dipped his head in farewell and strode from the room.

The dishes were finished at last. Sadie looked at her puckered fingers and swallowed the lump in her throat. Twice Nanna had taken the dishes she'd washed and rinsed, dried them and put them right back in the dishpan. She hadn't known how to stop her without hurting her feelings or confusing her more. If Poppa hadn't called for help, they'd be doing dishes still. How did Gertrude manage? Why couldn't she?

The helpless feeling in her chest swelled. What happened to Nanna? What made her forget what she had done so that she did it over and over again? Why did her grandmother's mind slip from the present to the past and back again? She wanted so much to help her, but how did you help a woman who forgot you? Who confused the child she had raised from a toddler with others?

She removed her apron, scooped some rose-scented oatmeal-and-beeswax cream from the small crock on the shelf over the washstand and rubbed it into her hands. If only she could tell when her grandmother was going to slip into the past, she might be able to prepare herself and do something to stop it…if one could.

The ache in her heart grew. She smoothed back her hair and scanned the kitchen to be sure all had been put to rights for Gertrude's return in the morning, then dimmed the lamp and walked out into the hall. If Nanna had remembered about Cole's suit coat and repaired that tear…

She sighed and grasped hold of the thought of Cole. She wished he would simply go away, but at least he was a distraction from her concern over her grandmother, the anger she felt toward him a welcome respite from the lost, hollow feeling that had settled in her heart since she'd come home.

Twilight showed outside the entrance hall window, and she hurried her steps. Cole would soon return to carry her grandfather to bed. Why had he not come for supper? It had been odd not having him sitting at the table sharing their meal. Though she was thankful. It was only that she had become used to him sitting across from her.

There was something too…*accepting* about his relationship with her grandparents. They treated him as they would a son. And what was truly disturbing was that she was responsible. If she had been here where she belonged when her grandfather had his seizure, none of this would have happened. Cole would not have set foot in this house. And he certainly would not be caring for her grandfather. Although, to be honest, he did an excellent job of it.

She stopped outside the sitting-room door, took a deep breath, squared her shoulders and stepped into the room. *Oh, Nanna...* Tears filmed her eyes, blurring the large stitches of crimson yarn her grandmother was using to sew the two sides of Cole's sleeve together.

"Sa...die..."

"Yes, Poppa?" She looked at her grandfather sitting helpless in his chair and clamped her lips together to hold back a cry of anger and frustration at her inability to help these two people she loved so dearly.

"Checkers. Bring...table."

Her heart sank. She didn't want to disappoint him, but she had no time to play a game of checkers now. She had to somehow get Cole's coat from Nanna and remove those stitches before he returned. She blinked her eyes and cleared her throat. "Poppa, I—"

He shook his head. "I play...Rachel." His gaze darted to Cole's coat in his wife's hands then came back to lock on hers, his message clear.

She read the love and care for her grandmother in his brown eyes, and the awful loneliness inside her eased. He might be limited physically, but he was still her poppa—and he had just given her the answer to her dilemma. She curved her lips into a trembling smile. "A perfectly lovely idea, Poppa. I'll be right back."

She hurried across the entrance hall to the library, lifted the small game table from its place in the corner and carried it back to set in front of his chair.

He reached for her hand, pulled her close and placed his mouth by her ear. "Distract...doesn't hurt...her."

The warm breath of his whisper tickled her cheek. She swallowed hard and gave him a quick hug. "Thank you, Poppa. I didn't know what to do. I'll remember." She straightened and stepped back.

He pulled the drawer in the table open and began placing the red and black wood disks on the inlaid game board. Memories of him teaching her to play the game caught at her throat. A deep breath steadied her and she moved a Windsor chair into place on the other side.

"Rachel. Come…play."

Her grandmother glanced up and shook her head. "Sadie will play with you, Manning. I'm mending Cole's coat."

"No. Want…you to…play."

Her grandfather waved her away. She stepped to the chair she'd occupied earlier and picked up her book.

"Let you…go…first."

Her grandmother laughed, laid Cole's coat on the settee, walked over to the game table and seated herself. "That is so very gallant of you, Manning. But we both know it will make no difference. You always win."

She watched her grandmother reach to slide a checker forward and moved quietly toward the settee. Her grandfather lifted his head and looked at her. She made sewing motions and pointed in the direction of the back porch. Grabbing Cole's coat with the threaded needle stuck in its sleeve, she snatched a skein of black embroidery wool and a pair of scissors from her grandmother's basket and hurried out the door.

Cole stopped and stared through the tree trunks at the glowing lamp on the Townsends' porch. His pulse jumped at recognition of the slender figure seated in its circle of light.

He frowned at the unwanted reaction, lifted his lamp high to give Sadie ample warning of his coming and walked out of the woods and up the garden path, stopping at the bottom of the steps. "Good evening."

She nodded, then glanced toward the kitchen door beside her, no doubt wishing she could flee his presence. Why didn't she? For that matter, as fearful as she was, why was she sitting outside at night? He climbed the steps, set his lamp on the railing and leaned his shoulder against the post as a signal that he would come no closer. "It's a hot night."

"Yes."

She looked at him but avoided meeting his gaze, as always. The tension, the wariness in her reached him from halfway down the porch. Clearly she wanted him to leave. His obstinacy rose. "Being so still with no breeze brings out the fireflies."

"I hadn't noticed. I'm busy."

A pointed hint. But for some reason she wasn't running away from him, and he intended to take advantage of it. Perhaps some time spent talking together would prove to her she had nothing to fear. "I used to run around and catch fireflies when I was a kid. I tried to see how many I could capture in one night. I guess everyone—" Something fluttered at the corner of his vision. A bat flew under the porch roof and swooped toward the lamplight on the table.

Sadie squealed and jerked to her feet. Her chair crashed over and something clanked against the floor.

He leaped forward and waved his arms through the air, driving the bat toward the railing. It swooped low between the porch posts and disappeared into the night. A smile tugged at the corners of his lips at the sight of Sadie pressed back against the house wall with a blanket over her head and shoulders. "You can come out, now. The bat is gone."

"Are you sure? I hate bats!"

His smile widened to a grin at her muffled words. "I'm sure." He set her chair aright and scooped up the objects that had fallen when she jumped up—a pair of scissors and a spool of black wool thread. She'd been sewing. He straightened and looked her way, eyed what he'd thought was a blanket now dangling from her hands. "That's my coat. What—"

"I'm mending it." She freed a hand and smoothed back her hair, straightened her collar.

He was rather sorry she did. She looked less self-contained and standoffish mussed up like that. Pretty, too, with her cheeks flushed and— He frowned, laid the scissors and yarn on the table. "That's kind of you, but not necessary, Sadie. It's not your fault it needs to be repaired."

"I'm afraid it is." She held the torn sleeve forward for his inspection. "Nanna sewed the sleeve together."

He looked at the large red stitches puckering the wool of his sleeve, then lifted his gaze to her face. "And you thought it necessary to fix the sleeve before I saw it?" How little she thought of him. And without cause. He took a breath to calm the anger tightening his gut. "I've grown to know your grandmother quite well in these past few weeks, Sadie. She's a wonderful woman. If she…mistakenly sewed my sleeve together, it doesn't matter."

"It would to Nanna…if she knew."

There was a glitter of moisture in her eyes. He looked into their brown depths and suddenly understood why she hadn't run inside when he appeared. "That's why you're working here on the porch in this heat, isn't it? So she won't realize what she's done."

She lifted her chin. "I'll have your coat finished by the time you're ready to go home."

There'd be no changing her mind, judging from her protective tone. "As you wish. You can lay the coat on the railing by my lamp when you're done. Now, if you'll excuse me, I'll go tend to Manning's needs." He turned and walked toward the other door.

"Cole…"

He looked back her way.

"I do thank you for your kindness to my grandmother and for the help you give my grandfather…no matter what your reasons."

He could have done without that reminder of her distrust. Would he always walk in the shadow of Payne's dark deed?

Chapter Seven

He was kind to her grandparents—she couldn't deny that. She simply wanted to know why. Sadie fanned her face with her hand and stepped closer to the window as Cole strode down the garden path toward the woods, his mended suit coat a dark shadow over his arm, his lamp lighting his way. Both Poppa and Nanna thought highly of him. It was clear they trusted him. They seemed to have forgotten that his brother had also been pleasant and helpful until—

She jerked her gaze from Cole's broad shoulders, his strong, powerful arms moving in rhythm with his long strides. She hadn't forgotten. She wished she could. But the memories, the nightmare never stopped, and coming home had made them more powerful than ever. There were so many reminders—chief among them Cole, so like Payne with his dark eyes and black beard. Every time she looked at him she remembered.

The yellow glow of his lamp swept forward, passed over the garden bench where he carried her grandfather to enjoy the morning sun every day, moved across the ground and slid over her grandmother's small, wood wheelbarrow sitting by the corner of the fence. Cold gripped her. Shivers coursed down her spine. She wrapped her arms about herself and absently rubbed her upper left arm, her gaze frozen on the small, painted cart. *If Poppa hadn't sent that logger to fix the split handle, no one would have heard her scream over the noise of the saws....*

She whirled from the window, tried to order her thoughts, but the unwanted memories flashed, one after another, into her head—Nanna asking her to pick berries for a pie…the smell of the warm blackberry patch… the sun-dappled path…Payne stepping out from behind the trees…

"No!" The protest burst from her constricted throat. She grabbed her skirts and ran from her bedroom, rushed down the stairs, across the entrance hall into the library and sagged against the door, shaking and gasping for breath. She drew in air, replacing the remembered scents of Payne's sweat, forest loam and the crushed blackberries beneath her as she fought him with the scents of wood smoke, leather and candle wax and a hint of bayberry—the smell of safety.

She closed her eyes and thought about Nanna teaching her how to cook and sew and do needlepoint, of Poppa teaching her to read and showing her how to play checkers and drive the buggy, of how wonderful life had been before her world had been torn apart.

Her ragged breaths evened and her pulse slowed. The quaking eased to an inner trembling. She opened her eyes and looked around the moonlit room, drinking in the sight of all that was dear and familiar. The settle with its hooked-rug pad and worn pillow. Poppa's chair by the hearth with the flat stone and hammer he used to crack open butternuts and hickory nuts close by. His desk.

The peace she sought fled. She stared at the gaping space on the desk's bookshelves where the green leather business ledgers should be and shoved away from the door. Payne Aylward had stolen her grandfather's money and robbed her of her dreams. She would not allow his brother to harm her grandparents.

But would he? Cole was so gentle with her grandmother and so thoughtful of her grandfather. And he had brought her the umbrella and left her his raincoat during the storm. And he'd saved her from the bat. Those were not the actions of a cruel man. Still…

Her breath shortened and she wrapped her arms about herself and rubbed her arm, thinking back to those moments on the porch. How foolish she'd been to blind herself in Cole's presence by throwing his suit coat over her head, but she'd been so afraid of the bat she'd forgotten to be frightened of Cole. Yet once again, he had not seized the opportunity to—

Oh, what she was *thinking?* Perhaps Cole was not cruel like Payne, but that did not mean he wasn't as dishonest. She mustn't allow herself to be swayed from her purpose by his acts of kindness. There had to be a reason why he was spending his time doing these things for Nanna and Poppa, and it was up to her to discover what it was. She was certain it had something to do with the books, else why would they be missing?

She moved to the settle and curled up in the corner, leaned back and closed her eyes to think. How would it profit Cole to have those ledgers?

Cole stepped behind the partition, hung his suit coat on its peg, lifted the lamp close and examined the sleeve. The mend was barely visible. Sadie Spencer was an excellent seamstress. Was she as good a teacher? He could well imagine her standing, all cool and contained, in front of a class of students and commanding their attention. Did any of them sense the vulnerability beneath her calm, quiet exterior? Likely not. She hid it well. Until you looked into her eyes. Her eyes tore at your heart.

He scowled, swiped the sheen of sweat off his forehead with the back of his arm and walked out of the hot, stuffy office into the sawmill. The metal handle of the lamp clinked softly as he hung it on the hook over his workbench, then moved to the edge of the deck and stood looking out over the pond silvered by the reflected moonlight. There was no breeze to disturb the water's calm, no sign of a ripple, but he knew the unseen currents that ran through the depths beneath the surface. He'd felt them flowing against his body, fought their surprising strength, and he had a hunch Sadie fought hidden currents every day. Fear lived in the depths of her eyes. And it was his brother who had put it there. His own brother.

What were you thinking, Payne! How could you *do* that? He clenched his jaw, turned to the workbench, wedged the gear he was making into the vise and picked up a chisel. The same old questions chased through his mind. Had something happened to change Payne? Or was it that their father's blood had some horrible flaw that had surfaced, the way a dead, rotting fish floated to the top of the pond? Would it happen in him? The sickening doubt rose, knotted his stomach. *God, please, I need to know.*

He placed the chisel against the walnut wood, then

picked up a maul and struck it a sharp blow. A quick yank freed it to be placed against the wood at a new angle and hit again. A small chip of wood popped off and dropped to the floor. He moved the chisel from side to side, hitting it again and again, driving it deeper toward the center of the gear, forming a vee. The questions with no answers flew through his mind like the wood chips flying through the air.

He measured the cog he'd formed, loosed the gear and repositioned it in the vise. If only he could have found Payne, he would know. He'd have beat the answers out of him if necessary, then dragged him back to face justice so he couldn't hurt anyone ever again.

Beat him. Like he had their father. Yes, that violence was in him. And what else?

The knots in his stomach twisted tighter. He wiped the sweat from his eyes, lifted the chisel and began the last vee on the gear. What had unleashed Payne's depravity? Where was he? Had Payne hurt anyone else? His face tightened, and he slammed the maul against the chisel, breaking a large chip of wood free. Too large for one hit. If he didn't rein in his frustration, he'd ruin the work. And it was likely he would never know the answer to the questions that haunted him anyway. It was sure Payne would never return to this area. His older brother was too smart to do that…or maybe he was only clever and cunning, like their drunken brute of a father.

He finished the vee, picked up his rasp and smoothed the work he'd done, then ran his hand over the gear to feel for any rough spots. Pounding on the chisel against the hard wood had made his bruised hand swell again. His fingers wouldn't fit into the bottom of the vee. He made a couple more passes over them with the rasp for good measure, then loosed the wedge and took the gear out of the vise. It was ready, unless the square center hole needed more work.

A quick comparison to the squared-off ends of the thick, round piece of walnut on the bench showed the fit was perfect, tight enough so that when he drove the gear onto the shaft there would be no slippage. He laid the shaft and gear back on the workbench and brushed his hands together to rid them of the clinging wood dust. Tomorrow he would drive the wagon into Pinewood and see if Nate had the wheels made. He needed them before he could do more on the chair.

The tension across his shoulders eased; excitement tugged his mouth into a smile. If this experiment worked… He quashed the thought, sat on the edge of the deck, removed his boots and socks and dangled his feet in the icy water. Shiver bumps prickled the flesh on his legs.

Could Sadie swim? She'd lived by this millpond all her life.

He frowned, pulled one foot from the water and leaned his back against a post, giving up his effort to keep thoughts of Sadie away. She sure had looked different tonight, all mussed and flustered and embarrassed over being frightened of that bat. And beautiful. Her cheeks had been flushed by the heat, that awful paleness that washed over her whenever he came near gone. If only she would really look at him—meet his gaze. Of course, it was probably best that she didn't. He could get lost in her brown eyes….

He scowled, leaned down and scooped up a handful of water and splashed it over his face and neck. He'd best keep his thoughts on business. He'd no right to be thinking wishful thoughts about Sadie Spencer.

The letters ran together and the words blurred. Sadie shook her head, laid the book on her bedside table and rubbed her eyes. It was useless to try and read to stay awake.

She slipped out of bed and crossed to the washstand, lifted her long, thick braid of hair off her neck and coiled it on top of her head. If only there were a cooling breeze. Or a hard rain. That would break the heat.

Her mind leaped back to that day in the stable with the rain drumming on the roof and the lightning flashing outside the window. She'd been cold and shivering then. Of course, she'd also been facing Cole alone in that dark building, with no one to come to rescue her if she'd screamed. She'd been terrified. And then he'd left her the umbrella and his rain jacket and gone out into the storm. She had been there all alone and defenseless, and he had walked away.

I am not my brother, Miss Spencer. You've nothing to fear from me.

The words Cole had spoken her first day home flowed into her head, stilling her hands. She could hear his voice as clearly as if he were in the room. She shook her head and reached for her hairpins. She'd be a fool to trust his words. Still, she'd been alone, and he'd walked away. And then again, on the porch...

She held that thought close for a moment, then jammed pins into her hair to hold the coiled braid in place, dipped a cloth into the pitcher of water and wiped her face and neck. The water was warm. So were the floorboards beneath her bare feet.

Even a small breeze would give some relief. She started toward the window, spotted bats darting and swooping through the moonlight outside and changed her mind at the thought of one of the horrid creatures flying into her room. She'd rather be hot.

Weariness pulled at her. Her nightgown clung to her moist skin. She grabbed its long skirt and fanned the fabric to cool her legs, gave up the struggle, wet the cloth again and waved it in the air to cool it as she crossed to her bed. She'd made a fool of herself tonight, throwing Cole's suit coat over her head like that. But the way bats swooped and darted around, she couldn't tell where they would go next or where they would land, and if one got in her hair—

She shuddered, lifted her nightgown above her knees and rested back against the pillow. The cool, wet cloth she placed over her eyes closed out the dim light. Cole hadn't laughed at her silly behavior. He'd simply come to help her. A gentlemanly thing for him to do. But confusing. She wished he'd stop doing things that were contrary to her opinion of him. It made things more difficult. And proving her suspicions true would be hard enough.

Oh, Poppa, I'm trying.

She yawned, thrust away an image of Cole driving the bat away, and slipped over to a cooler spot on the bed. It would be all right. All she had to do was locate those ledgers.

Please, Almighty God... I have to...find the truth. Please...don't let me...fail....

Chapter Eight

The sun was up and shining in a clear, bright blue sky. There would be no relief from the heat today.

"Some…thing wrong, Sa…die?"

She turned from the window and looked at her grandfather being carried by Cole to his chair. Thoughts of the dream she'd had last night rushed into her head. Warmth crawled into her cheeks. "No, nothing, Poppa. Why do you ask?"

"You…sighed."

"Did I?" She resisted the urge to unbutton the collar on the embroidered waist of her pale green cotton gown and smiled. "I was wishing for the sight of a nice, dark thundercloud this morning."

"Me…too." He nodded and settled himself as Cole lowered him into his chair. "Too hot to…sit out…side."

"Or to work in the garden." Her grandmother reached for the sewing basket beside her chair. "I was going to weed the tansy and moon pennies today, but I'm afraid my poor flowers will have to fend for themselves."

A rush of thankfulness for the clear, alert expression

in her grandmother's eyes tightened her throat. Nanna was having a good morning. "I'm sure your flowers would like a nice, cold drink of rain, Nanna. They're looking a little wilted."

"Everything looks a little wilted." Cole straightened and tugged his sleeves into place. "I would welcome a rainstorm myself—even if I am taking a wagonload of clapboard into town this morning."

He made clapboard at his shingle mill? She looked at Cole, found his gaze on her and glanced away, thankful for the heat that would explain her flushed cheeks. Why should a dream make her so unsettled?

"Big…sale?"

"Yes. And we could have had another order equally as large in Olville, but they need the clapboard now. And we can't make enough fast enough to cover both orders."

We? He had a partner? A chair scraped. She turned her head slightly in order to see better. Cole had seated himself and was leaning toward her grandfather.

"Manning, have you given any more thought to purchasing the clapboard machine?"

Her grandfather frowned, shook his head. "Expen… sive."

"You can get a note at the bank to pay for it. I could make the arrangements this morning."

Cole wanted her grandfather to buy him a clapboard machine? All thought of the dream fled. So that's what he was after. No wonder he hadn't wanted her to hire a man to replace him.

"Don't like…debt."

She snagged her bottom lip with her teeth to hold

herself from telling her grandfather not to do it. Perhaps buying Cole the machine was the arrangement her grandfather had made with him for his care, but he didn't yet have enough money. So much for Cole's kindness. She fought off an unwarranted sense of disappointment. Guilt soured her stomach. If she had been here, there would have been no need for such a bargain.

"Why don't you give it some more thought, Manning? I wrote the man who makes the machines—a Robert Eastman in Brunswick, New Hampshire. We'll talk more when he writes me back with the particulars." Cole rose, slid the chair back by the game table and headed for the doorway. "The men are loading the wagon now. I'll be back from making my delivery in time to take you in for dinner." His footsteps faded away down the hall.

Did her grandfather signing a note to buy the machine have something to do with the missing ledgers? And what of the empty cash box? Should she ask about them? She drifted across the room, her long skirts swishing over the tops of her slippers, her ears tuned for the closing of the back door. What was keeping him? She couldn't—

"Sit down and busy yourself at something, Sadie." Her grandmother smiled, freed a hand and patted the settee cushion. "Come and help me edge these handkerchiefs. It makes me feel hotter watching you move around."

"It's too hot to sit, Nanna. At least when I walk about the air moves." She smiled at her grandmother then stiffened when she heard Cole's footsteps again, grow-

ing louder. He was returning. What did he want now?
She frowned and picked up the book her grandfather
was reading. *The Prairie*. The pages rustled softly as
she opened the cover. "I see you're reading about Natty
Bumppo's adventures again, Poppa."

"Excuse my intrusion..."

Cole's tall, broad-shouldered form filled the doorway.

"I forgot to ask if there is anything you need from
town, Mrs. Townsend."

"I should like some lemons, if they're not already on
Gertrude's list. Some cold lemonade will be refresh-
ing with supper."

He did their shopping, too? He certainly had in-
serted himself into the family's business. And her absence when they'd needed her was responsible. Her
guilt deepened. She shoved her dread of facing the
villagers aside. They would greet her with welcoming
smiles, but the knowledge of what had happened to her
would be in their eyes. The memory swarmed back.
She forced it away and handed the book to her grandfather. "There's no need for you to burden yourself,
Cole. I'm home now. I will do the shopping."

"Very well." He crossed the room and held out a
piece of paper. "Here is the list."

She drew back at the touch of his large, scarred
hand. Memory flashed. Her cheek prickled.

"Don't scream!"

*His arm flashed toward her. His dry, rough hand
landed against the side of her face, scraped across her
cheek. Her head snapped back. A salty, sweet taste
burst onto her tongue—*

* * *

"Sa…die!"

She swallowed, opened her eyes and looked down at her grandfather.

"You all…right?"

"What's wrong with her?" Her grandmother's skirts rustled as she rose and hurried over to peer up at her. "Why, Sadie, you've gone all pale. Are you ill?"

Her grandmother's hand touched her cheek checking for fever, dispensing comfort as it had so many times. The prickling sensation stopped. She drew a steadying breath and forced a smile, realized she was clutching at her throat and relaxed her hand, pretending to loosen her collar. "I'm not ill, Nanna. It's the heat…."

Cole's boots moved out of her vision. She glanced his way and watched him place Gertrude's list on the game table then head for the hall.

"I'll hitch Sweetpea to the buggy for you."

"Please don't bother. I'll do it when I'm ready to leave."

He stopped, turned and looked at her. She stared at the black beard, at the lips pressed so tightly together they had all but disappeared and fought back images of Payne's cruel face hovering over hers. *I am not my brother, Miss Spencer. You've nothing to fear from me.*

Silence stretched between them. Cole's chest swelled with a deep intake of air she could hear even from where she stood. His lips parted then closed again. He nodded and left the room, his boot heels striking hard against the wood floor in the hall.

He was gone. She stepped to the game table, turned so her trembling hand would be hidden from her grandparents and picked up the shopping list. *She had to go to town.* Dread tightened her stomach. "Well, it seems I shall be going into town today. Would you like to accompany me, Nanna?"

Her grandmother narrowed her eyes and peered up at her. "I would, Sadie, but I don't believe you should go. You said the heat was bothering you. Why don't you hurry and catch Cole and give Gertrude's list back to him, then go and lie down?"

She took a breath and shook her head. "I'm fine, Nanna. And the outing will do me good. Now, if you'll excuse me, I've a few things to do before we leave."

She hurried out of the room, lifted her skirts and climbed the stairs, her heart pounding, the list clutched in her hand. Perhaps she wasn't yet ready to face going into Pinewood, but she would manage. And now she wouldn't have to find the courage to walk that path. She would wait a short while until she was certain Cole had left for town, and then she would hitch up the buggy and drive to his shingle mill and get the ledgers. She would think of some excuse to give Nanna.

The shingle mill. His partner!

Her chest tightened. She stopped, pressed her hand to the pulse throbbing at the base of her throat and forced her constricted lungs to take in air. It would be all right. She would be safe as long as she was not alone. Nonetheless…

She crossed to her dresser, picked up one of her long hair picks and slipped it into her purse, then sat on the edge of her bed to wait. She knew for certain now. Cole wasn't caring for her grandfather out of kindness; he was being paid to do so. But that didn't explain the empty money box and the missing ledgers. He had some sort of scheme afoot. How foolish of her to let down her guard because of a silly dream.

And he had thought *he* was stubborn. Hah! He couldn't hold a candle to Sadie Spencer when it came to stubborn! Cole scowled and drew back on the reins. "Whoa, boy."

He set the brake and leaped from the wagon, tied Plug-ugly to the hitching rack in front of the wagon shop and strode toward the open doors. He understood that Sadie was frightened of him, but why wouldn't she let him help her? There was no reason for her to refuse his offer to hitch up the buggy for her. None. She didn't have to be in the stable with him. He would have hitched up and gone on his way while she stayed in the house. Maybe if she would give him a chance, she'd learn he wasn't like Payne. He was tired of telling her so.

He stepped into the barn, blinked away the momentary blindness caused by coming in out of the bright sunlight and nodded to the man fitting an axle on a wagon. "Morning, Carl. Nate here?"

"He's in the back." The wheelwright straightened and swiped his forearm across his glistening brow. "Hot enough for you, Cole?"

"It'll do."

And that was another thing. Horses were just like people. They could get fractious and out of sorts in this heat. And Sweetpea hadn't been used much since Manning had taken ill. What if the mare went mulish and took it into her head to act up? She'd tried to wedge him into a corner once. If she tried that trick on Sadie… He stopped and glanced back toward the open doors. He should have told her to bridle Sweetpea and snub her close while—

"Hey, Cole. If you're here for the wheels, I'm just about to start the small one. The others are finished, though. They're leaning against the wall over there." Nate Turner nodded his head to the left.

Cole corralled his thoughts, crossed to the wheels and ran his hands over them. Not a flaw or a burr to be found. "Good job, Nate."

The older man nodded, fitted a round piece of wood to the lathe and pumped his foot against the pedal, drawing the rope tight and turning the spindle. "I'm not used to doing fancy-type work. I hope they suit."

"The turnings on the spokes are exactly what I wanted. When do you expect to have that one finished?"

"Shouldn't take long. Quarter hour or so. I'd have had it done by now except for that extended knob axle you want made in it."

Wood dust clung to his hands. He brushed them together and turned to go. "I've got a load of clapboard to deliver. I'll stop for the wheels on my way back through."

He hurried out to the wagon, climbed aboard and slapped the reins against Plug-ugly's rump to start him moving. A quarter hour or so, plus the time it would take to unload the clapboard and then drive the wagon back to the sawmill, was too long. He would leave the load at the livery and rent a horse. He could come back and unload after he knew Sadie was all right.

"Good, girl, Sweetpea." Sadie stroked the mare's side as best she could from her confined space in the corner. "Move over, now." The mare snorted and tossed her head. "Come on, girl, move over." Not so much as a twitch. Obviously, cajoling would not work. She pulled in a breath and fanned her face with her hand. The heat radiating from the mare made the corner stifling. Enough was enough.

"Move *over!*" She placed the palms of her hands against Sweetpea's haunch, pressed her back against the stable wall and pushed with all of her strength. The mare stood. If only there were space enough to draw her hand back for a good slap. She looked longingly at her purse sitting on the grain chest by the door. If she had that hair pick, Sweetpea would move! Perhaps... She stiffened her finger and poked the bay with her fingernail. The mare's muscle rippled beneath her skin.

She glared at the stubborn mare, gritted her teeth, then reached up and swiped back a tress of hair stuck to her clammy forehead. "I don't want to hurt you, Sweetpea, but you leave me no choice." She reached under the mare's belly and pinched as hard as she could. The horse grunted and stomped her right rear leg. The hoof barely missed the toe of her slipper and landed solidly on top of the harness she'd dropped when Sweetpea had crowded her into the corner. Now what?

Tears threatened. She sagged back against the wall and assessed her situation. If the horse moved any closer her way, she would be crushed against the wall. Alarm tingled along her nerves. She couldn't move past the mare, couldn't climb on her back and dared not try to crawl out beneath her belly. If she brushed against one of her legs...

Perhaps Nanna would come to the stable to find out why it was taking her so long to hitch up the buggy.

Her spirits lifted with hope, then sank as quickly. It was just as likely Nanna would forget they were going to town. But surely Poppa would remember and send Nanna after her—if he had not fallen back asleep. No, she could not depend on someone coming to rescue her. She would just have to wait until Sweetpea moved and she could slip free.

It was so hot and still! Perspiration moistened her neck beneath the hair that had pulled free from the thick coil at the crown of her head. She ran her fingers through the long, heavy strands, searching for the missing hairpins. *A hairpin*. No. If Sweetpea reared…

Panic pressed in. She turned her head away from the mare in front of her and eyed the stall that formed one wall of the corner where she was trapped. If she could manage to turn… And if she could find a foothold so she could boost herself up and over… But if she fell, and Sweetpea kicked…

She took a calming breath, pressed back against the stable wall and inched around, careful not to touch the mare. Now to get out of here! She reached up and grabbed hold of the top of the stall wall, found a place to put her foot and boosted herself up.

The door squeaked.

Nanna!

The door opened. Light flooded the stable. She tightened her grip on the stall wall and tried to look over her shoulder. "I'm here, Nanna. Sweetpea—"

Boots thumped against the plank floor. "Ho, girl. Come on, now."

Cole.

Hoofs thudded. So did her heart. Sweetpea's rump and tail disappeared from her view. She reached her foot back down to the floor, released her grip and turned to face him.

"Are you all right?"

"Yes." Her voice quavered with the trembling that was setting in. "But I'm grateful to be free. Sweetpea had me trapped in the corner. She…wouldn't move."

He nodded, bent down and picked up the harness she'd dropped. "Next time, snub her tight to the post while you harness her. She can't back you into the corner that way."

He'd rescued her, again. An odd sort of tingling warmth hit her stomach. "I'll do that." She brushed a lock of hair that had fallen forward back over her shoulder and remembered her disheveled appearance. Heat crawled into her cheeks, though she wouldn't have thought it possible they could get warmer. She headed for the door.

"Do you want me to hitch Sweetpea to the buggy for you? Or will you be waiting until after dinner to go to town?"

She stopped dead in her tracks and looked back at him. "Surely it's not dinnertime?" How long had she been trapped by that miserable mare?

"No. Not for another hour."

An hour? The warmth in her stomach turned cold. "Then why—" She clamped her lips together, leaving the question unasked. There was no sense in letting him know she—

"Because I got to thinking about Sweetpea's little trick and that there would be no one to help you if she got you cornered."

The answer rolled off his tongue easily enough, but he sounded irritated. Had he realized she knew he'd not had time to deliver clapboards to Pinewood and return? Why had he lied about the sale? To make her grandfather agree to sign the bank note? She nodded and what was left of her coil slipped. She shoved the loosened knot of hair back toward the crown of her head. "I see. Well, whatever the reason you're here, thank you for saving me from my…predicament."

He shrugged and raised the harness he held. "Shall I hitch up?"

Her plan had been ruined. He would be at his mill now. She shook her head and the coil came wholly undone; hairpins pinged against the floor. Heat flared into her cheeks again. "No. I believe I'll wait and go to town tomorrow."

"As you wish." He pivoted, hung the harness on its peg, then led Sweetpea toward her stall.

His voice sounded strained. Was he angry? She grabbed the drawstrings, yanked her purse off the grain chest and hurried out the open door onto the graveled carriageway. There was a strange horse tied to the hitching post. Just what she needed, a caller— and she all dirty and undone. She looked at the porch but spotted no one. Good. Whoever it was had already gone inside. She could sneak upstairs and repair her appearance before she was seen.

She ran for the porch, hurried to the kitchen door and stepped inside.

"Oh my! What happened to you?"

She looked at Gertrude's startled expression and shrugged. "Sweetpea got ornery and trapped me in the corner when I tried to put the harness on her." She shot a glance at the door to the hallway. "Where is our caller?"

"What caller? There's no one here."

"Well there's a strange horse tied—" She whipped around, opened the door and stepped out onto the porch in time to see Cole mount and ride away.

Chapter Nine

It's only a path.

Sadie stopped behind the garden fence and forced her gaze to the hard-beaten, boot-trodden soil that stretched from the gate to the edge of the woods, so close the branches of the near trees hung over the weathered chestnut pickets.

Shivers chased up her spine. She wrapped her arms about herself and rubbed her upper left arm, found the hidden lump, remembered the sickening snap of the bone when Payne threw her to the ground.

Stop it!

She whirled and started back up the garden walk, the heat of the sunbaked slate warming her feet through the soles of her slippers. She couldn't do it. No matter how badly she wished to find those ledgers, she couldn't go into those woods.

But she refused to run, though everything inside her was crying to do just that. She was through running away. She'd been doing so for four years. She lowered her hands to her sides and clenched them into fists.

"You *will* conquer this fear, Sadie Spencer! You *must*. You have to be ready when another opportunity arises."

Her low, tense words hung on the hot, still air, quivering and useless. She turned onto the path to the stable and walked toward the hitching post at the end. Cole had lied about that big sale. He'd not taken a wagonload of clapboard to Pinewood as he'd claimed. He'd been riding a horse. But there was no sense in telling Poppa until she got those ledgers and could refute any lie Cole might tell to cover what he was really doing.

"Almighty God, please give me the courage to go to the shingle mill the next time I learn Cole is gone— even if I must walk that path. And please expose Cole's scheme to me, whatever it may be, that I might help Poppa. Amen."

An image of the horse flashed into her head. She could see it as plainly as if it were still standing there. A golden chestnut with flaxen mane and tail. Cole's horse was gray. She frowned and moved on to the stable. Why had Cole been riding a strange horse? And why had he *really* come back from wherever he had gone yesterday? The reason he'd given was ridiculous. Did he truly think she would believe it was in case Sweetpea had pinned her in the corner? Not for a moment! Though it would be nice if it were true.

She opened the stable door and stepped into the dim interior, paused as the memory of Cole standing there looking at her with Sweetpea's reins in his hands flashed into her head. For that moment she'd felt…safe. No. That was foolishness. She was letting her gratitude and relief at being freed from Sweetpea's tyranny run away with her imagination. She mustn't let Cole's act sway her from her purpose, lest she never discover his.

Still, it was odd that she hadn't felt frightened, only… nervous.

Sweetpea stretched her head out over the stall door and whickered, thumping her hoof against the floor.

Her thoughts returned to the task at hand, and she hurried to the stall and stroked the mare's nose. "Oh, no, Sweetpea. You can't fool me again with your pretense of friendship. Nanna and I are going to town—" she reached up and snatched the halter from its peg on the post "—and this time, you're getting snubbed to the post while I harness you."

The vertical blade screeched through the log as the pitman arm lowered the sash, chattered as the arm raised it again and the log carriage inched forward. Cole put down his pen and crossed to the office door, looking out at the sawyer running the saw and the joiner fitting the rough-sawn boards for the smoothing plane. The plank floor vibrated beneath his feet.

A frisson of satisfaction spurted through him. The mill was turning out sawn stock faster than ever. Simply having the sawyer take a cut off both sides of a log, then turn it onto one of the flat sides before he began cutting boards saved them the time and labor spent having to hand-edge them after they were cut, as was the usual method. And that idea had enabled him to lower the board-foot cost and still increase Manning's small profit because of greater sales. The other improvements he'd made had also proved worth both the time and money he'd expended. And, due to the changes he'd implemented, there were fewer accidents now.

He shifted his gaze to where four men worked with froes and mauls, draw shaves and planes riving out clapboards. He'd begun filling all the shingle orders at his own shingle mill so he could put Manning's shingle weavers to work making clapboards, and they still couldn't turn out the work fast enough to fill order requests.

But that machine could. If the clapboard machine was as fast as his shingle machine, it would turn out ten times the work those men could in the same amount of time. And the clapboards would all be of a size and superior to man-made ones.

Still, he could make no further plans until he heard from Eastman and learned the dimensions and installing requirements, but he hoped the water-powered machine would fit where the men now worked. If he didn't have to build an addition to hold it, they could have the machine in place a few days after it arrived. It wouldn't take long to teach the men to operate it. Then Manning's mill would have the advantage of being able to make superior clapboards faster than all the other sawmills in the area. *If* he could convince Manning to sign a bank note to buy the machine.

He shoved doubts away and strode to the open edge of the deck, skimmed his gaze over the workers picking up and stacking to dry the sawn stock that had been slid down the skids to the yard. He focused on the men who were loading already dried wood on a wagon. After today's delivery, he would have more money to put in the profit column—even after he paid the men. It felt good. Manning's business had been shakier than the floor beneath him when he stepped in to manage it.

He lifted his lips in a grim smile. Having put Manning's business back on a solid basis eased a bit of the guilt he carried for the hurt Payne had caused the Townsends—and Sadie.

Sadie.

The screech of the saw and the smack of the boards slapping against one another as they were loaded faded. He jammed his hands in his pockets and looked out at the distant forested hills. She'd had a smudge on her cheek. Her *pink* cheeks. And a piece of straw stuck in her hair that was half caught up in a skewed pile on her head and half hanging down her back. His fingers twitched. The shiny acorn color and the silky look of her hair had him hard-pressed not to pluck the piece of straw away as an excuse to touch it. And her eyes— He'd stood there hoping she'd lift her long lashes so he could look full into their brown depths, all shadowy with embarrassment and sparking with indignation at the same time.

He blew out a breath, yanked a hand free of his pocket and ran it over the back of his neck. She'd been mad as a hornet at that mare. But even angry, dusty and dirty, disheveled and disgusted as she'd been yesterday, Sadie was flat-out beautiful, with an inner dignity and queenly grace that set his thoughts to traveling down paths they had no business to tread. None. But he found them trotting along anyway. Heading for nowhere. Like now.

He frowned, turned and headed back to the office. He had men's pay to figure and record before he drove that wagonload of lumber to town. That should keep his head where it belonged.

"Good day, Rachel. Welcome home, Sadie!"

"Thank you, Mrs. Braynard." Sadie shifted the reins

into one hand and waved at the plump woman sweeping the board path in front of her cabin. The news of her return was out now. The entire village would probably know before she reached the mercantile. Her lips twitched.

"What is amusing you, Sadie?"

She glanced over at her grandmother and grinned. "I was just remembering how, when we were young, Daniel, Willa, Callie, Ellen and I would run as fast as we could from Willa's house to the Sheffield House to see if we could get to the hotel before the news of our coming reached Mrs. Sheffield."

"Sadie Spencer! You be respectful of your elders!" Her grandmother huffed, looked down and smoothed her skirt. But it was too late; she'd already seen her smile.

"I'm only being honest, Nanna. Daniel's mother is a kind, warmhearted woman, but she does like to spread news."

"Well, someone had to spread the alarm when Daniel led you girls off on an adventure."

How wonderful it was to have her grandmother acting normal. Tears stung her eyes. "You do Daniel a disservice, Nanna. He used to try and get away from us." She laughed and shook her head. "Poor Daniel, he never could have any solitude. I wasn't fast enough to keep up with him when he ran, but I was always right on his heels and would discover where he was hiding. He called me Quick Stuff." Memories bubbled up from a forgotten well of happiness. She'd had a wonderful childhood.

A wheel dropped into a rut, jolting her back to the present. She reined in Sweetpea at the end of Brook

Street, then made the turn onto Main Street, and the buggy rumbled over the Stony Creek Bridge. One of their favorite places to play…

"Oh, my. Look at that." Her grandmother grabbed the leather hold strap and turned her head toward the side of the road. "Mr. Dibble is enlarging his establishment. I shall have to tell your grandfather. He'll want to know all about it."

"Yes, he will." She drew back on the reins, leaned forward and peered beyond her grandmother at the timber skeleton of an addition being built on the back corner of Dibble's Livery. Two men were working on the partially finished roof. Another stood on a ladder, handing a board up to them. Two others were nailing boards on the sides.

She dragged her gaze to the ground and looked at the pile of clapboard waiting at the base of the new structure. Had Cole told the truth? Was this the sale he'd spoken of? No, of course not. This clapboard had to be from another sawmill. A man couldn't deliver a load of wood on horseback.

"Why are you frowning, Sadie? Does something displease you?"

Why *was* she frowning? What had she to be disappointed about? That Cole had lied? What had she expected from a thief? She'd let his kindness and his protective ways sway her good judgment—kindnesses he was being paid for! She straightened on the seat and shook her head. "No, Nanna. The sun is shining in my eyes. Shall we move on?"

She glanced at the road behind them to make sure the way was clear and snapped the reins to start Sweetpea moving again. As soon as she was finished with the shopping, she would go to see Willa and ask her to come to Butternut Hill and accompany her to Cole's mill. She had to get those ledgers before Cole had her believing his lies.

Chapter Ten

"Oh, my. The dining room looks lovely with flowers on the tables. And the tea cakes look delicious. No wonder your new restaurant is such a success, Mrs. Sheffield." Sadie stepped back from peeking into the dining room and eased the door she'd cracked open closed, lest one of the townspeople enjoying their tea or coffee notice her. "Callie wrote me all about it, but I didn't picture it being so elegant. I shall have to stop in for tea the next time I come to town."

"And deprive me of the pleasure of a visit? You'll do nothing of the sort, my dear child." Sophia Sheffield's hands gripped her shoulders. She turned her to face the bustling activity of the maid loading a tray with more cookies and cakes for the present diners while the cook prepared the midday meal, then pointed across the room. "You will come barging through that back door into this kitchen begging treats, the same as you girls and Daniel have always done."

"They never could seem to get enough cookies, Sophia. Especially the molasses ones." Her grandmother gave her a mock frown. "The brown cookies disappeared quite regularly from the tin in my kitchen."

Nanna had remembered what she had called molasses cookies as a child! And her eyes had been clear and alert all morning. Hope that whatever had been wrong with her grandmother was gone brought an ache to her chest.

"And from my kitchen, also, Rachel. As well as the white cookies that were Willa's favorites." Sophia laughed and shook her elegantly coiffed head. "My, that takes me back."

"And me." Her grandmother sighed. "How quickly the time passed."

"Indeed." Sophia led them to the far end of the large kitchen, out of the way of the cook and serving maid. "But we have our memories."

"Yes, we do, Mrs. Sheffield." Sadie laughed and moved to the eating table by the back door. "I remember you sitting us down in these very chairs and lecturing us about taking cookies instead of asking for them." She shifted her gaze to her grandmother and grinned. "And I remember receiving a few similar lectures from you at home, Nanna."

"Well, they never *worked*."

"Of course not." She giggled, feeling young and unburdened being in Callie's aunt's kitchen with Nanna again. "We children knew perfectly well that if we asked one of two things would happen—either we would be told to wait until after we had eaten, *or* we would be given one cookie each instead of the two or three we wanted. We all decided early on that the extra cookies were worth the lectures."

"Why, Sadie Elizabeth Spencer! I raised you better than that!"

She dissolved into laughter at her grandmother's feigned indignation.

"Evidently we adults all failed to impart that particular moral lesson, Rachel." Sophia's lips twitched.

"Oh, no, Mrs. Sheffield, you're wrong." She tamped down her laughter and looked into Sophia's violet eyes. "We all knew that taking things was wrong. And we were careful not to do so—except for the cookies." The laughter bubbled up her throat and burst free again. "We reasoned that since you had baked them for us, it didn't really count as taking what was not ours."

"A child's logic…" Sophia laughed and walked to the cookstove, pulled the teapot forward onto the front plate. "Well, you and your friends were wrong, young lady. Now, I suggest you run over to Willa's for a visit during which you repeat this conversation so you can both repent of your ill-conceived childhood deeds."

How kind Sophia was. She'd been longing to go see Willa and ask her to come to Butternut Hill. Did she dare? She cast a glance toward her grandmother. If she lapsed into the past… "That's a lovely idea, Mrs. Sheffield, but…I'll visit Willa another time."

"There's no time like the present, Sadie." Sophia lifted a tin of tea from off the shelf by the stove, turned and looked straight into her eyes. "You go on, dear. Rachel and I are going to have a nice chat over a hot cup of tea. I haven't seen her since they moved back home, and I've lots of village news to tell her."

The message in Sophia's beautiful eyes was clear: *your grandmother will be fine here with me.* Still…

"Oh, lovely, Sophia! I've missed out on so much

since Manning was taken ill by that seizure. Let me help with the tea." Her grandmother waved her toward the door, turned and reached for the china teapot on Sophia's stepback cupboard.

She opened the door onto the large, familiar back porch, uncertain of what to do. Perhaps she should stay out here and wait. In spite of Sophia's kindness, her grandmother might need her. She seated herself on one of the two settles that faced each other on either side of the kitchen door and looked around. How often she had played here on the porch with Callie and Willa. And beneath it.

A smile curved her lips. She rose and walked to the far end of the porch, braced her hands on the railing and leaned out to look down at the board they had slipped behind to sit in the dim light and listen to the footfalls overhead while they made plans and whispered their childhood dreams to one another. Except one. She'd never confessed to Callie or Willa the love for Daniel she'd carried deep in her child's heart.

She straightened and looked out beyond the hotel's stable, resting her gaze on the calm, flowing waters of the Allegheny River. One day the men who worked in her grandfather's logging camps would come into town and she would see Daniel again. "Please Almighty God, please. Don't let...what happened...have made me afraid of Daniel too. Not Daniel..." She would never marry him. That dream was dead. But she couldn't bear to have her friendship with Daniel ruined.

She caught her lower lip with her teeth and hurried back to the kitchen door. A muted burst of laughter from her grandmother and Sophia came through the painted wood, freezing her hand on the latch. She shouldn't interrupt their visit because she suddenly needed comforting.

A long gash in the top left panel of the door snared her gaze. Daniel had told them it was made by an Indian trying to chop down the door with his tomahawk. How he had scared them! Deliciously so.

The desire to see Willa surged like the Allegheny's waters during the spring flood. She shot a look at their buggy tied behind Barley's grocers. She had to make haste. It wouldn't take Lehman Barley long to gather the items on Gertrude's list.

She lifted her hems and rushed down the stairs and along the path to the graveled carriageway that ran beside the hotel, hurried down it to Main Street, waited for a wagon loaded with bundles of bark to pass and dashed across the hard-packed dirt.

"And this is the side porch. Joshua and Sally like to have their midday meal out here. Matthew and I join them when he's home."

Sadie followed Willa out of the kitchen door onto a deep porch cooled by the shade of a large elm tree. "You have a lovely home, Willa. It's so…peaceful."

"At the moment, perhaps." Willa laughed and shook her head. "I assure you, it is considerably livelier when the children and Matthew are home."

Willa fairly oozed happiness. Sadie looked around for a way to change the subject from a husband and children. "And who is this?" She leaned down and petted the dog that bounded up the steps to greet them, smiled and scratched behind his ears when he wagged his tail.

"That's Happy—Joshua's dog. He got him the same day Sally got her cat, Tickles."

A smile she'd never before seen settled on her friend's face. A happy, secretive sort of smile full of contentment that made her stomach tighten. She'd never know the joy of having children.

She took a deep breath, walked to the railing, looked toward Main Street. "This was all an open field when I left. Now there is a bank—"

"Owned by Callie's husband."

"Yes." *Stop talking about husbands!* She smiled to cover the revulsion the idea of marriage brought and slid her gaze to the right. "And the church. And this parsonage. All of them standing where we used to play puss in the corner…and touch wood…and I love my love with an A." Her throat closed.

"What's wrong, Sadie?"

She shook her head, gave a little shrug. "Everything is so…different."

"You're not talking only about the village, are you?"

Understanding shone through a shimmer of tears in Willa's blue-green eyes. "No. It's Nanna, and Poppa, and—" She stiffened, her defenses rising at Willa's touch on her arm. She swallowed back the sudden rush of tears that threatened and moved away.

"Stop it, Sadie."

Her heart squeezed at the hurt in Willa's voice. "I'm sorry, Willa. It's—" She stopped, looked down at her trembling hands and hid them in the folds of her long skirt. She couldn't admit, even to Willa, that she'd been alone so long with no one to care about her troubles or comfort her that a simple act of kindness made her come undone. No wonder Cole's actions had made her doubt her original opinion of him. She pasted a smile on her face. "I'm a little shaken by all I've faced since coming home. The memories…" She blinked her eyes and turned to look out at the field that was no more.

Willa stepped to her side, took her hand and tugged her toward the steps. "Come on, Sadie."

There was no time to protest. It was either hurry along with Willa or fall down the steps. "Where are we going?"

"To the gazebo. Last one there is a stinky old skunk!"

Her arm jerked as Willa dropped her hand and broke into a run.

"That's cheating!"

Willa glanced back and stuck out her tongue, laughed and ran on.

"Very well, Willa!" She lifted her hems and ran, the toes of her shoes flashing in and out of view as she caught up to her friend and raced on through the park next to the parsonage and up the steps of the gazebo. Willa clambered up them right behind her and they both collapsed, laughing and panting, on one of the benches.

"Oh, my, that felt good. I haven't run like that since—" She coughed, pretended to lose her breath.

"Me either." Willa shoved back the hair that had jostled free onto her forehead. "I never could beat you in a race, Sadie. None of us could. Not even when we cheated. But losers get to go first. So…" Willa rose and stood in the center of the gazebo floor, her shoulders squared, her hands held straight down at her sides as they'd been taught to do when reciting in school. "I love my love with an A because he is *amiable*. I hate him with an A because he is…er…*antagonistic*. His name is *Allen,* he comes from *Africa* and I gave him an *antelope*. Your turn."

She laughed and stepped to the center of the floor

while Willa sat down. "I love my love with a B because he is *beneficent*. I hate him with a B because he is *boastful*. His name is *Benjamin,* he comes from *Buffalo.* And I gave him a *buggy.* No pauses, I win." She wrinkled her nose at Willa and sat down.

"Well, I shall win this time!" Willa jumped up and stood facing her. "I love my love with a C because he is *caring*. I hate my love with a C because he is *cautious*. His name is…"

Cole. The image of Cole standing in the stable looking at her flashed into her head. How ridiculous! She ignored the skip in her pulse and returned her attention to Willa.

"…a *cracker*. No pauses! You can't beat me this time."

"I can if I'm able to name two gifts."

"No fair taking time to think!"

She hopped to her feet, feeling ten years old again. "I love my love with a D—" *Daniel* "—b-because he is *daring*. I hate my love with a D because he is *daunting*. His name is—is…"

"Daniel, Sadie. His name is Daniel. It always has been." Willa's eyes warmed with compassion. She rose and came to stand facing her. "We're no longer children, Sadie—you can say it aloud."

Not now. The truth of what was closed in. Bitterness washed the sweetness of Daniel's name from her tongue. Love was something that could never be for her. She raised her chin. "As you say, Willa. We're no longer children. And we're too old to play this childish game."

She took a breath, glanced back toward the Sheffield House and the block of stores standing shoulder to shoulder above the raised wood walk on the other side of the hotel's gravel carriageway. "I have to be getting back. Mr. Barley will have gathered up the items on Gertrude's list by now—and Nanna may need me. But before I go, I'd like to ask you a favor."

"Of course, if I am able to help, Sadie."

"Will you come out to Butternut Hill and go to—" she had no reason to offer for going to Cole's mill! "—Poppa's sawmill with me? I want to go there, and I haven't the courage to go alone."

"Oh, Sadie, of course I will. I'll try to come tomorrow or the next day."

"Good." She smiled and squeezed the hand Willa had placed on her arm. "Thank you. I shall look forward to your coming. Now I must get back to Nanna. Good afternoon, Willa."

She hurried from the gazebo and walked out to Main Street, feeling Willa's puzzled gaze on her all the way. Perhaps she should have told her she wanted to go to Cole's mill and why? No. There would be time enough for that when they got there and she had Poppa's business ledgers in her hands.

Chapter Eleven

Sadie ducked her head and hurried across Main Street, then paused in the shade of the hotel and skimmed her gaze over the line of stores that formed Pinewood's village center. Rizzo's barber shop, Evans's millinery, Hall's shoemaker and seamstress shop, Barley's grocers, Robert's apothecary, Cargrave's mercantile and Brody's meat market.

Every name, every window and doorway of the stores brought a memory leaping forward. A piece of her favorite candy slipped into Nanna's shopping basket, a length of hair ribbon tucked into the package with a new dress, the taste of stomach bitters, choosing valentines…

The storefronts turned into a watery blur. These were good, kindhearted people who had known her all of her life. She was safe with them. But the shame…

She started for the hotel's back door, then stopped. She had to stop hiding. She could not let what had happened rob her of a normal life any longer. She blinked her vision clear, set her jaw and climbed the steps to the wood walkway that stretched along the front of the stores.

"Sadie! Sadie Spencer, is that you? I heard you were back."

Ah, Mrs. Braynard had been about her work. But it was just as well. She forced a smile and turned toward the woman exiting Lillian Evans's millinery shop with a parcel in her hands. "Mrs. Colmes, how nice to see you again. How are Mr. Colmes and Judith and Susan?" *Please, let that distract her from asking about me.*

"They're fine, Sadie. Judith is married and soon to make me a grandmother. And Susan is teaching. She took over at the Oak Street School when Willa married. But Willa probably wrote you of that." The pride in the older woman's eyes gave way to sympathy. "It's so good to see you home, Sadie. How is your grandfather faring?"

"Poppa is—" her throat squeezed "—it's difficult for him to…manage things."

"I'm so sorry, dear. I know it's hard to watch someone you love suffer the ravages of ill health."

"Yes." She looked away from the compassion in Myra Colmes's eyes lest her next question be about Nanna and she start sobbing. "You've bought a new hat."

"I did. I saw it in the window as I was passing and simply had to have it. I'll be wearing it Sunday." Anticipation warmed the older woman's voice. "Will I see you in church?"

She shook her head, curved her lips into a smile. "No. Sunday is Gertrude's free day, and I stay at home with Poppa and Nanna."

"Oh, yes, of course. I should have thought of that.

Well, I hope I will see you again before you return to your teaching position in Rochester."

A gentle probe. She took a breath and let out the news. "I'm not going back to the seminary, Mrs. Colmes. I'm staying with Nanna and Poppa."

"Oh, Sadie, how wonderful! Rachel must be thrilled. She's missed you terribly. And Manning has too, of course. Well, I must be off. Mr. Colmes is waiting for me at the hotel." The lines around the woman's eyes and mouth deepened as she smiled and lifted her wrapped parcel. "Sophia's new restaurant is a true blessing. Frank used to be so cranky when I shopped, but now he goes and gets coffee and a bite to eat when he's through with his business. He loves their plum cake. Goodbye, dear. And welcome home." Myra Colmes touched her arm, then hurried off toward the Sheffield House.

She had survived. She was a bit trembly but unscathed. The knowledge of Payne's attack on her had been there between them, had manifested itself in Myra's sympathetic touch—but it had remained unspoken. No questions had been asked—except the oblique one about her future plans.

The tension drained from her. She smoothed the front of her gown and hurried down the walkway to Cargrave's. The bell over the mercantile's door jingled its familiar, friendly sound. She paused and took a breath. Everyone in the store would be watching to see who entered. She stepped into the interior, dark and cool after the bright, hot sunshine, and breathed in the blended aromas of leather, coffee and molasses that had always greeted her.

"Why, Miss Sadie! Welcome home. It's good to see you again."

The proprietor didn't say, *after so long,* but she heard it in his voice. "Thank you, Mr. Cargrave." She looked down to avoid meeting the gaze of the man standing by the scale and cash box at the end of the long counter laden with various tins and boxes.

"Sadie! Welcome home, dear."

She turned toward a woman hurrying her way from the dry-goods shelves with another woman following behind her and smiled. "Mrs. Wright!" She rushed into Willa's mother's open arms and fought back tears as she was enfolded in a warm hug. "Or, I should say, Mrs. *Dibble.* Willa wrote me of your marriage. I'm so happy for you." She stepped back and squeezed Helen Dibble's hands, shocked at the softness of them. They had always been so rough and dry from doing laundry for loggers.

"Thank you, dear. My, how pretty you are!"

"She is indeed. Welcome home, Miss Spencer."

She glanced at the other woman. Tall, slender, dark hair… "Miss Brown! How are you?"

"I'm fine, Sadie. And it's Mrs. Grant now."

"Oh, I'm sorry, Mrs. Grant. I didn't know."

"Nor could you. A lot has happened since you—"

The bell jingled. Ina Grant looked toward the door and went silent. Helen Dibble's hands tightened on hers, pulled her close. She glanced over her shoulder.

Cole.

That odd warmth spread through her at the sight of him, then everything rushed back. Her chest tightened. Everyone would be thinking of what had happened to her. She looked at the women, read the dismay and sympathy in Willa's mother's eyes, the curiosity in Ina Grant's, smiled and tugged her hands free. "It was so good seeing you both again, but I must hurry. Nanna is waiting for me at Mrs. Sheffield's." She snatched a spool of needlepoint wool from a nearby table and walked over to the counter before Ina could ask any of the questions that hovered behind her twitching lips.

"How may I help you, Miss Sadie?"

There was kindness and understanding in Allan Cargrave's eyes. She took a breath and spoke clearly for the benefit of the proprietor, Ina and anyone else who was interested. "I'm not returning to Rochester. I am staying home to care for Nanna and Poppa, so if you would open an account for me, please. And I'd like you to order Mr. James Fennimore Cooper's new book titled *The Pathfinder*. Please charge the book and this needlepoint wool on my new account, not on Poppa's."

Approval flashed into Allan Cargrave's eyes. He nodded and dipped his pen. "As you wish, Miss Spencer." The nib scratched softly across the paper as he wrote her name in his account book and added the items she'd purchased.

There was a respect inherent in the new name he called her. She was no longer the young girl who had fled Pinewood. She lifted her gaze over his bowed head to her reflection in the glass-fronted cabinet behind the counter, suddenly seeing herself with his eyes. She *wasn't* that young girl anymore.

"Thank you, Mr. Cargrave." She clutched the spool of wool and headed for the door, acutely aware of everyone watching her, especially Cole.

He opened the door and stepped back, then dipped his head in a polite bow, his black beard grazing his red shirt.

The ugliness of the past resurrected, and her new-found confidence faltered. She returned his polite nod, swept her long skirts aside and stepped out into the narrow entrance, wishing the Allegheny were in flood and the waters were lapping at the raised wood walkway so she could throw all the bad memories into it and watch them float away. Her lips curved into a tight little satisfied smile. She was getting better. Even if she *was* trembling like a leaf in a windstorm. At least she hadn't thought about running away to hide.

Of all the misfortune... Cole closed the door instead of running after Sadie to apologize. For what? Coming to the post office? He hadn't known she was in the store until he stepped inside. *The silence.* No one had moved or spoken or— They were still frozen. Still watching.

He dragged his gaze from the window, put on a polite smile and turned. "Good morning, ladies." He dipped his head the women's direction and strode calmly to the glass-fronted nest of pigeonhole mailboxes. There was murmuring and a stirring of movement behind him as the shoppers went about their business. Good. *That* was over. Except for the talk that would start to circulate.

He looked full at the stout, gray-haired postmaster, who was leaning on the shelf at the narrow, waist-high opening in the center of the glass box wall, unabashedly taking in the proceedings. *Poor Sadie. Poor him!* What would seeing them together do to his acceptance by the villagers? His fingers twitched with the desire to snatch the wire-rimmed glasses off the end of Zarius Hubble's nose. If he said one word about—

"That letter you've been waiting for's come."

The postmaster leaned sideways and pulled a folded paper from one of the small cubicles, tapping it against the palm of his hand. "I believe it's the first letter we've ever got from New Hampshire. Been waitin' for you to come in. I know you been anxious about getting it."

"A bit." He ignored the curiosity in the older man's eyes and looked pointedly at the letter. "Is there money due?"

"Noooo…"

"Then I'll wish you a good day, Mr. Hubble. I've got to get back to the mill." He held out his hand.

"You can't blame a man for trying." The postmaster grinned and handed him the letter. "Give Manning my regards."

"I'll do that. Ladies…" He turned and bowed toward the women standing by the dry-goods shelves, then strode to the door. The bell jangled his departure.

He trotted down the steps to the road and strode diagonally across to pick up his wagon at Dibble's Livery. It should be unloaded by now. He'd read the letter on his way back to the mill.

The clapboard machine would fit the space.

Cole shot another glance toward the place where the machine would sit, then turned the armchair he was working on onto its back, picked up the handsaw and placed the blade on the mark he'd made on the front leg.

He would move the benches and stools the men used now to the far end of the deck….

He drew the saw back to start the cut, then leaned his shoulder into the action, his thoughts switching between his two projects as quickly as his arm pumped up and down.

…and he'd build a new slide to roll in the bolt logs.

That would avoid a jam with the other unloading wagons.

The end of the chair leg fell off, and he moved to the other front leg and cut it to length. He picked up the short, wide board he'd sanded and waxed, nailed one edge to the bottom of the shortened legs, then attached the iron brackets David Dibble had made to hold it solidly in place.

Now for the back legs…

He turned the chair over, cut off both legs, smoothed the cuts with his fine rasp, then rubbed them with wax, careful not to touch the leather covering the padded seat. The chair was ready. All he had to do was measure for the hangers and have David Dibble make them tomorrow.

A grin tugged his mouth awry. If this worked Manning would— No. It looked good so far, but he wouldn't start celebrating yet. He picked up the chair and carried it back to his private quarters, went back for the axle and wheels, then tossed an old blanket over them all to keep out the sawdust that permeated every nook and cranny of his small living space.

The fresh air lured him back out onto the open deck. He leaned against one of the roof support posts and gazed out at the pond, listening to the water whispering and chuckling along beneath his feet. Perhaps if he could reduce the amount of money Manning would have to borrow, he could convince him to invest in the clapboard machine. The logging operations had been going well. And the sawmill had been making a profit. Small, but— No, there wasn't enough money to use for anything other than Manning's family's expenses and the men's salaries, though he hadn't yet figured the shingle sales this month. And they should have increased since he'd been using his shingle machine to make them. That might be enough to convince Manning. Yes, that might do it. He'd take the ledgers to his mill tomorrow morning and make the entries.

Chapter Twelve

It was jump or be jumped. Her chance had come. Sadie smiled, hopped her checker over her grandfather's and removed his black one from the board. "King me, Poppa." She looked from the game board to her grandmother, busy sweeping the hearth again. Her repetitious behavior was harmless enough, but she couldn't stand to watch it any longer.

"Come take my place, Nanna. I've just got a king. I'm winning."

"Not…yet." Her grandfather grabbed a black checker she hadn't noticed in a corner, jumped it over the three red ones she had left on the board and landed square in front of her new king.

"Poppa!" His chuckle warmed her heart. She looked at her now-lonely king trapped in the corner by two of his checkers and wrinkled her nose at him. "All right, I concede. You're too good for me."

"He always wins, Sadie. You should know that by now." Her grandmother smiled at her, then resumed her sweeping.

She rose and put her arm around her grandmother's

soft shoulders. "It's too hot for you to work so hard, Nanna. Why don't you rest a bit? I'll finish sweeping later, after it cools."

"Well…" The swish of the broom against the clean hearth stopped. "I am warm."

She grasped the broom handle and urged her grandmother forward. "You come and play a game with Poppa, Nanna. And I'll go to the springhouse and get some lemonade."

"Oh, lovely! I do enjoy Ivy's lemonade. She makes it just right…not too sweet." Her grandmother seated herself and slid a checker forward. "Be sure to bring a large pitcherful and enough glasses for Sarah and Edward, also. They're stopping by this morning."

Oh, Nanna. Mother and Father have been dead since I was three years old. She glanced at her grandfather, saw the pain in his eyes and hurried out of the room, carrying the hearth broom with her and struggling to hold back tears. She was becoming more accustomed to her grandmother's lapses into the past, but there were still moments when—

"Saaadie…I'm heerrre…" Willa came rushing out of the kitchen and crashed straight into her.

"Oh!" She dropped the broom and grabbed for the wall to steady herself. They stared at one another, then burst into laughter.

"I'm sorry, Sadie." Willa reached up and pulled her hat back into place. "Gertrude said you were in the sitting room."

"I was." She looked into Willa's twinkling blue-green eyes and leaned down to pick up the broom, sobered by the reason for her friend's visit. "I was on my way to fetch lemonade for Nanna and Poppa."

"Oh, good. That gives me a chance to visit with them a moment before we leave for the sawmill."

"No!"

Willa's eyes widened and her brows arched. "What?"

"I mean…I'd like to go to the mill right now—while Nanna and Poppa are playing checkers. I'll have Gertrude take them their lemonade, and you can visit with them when we come back." *Please, Lord. If Willa mentions the sawmill to Poppa…*

"Oh. Well, whatever you think best." Willa grinned and motioned toward her hand. "But I suggest you leave the broom behind. If you arrive at the mill carrying it, they might think you've come to clean up all that sawdust."

"Indeed." She smiled, ignored a twinge of guilt at not being entirely forthright with Willa and led the way into the kitchen to give Gertrude her message on their way out the door. After all, she was doing this for her grandparents' sake. And it was Cole's fault she had to be secretive about it. So why didn't her conscience ease?

Guilt rode her shoulders as they left the porch and walked to Willa's carriage. Should she tell her their real destination was Cole's shingle mill and why? No. Willa might refuse to go with her if she knew she was searching for—

"Does it bother you that Cole Aylward is managing your grandfather's businesses, Sadie?"

She froze, gaping at Willa, who was freeing the reins from the hitching post. *Cole was running Poppa's businesses?* Her stomach clenched. She snapped her mouth closed, put her foot on the iron rung, gripped the side of the phaeton and climbed in. No wonder Cole had taken the ledgers. He could do what he would, when he would, and her grandfather would be none the wiser. At least she now knew where to find the books.

"You didn't answer me, Sadie." Willa climbed to her seat and looked over at her. "Does Cole managing your grandfather's businesses bother you?"

"I'm getting used to the idea." Willa's eyebrows shot skyward again at her acerbic tone. She settled back on the padded leather seat, pressed her hand against her roiling stomach and stared straight ahead, chiding herself for believing, for even an instant, that Cole Aylward's kind actions had sprung from his heart.

Cole rode into the mill yard and eyed the horse and rig tied to the hitching rack outside the office. Must be the pastor needed more lumber for that tree house he was building for Joshua. Regret rammed a fist into his gut. He'd never have that pleasure. He had to have a wife to have children, and he wouldn't marry—not if there was a chance he might someday turn violent and hurt the woman he loved. Or the children born of their marriage.

He buried rising thoughts of his father and brother and slipped from the saddle, looped Cloud's reins over the rail and climbed the steps to the deck. A quick glance around told him Matthew Calvert was not in the mill. The clang of the sawyer's hammer against the iron dogs he was using to spike a log into position for the next cut rang in his ears as he strode to the office and opened the door. "Sorry I wasn't here when you arrived, Pastor. What can I do—"

"Oh!" Two women whirled about to face him. Willa Calvert, who looked upset and abashed, and Sadie, who looked…defiant. His heart jolted at the sight of her.

The saw blade in the mill started screeching and chattering its way through the log spiked to the carrier. He stepped into the office and pulled the door closed to dull the noise and shut out the flying sawdust. "Good afternoon, ladies." He glanced down at the open drawer in the desk in front of Sadie. "May I help you?"

Willa Calvert's cheeks turned pink. Her mouth opened, then closed. She clasped her hands together in front of her and looked at Sadie. He followed her gaze.

"I've come for Poppa's business ledgers."

So that was it. Manning wanted to check the accounts to see if they could afford to buy the clapboard machine. He smiled and stepped closer to better hear Sadie's soft voice over the noise of the saw. "There was no need for you to come after them. All Manning had to do was ask and—" A sudden flash of guilt in her eyes stopped him cold. Manning didn't know she was here. *She* wanted the books. Why? For the second time in as few minutes, that fist rammed into his gut. What did she think he was doing—stealing her grandfather's money?

"Nonetheless, I'm here."

Sadie closed the desk drawer and stepped over beside the pastor's wife, who looked decidedly uncomfortable. What had Sadie told her?

"If you will give me the ledgers, I will leave."

Sadie's voice was steady, but her hands weren't. They'd been trembling when she closed the drawer. He glanced down to where she had them tucked out of sight in her long skirts, then raised his gaze back to her face. Her eyes were focused somewhere in the vicinity of his chin. Would she ever *look* at him? You could read so much in a person's eyes. If she would give him a chance… He shrugged off that hopeless wish and shook his head. "I can't do that. They're not here." Her shoulders jerked and her back went as straight as one of the rods they used to roll the logs around.

"What do you mean they're not here? Are you saying you don't have them?"

Her tone called him a liar. His hands flexed. He could cheerfully have choked an apology for stealing Manning's money out of Payne had he been there. Maybe then she'd see him as his own person, not an extension of his brother. He sucked in air to quell his rising anger. "No. I'm saying the ledgers are not here. They're at my shingle mill."

"At *your* mill."

She was so angry she actually looked into his eyes an instant before her gaze skittered away from his and landed back on his chin. It shook him. So did the look of confusion that swept over Willa Calvert's face. He held back a frown and nodded.

"Why are they at *your* mill?"

He took another breath and a strong grip on his patience. "Because I'm filling all of the shingle orders there." Whoa! And he'd thought her posture was rigid before. "Look, if you think—" He clamped his lips tight and shook his head. No point in putting such thoughts in Willa Calvert's head if Sadie hadn't accused him to her.

"Let's go, Sadie. I'm sure Mr. Aylward has work to do."

He looked down at Willa Calvert's hand tugging on Sadie's arm.

"We might as well. My quest here is fruitless."

He scowled as Sadie yielded to her friend's urging and turned toward the door that led outside, stepped forward in time to open it. Sadie's unspoken accusations hung on the air like the sawdust drifting from the open mill deck as she swept by him and followed Willa down the steps.

His fingers clenched on the latch. There was no sense in following to hand them into the phaeton. Willa Calvert was already climbing in, and Sadie wouldn't want him to touch her. And he shouldn't. He looked down at his large, callused, *empty* hand. Fool that he was, he wanted to touch her hand too much.

The thought drove him inside. He stepped to the window and stared out at the rippling water of the pond, listened to the rush of water through the flume beneath the floor. Not only was Sadie afraid of him, she thought he was a thief. The thought sickened him.

What did he expect? His name was Aylward. Sadie would always see him through the prism of Payne's vile attack on her. Unless—he took a breath, raised his gaze to the forested hills beyond the pond—unless he could find Payne and bring him back to Pinewood to atone for what he'd done. It wouldn't change what had happened. Nothing could change that. How he wished he could! But it might make Sadie see him for who he was.

Help me, Lord, to find Payne that justice might be done and Sadie will know I'm not like him. Oh, God, don't let me be like him. The possibility knotted his stomach. It wasn't only for Sadie's sake he had to find Payne.

He strode to the desk, took out paper and unstoppered the inkwell. His search for Payne had slowed when he started his shingle business, and it had ceased altogether with Manning Townsend's seizure. He could not be gone all day with Manning depending on him to be his legs. But he could send letters to the authorities in the towns he'd not yet visited. It had been four years, but perhaps he could pick up Payne's trail and track him to his present location by the responses. He dipped a pen in the ink, thought a moment, then bent over the paper.

Most Honorable Sirs:

I am seeking information about my brother, who disappeared four years ago. His name is Payne Aylward, though he may be using another at present.

Mr. Aylward is a logger, robust in appearance and manner. He is tall (approaching six feet) with broad shoulders, black hair and beard, dark gray eyes and a broken front tooth.

If you have seen or heard of this man in your area, no matter how long ago, please write me, postage due on receipt, at the direction following my signature. I will tender a recompense of ten dollars for any information that proves to be true and useful in locating my brother.

Respectfully,
Cole Aylward
Pinewood Village, New York

He scanned what he had written, blotted the paper and set it aside to begin another.

Sadie gripped the hold strap so hard her fingernails dug into her palm as the buggy rocked across the rutted sawmill yard and swayed out onto the dirt road. "I don't know what to do now." She blew out a breath and glanced at Willa. "I can't go to Cole's mill and—"

"Certainly not! I'd like an explanation, Sadie." Willa shot her a look, then turned her attention back to the road ahead and urged the horse to greater speed. "You *embarrassed* me back there. I can't imagine what Cole Aylward must think of our actions. Sneaking into his office and—"

"We did *not* sneak. We walked up the steps the same as anyone." She huffed out a breath and released her grip on the hold strap. "And it's *Poppa's* office."

"Not while he is unable to run his business. Cole is his manager and the office is his to use now. And as for the ledgers…" Willa shot her another look. "Why didn't you tell me you were going after them? Better yet, why didn't you simply ask Cole for them instead of sneaking around trying to find them?"

"Because he's a thief."

"What?"

She grabbed for the strap again as Willa drew back on the reins. "I said, Cole's a thief. And a liar." The carriage stopped. She let go of the strap and massaged her reddened palm. "He has a scheme afoot to steal Poppa's money, or his businesses, or something."

Willa stared at her, shock and dismay clear on her face. "Oh, Sadie, are you certain? Cole seems so nice and honest and upright."

"So did Payne." Saying the name brought a bitter taste to her mouth. She stopped massaging her palm and wrapped her arms about herself, rubbing her upper left arm.

Willa's hand covered hers. "Does your arm still pain you?"

She looked into Willa's eyes, moist with tears, and shook her head. "No. It's only…memories…" Willa's hand tightened on hers.

"Is it still so bad, Sadie?"

"No. It's only that there are so many reminders here at home they strike unexpectedly." She took a breath and lowered her hands to her lap. "The nightmares are the worst. They're so…vivid." She shuddered and wrapped her arms about herself again.

Willa cleared her throat, snapped the reins and started the horse moving. "So tell me, what is Cole's scheme? How is he stealing your grandfather's money?"

"I don't know." She sighed and looked over at Willa. "That's why I need the ledgers, so I can find out and tell Poppa. Then he will dismiss Cole, and he'll never come to the house again." A hollow feeling struck her stomach. She took a breath, refusing to think of how empty the house would seem without him there.

"Is that what this is about, Sadie? Your fear of men? Of Cole in particular? He's very like P—his brother in appearance." Willa's voice was cautious, caring.

She stiffened, jerked her gaze from Willa to her home as they turned into the carriageway. "This is about saving Poppa's businesses, Willa. He is helpless. And you heard Cole—he is filling all the shingle orders at *his* mill. Who knows what else he is doing? I have to be Poppa's eyes and ears." *Cole is his legs.* She shoved the thought away and gripped the edge of the seat.

"Perhaps Cole has a good reason for filling those orders at his mill, Sadie." Willa reined in and turned to face her. "If you don't know what *scheme* Cole is working against your grandfather, how can you be certain there is one?"

She wiped moisture from her cheeks and thought about her reasons. "Why else would he be so thoughtful and helpful to Nanna and Poppa after what happened? I should think our home is the *last* place he would want to be. That my grandparents are the *last* people he would want to be around."

"I don't know Cole well, Sadie. But Matthew does. And he likes him very much. I do know Cole is thoughtful and helpful to everyone. He has been ever since he came to town. He felt terrible about what happened. He even joined the search for Payne."

"He probably wanted to help him get away." Memories swarmed and brought the acrid taste back to her mouth. "Not that Payne needed help. He managed to escape while Poppa was carrying me to the house and the logger was running to fetch Dr. Palmer." She climbed from the phaeton, turning her back toward the path leading through the woods. The memories were too strong, her emotions too raw to look at it. "Payne— I mean, *Cole*—is trying to get Poppa to sign a note at the bank."

"For what reason?"

"To buy him a clapboard machine. And he keeps insisting, even though Poppa has said no." She placed her hand on the hitching post, the warmth of the wood so different from the cold inside her. "And he lied to Poppa about delivering a large order of clapboards to someone in Pinewood the other day."

Willa shook her head. "That wasn't a lie, Sadie. Cole delivered a load of clapboard to the livery the other day. The day you came to visit me. I know because Joshua and Sally were visiting Mama at the time and they went out on Mama's porch to watch the wagon being unloaded. It was the second load of clapboard he'd delivered. The first was delivered the day before."

She stared up at Willa, her certainty about Cole's lying shaken. *Had* he come back to rescue her? The image of him standing in the stable holding Sweetpea's reins and looking at her flashed into her head. She tightened her grip on the hitching post and ignored the sudden traitorous hope that made her stomach tremble. "Did you see Cole deliver the load on the first day?"

"No."

"Did the children?"

"No. But we all saw the pile of clapboard."

She nodded, smoothed the front of her skirt, then pressed her hand against her stomach to ease its painful spasm. It served her right for allowing her wish for someone to protect and care for her to sway her common sense. "It had to be someone else, then. Cole came to the house shortly after he said he was leaving to make the delivery and he was riding. You can't deliver a load of lumber on horseback." She swallowed the disappointment and glanced toward the house. "Will you come in for some lemonade, Willa?"

"Another time, Sadie—if you're all right? I should get back and rescue Mama. Joshua and Sally are visiting her again, and as much she loves them, they *are* energetic."

"I'm fine, Willa." She stepped back, thankful to have left the subject of the Aylward brothers behind. "Remember me to your mother. And tell Joshua and Sally I am eager to meet them." She frowned and stole another glance at the house. "I don't like to leave Nanna and Poppa for long. Perhaps you could bring them with you when your husband comes to call on Sunday? I'll make white cookies."

"In that case, it will be our pleasure." Willa laughed and urged the horse into a turn, waved as the buggy headed back toward the road.

Sadie returned Willa's wave, then stood staring after the buggy and thinking of the long, empty years ahead. They would be penurious years for her and her grandparents unless she could think of another idea to get those ledgers and thwart Cole.

At the moment, that idea escaped her. But there was one from whom nothing was hidden—including Cole's scheme. She climbed the porch steps, rested her hand on the post at the top and looked toward the cloudless, blue sky. "Almighty God, please help me find the truth."

Chapter Thirteen

Supper seemed as tasteless as the sawdust floating on the air at the sawmill earlier. Sadie put down her fork and glanced across the dining room table at Cole, watched him butter another biscuit. Their confrontation at the mill that afternoon hadn't affected *his* appetite. Of course, he still had the ledgers. And now that he knew she was after them, he could do what he would with them. She had failed.

Her mouth went as dry as it had that afternoon when Cole had walked into the office and found her going through the desk. She lifted her glass and took a swallow of lemonade. Perhaps she should ask him for the ledgers right now, in front of Poppa. He couldn't deny having them. He'd admitted he had them in front of Willa. And she could prove he was lying about delivering the clapboard.

She put down her glass and took a breath, then swallowed back the words forming on her tongue as Gertrude stepped into the dining-room doorway.

"Begging your pardon for interrupting your meal,

but there's a logger says he has to see Mr. Aylward right away."

She glanced back at Cole, saw the look that passed between him and her grandfather. A problem at the sawmill?

Cole tossed his napkin on the table and rose. "If you'll excuse me…"

She stared after him as he followed Gertrude from the room. What would she say when he returned? She had to frame her request carefully or Poppa—

"Sa…die…"

"Yes, Poppa?" She looked his way and saw the concern in his eyes.

"Go…see." He dipped his head toward the hallway.

She nodded and laid her napkin beside her plate then headed for the door.

"Rachel…you…pray?"

Pray? Her stomach flopped.

"Lord God Almighty, we come before You to ask that if any of our loggers or sawyers are injured, You will heal them in Your mercy. And, that if they are… beyond healing, You will receive them into Your loving arms. We ask for peace for…"

Loggers. She hadn't thought of the loggers, only the mill. Fear burst upon her, settled in her heart. Daniel worked at one of her grandfather's logging camps. She took a deep breath and rushed across the hall into the kitchen. Gertrude was alone at the work table slicing cake for their dessert. "Cole has gone?"

"He's on the porch."

She nodded and hurried to the door, pausing as running footsteps pounded away down the porch. "The logger must be leaving." The door latch clicked and she stepped back. "Cole, Poppa wants—" She stopped, looked at the dirt-spattered man who entered and took another step back.

"Cole left. He told me to—" The logger blinked. A grin slanted his lips. "Hey, Quick Stuff. I heard you were home."

"Daniel?" Disbelief, hope, doubt and joy quivered in her whisper.

"For sure!"

Two long strides closed the space between them. Her hands were swallowed by his big, strong ones. *Daniel.* She searched his mud-streaked, bearded face for the boy she remembered. She found him in the green eyes smiling down at her. "Daniel…" Her voice wobbled. She gave him a shaky smile. "It's so good to see you again."

"And you, Quick Stuff." His hands squeezed hers. He studied her for a moment, then shook his head. "You've grown up as pretty and delicate as an arbutus vine trailing across the forest floor." He looked down at their joined hands, scowled and looked back up. "You're shaking."

"I know." She gave a little laugh. "I do that sometimes."

His eyes darkened. He glanced toward the porch, then looked back at her, his gaze piercing, intent. "Are you all right, Sadie? Cole being around isn't bothering you or…anything?"

The memory of what had happened four years ago hung between them, manifested itself in the compressed line of Daniel's lips, the rigid posture of his wide shoulders. Tears clogged her throat. Daniel had always been fiercely protective toward her and the other girls, in spite of their pestering him mercilessly. She hadn't even had a chance to tell him farewell when she left town because he'd been out combing the woods, intent on finding Payne Aylward and making him pay for what he had done to her.

She shook her head and smiled. "I've become accustomed to Cole's presence. He comes often to help Poppa. He's very kind to my grandparents."

"I've heard. Still..." His gaze drifted toward the porch again and his chest swelled with a deep, audible breath. "You send word if you need me, Sadie." He released her hands. "Cole told me to stay and carry your grandfather into the sitting room when he's finished his supper. Will that be long?"

"Supper!" She caught her breath. "I'm sorry, Daniel. I've forgotten my manners in the excitement of seeing you again. We're still at the table. Will you join us?"

"With all this mud on me?" He grinned, and his eyes flashed with a mischievous look that took her straight back to their childhood. "Do you think your grandmother would allow me to share her dining table?"

She returned his grin. "You could wash up. There must be a clean face somewhere under those muddy streaks."

He lifted a hand, rubbed it over his face and grimaced. "I must look a sight. I had to ride for Doc Palmer as soon as we got the men free. There wasn't time for niceties."

"Of course not. Are the men...all right?"

His shoulders lifted in a shrug that said more than words. "Can't say until they wake up or Doc has a look at them."

She nodded, saddened for the injured loggers, but

thankful Daniel was unhurt. "Poppa is waiting to hear what happened." She turned toward the door to the hallway, then paused. "I must warn you, Daniel, Nanna might not understand. She is…unwell in her mind. She slips in and out of the past, and even forgets who I am—though she seems to remember you." She tried for a cheeky smile, but her lips trembled and she wrinkled her nose at him instead.

"I'm sorry, Quick Stuff." He reached for her hands again and gave them a gentle squeeze. "Ma told me your grandmother was forgetful, but I didn't know how bad it was."

She nodded and stepped toward the pantry. "I'll get a plate for you. Nanna will do what Poppa wants, and Poppa wants to hear what calamity brought you seeking Cole. And after that we can visit."

"Don't bother with the plate, Sadie." He touched her shoulder and turned her back to face him. "I can't stay, much as I want to. I'm only here because of the accident. I had to let Cole know what had happened. As soon as I get your grandfather settled, I have to get back to camp and help clear up the tangle of trees. We're shorthanded now."

She swallowed her disappointment and nodded. "I understand."

"But…the next Sunday I have off, I'll ride into town to see Ma, and then I'll come get you and we'll go up to the big rocks and watch for deer like we used to do."

She couldn't quite match his smile. And she couldn't tell him she wouldn't go into the woods. She groped for an evasive answer. "I'd forgotten about the big rocks. Now, we'd better go in to Poppa. He'll be getting anxious."

* * *

Cole slid from the saddle, looked at the star-strewn sky overhead and frowned. He'd spent more time at the lumber camp than he had anticipated, and Manning was still sitting in his chair waiting to be carried to his bed. The man must be in misery by now. He *had* to get that chair finished. His frown deepened to a scowl. He'd have time to work on it tomorrow evening now that the accounts were current.

He wrapped Cloud's reins over the hitching rail, unfastened the bag lashed to the pommel and strode toward the house and up the steps. His footsteps echoed across the porch, loud in the quiet of the night.

The light from the oil lamp in the window lit his way through the dining room and out into the hall. He placed the bag out of sight at the base of the center table in the entrance and stepped into the sitting room.

Manning glanced up from the book he was reading. "How are…the men?"

"Doc Palmer says Morse will make it. He's not as certain about Simmons. He says if he makes it through the next two days, he should be all right." He scrubbed his hand over the back of his neck, willed himself not to look at Sadie and lost the battle. She looked tired, sad and beautiful.

"Need someone…take care of…them."

"Morse's mother is going to stay at the camp and nurse them both." He walked to Manning's chair, watched Sadie rise and go to the settee and urge her grandmother to put away her needlepoint.

"Paula Morse is…good woman."

"Yes." He dragged his gaze away from Sadie and leaned down. "I'm sorry I'm so late, Manning. I'll get you to your room." He lifted the elderly man into his arms and headed for the entrance hall, Rachel scurrying out the door ahead of them to turn down her husband's bed. He glanced back at Sadie, now sitting on the settee and removing her grandmother's careless stitches. Good. She'd be there when he returned. He took a firmer grip on Manning and quickened his steps.

"Sadie." Cole spoke softly so he wouldn't startle her, but he might as well have shouted. She jerked her head up, looked his way and rose to her feet. Ready to run from him? The thought tightened his chest.

"Yes?"

The tremble in her voice caught at his heart. He'd give anything to stop the fear she felt for him, but how did you fight a memory? "I'd like a word with you. About this afternoon." He stepped into the room.

She placed the needlepoint she was holding on the settee and backed toward the fireplace, stopped and stared at the bulging bag he held. "Is that…"

"Your grandfather's ledgers, yes." He pulled the two green leather-bound books from the bag, stepped forward and laid them on the game table. "I had intended to give them to you after supper, but, as you know, I was called away."

He glanced over at her, caught a breath at the tightening in his gut. She looked so fragile, so vulnerable. He ached to hold her, to comfort her. He took a firm grip on his emotions and rolled the empty bag into a tight cylinder. "You'll find the accounts are current. All transactions are entered up to yesterday's date."

He tried again to catch her gaze, but she was looking at the books with a bewildered expression on her face. "I will be happy to stay and explain them to you if that will help."

The puzzled expression disappeared, and her face went taut. "That is…generous of you, but it is not necessary. I helped with the accounts at the seminary and am familiar with how income and expenditures are recorded."

"I see. Well, that is fortunate." He dropped his gaze to her fingers, nervously toying with the button closing the lace collar on her purple gown. Was her fear of him making it hard for her to breathe? Would she never trust him? Irritation pierced holes in his compassion. "Your experience with the seminary's accounting should help you find whatever you are looking for." The vexation roughened his voice.

She lifted her chin and rested her gaze in the vicinity of his chin. "I'm certain it shall. And if I *do* find I have a question, I can ask Poppa. He will understand everything."

There was a threat implied in her words, but he couldn't begin to imagine what she was accusing him of. He'd done nothing but help Manning Townsend. His ire rose, overcoming his good sense. "I'm sure he will. Perhaps then he will be able to satisfy your suspicions, whatever they are." He lifted his lips in a tight little smile and dipped his head. "Good evening, Miss Spencer. And good hunting!"

He slapped the rolled bag against his thigh, pivoted on his heel and strode from the room.

Chapter Fourteen

He was clearly angry. Sadie watched Cole stride from the sitting room, waited until his footsteps faded away, then stepped to the game table and picked up her grandfather's business ledgers. The back door opened and closed.

She wrapped her arms about the large books, pulled them against her chest and walked to one of the windows facing the carriageway. She couldn't see the horse.

Her grip tightened on the books, her thumbs moving in small circles against the smooth leather. Cole knew she was suspicious of him. He'd said as much. So why had he brought the books? Because he thought she would tell her grandfather he had them?

I will be happy to stay and explain them to you if that will help.

Her nerves tingled; her body tensed. He hadn't expected her to understand the ledgers. That's why he'd brought them. No wonder he'd looked taken aback and angry when she told him she'd helped with the seminary accounts.

Horse's hoofs crunched on the gravel outside the

window and she stepped to the side. Cole rode by on Cloud, tall and straight in the saddle, his red shirt and brown twill pants silvered, his gray gelding looking like its name in the wash of moonlight. No golden chestnut with flaxen mane and tail tonight.

She wished she'd never seen that horse. But she had. And that gave her another puzzle to solve. Why had Cole been riding the chestnut when he'd rescued her from Sweetpea? And why had he come back so soon? The truth of where Cole had been and what he had been doing that day was linked to that horse. She was sure of it. She had tried to think of a reasonable explanation but had been unable to do so. Perhaps the answer would be found in one of the entries in the ledgers.

She looked down at the books, suddenly reluctant to examine them, wishing she could simply forget the questions that nagged at her. But she couldn't. She sighed, shifted the books to one arm, lifted the oil lamp from the table by the settee and crossed the entrance hall to the library.

Cole drove the last pin into place to secure the iron brace centered on the bottom back rail of the chair seat, laid down the hammer and gave the small wheel at the other end of the brace a spin. The quiet whir blended with the murmur of the creek flowing beneath the deck, the peaceful sound at odds with his mood.

He frowned, caught hold of the wheel to stop its spinning, lifted the chair upright and stood back to look it over, much as Sadie was, most likely, examining the books he had left with her. But she wasn't looking for mistakes—she was looking for deliberate theft. He was sure of that. Why else would she want the ledgers? Well, she would find neither theft nor error!

His fingers flexed against the chair and he rolled it backward and forward to make certain the axle turned the two large side wheels in unison, then wiggled the chair sideways and backward, trying to tip it over. The small third wheel angled out from the back balanced it perfectly. Manning would not have an accident due to a flaw in his design. And Manning's granddaughter would not find a flaw in his accounting.

He scowled and took hold of the chair's back rail, his fingertips brushing against the smooth heads of the studs that held the padded leather inset in place. Tomorrow night he would attach the gears and test the chair. If it worked right, he would take it to Manning the next morning. He snorted out a breath. What nefarious purpose would Sadie attach to his gift? She thought him incapable of any altruistic motive.

He pushed the chair through the office to his private quarters and draped the blanket over it, crossed to his bed and flopped down on his back, staring up at the rough wood ceiling. The wariness in Sadie's eyes, the way she backed away when he neared her, sickened him. All his life he'd seen his mother do that with his father. *He'd* done it before he'd grown strong enough to make his father hold his temper in check when he was sober. Nothing could stop his father's cruelty when he was drunk.

His body tensed and his hands fisted in memory. He'd taken a good many beatings to protect his mother from his father's drunken rages. And it had gotten worse after he'd started secretly making shakes. No one in Pigeon Woods would hire an Aylward, and making and selling those shingles was the only way he could earn money to get his mother out of the village and away from his father.

He opened his hands and lifted them, staring at the scars where he'd missed a time or two with the froe and maul, and thought about his mother's gentle touch as she'd doctored his cuts, the hope that would glow in her blue eyes as she'd talk about their secret. He'd have died to keep that hope alive for her, so he'd sneaked off and made shakes and hid the bundled wood shingles in the back of a deep cave where his father—afraid of closed-in places—wouldn't find them.

A bitter smile twisted his lips. The cave had been the perfect hiding place. His father had followed him a time or two trying to discover what he was doing, but he'd easily eluded him in the woods. He should have known that wouldn't stop a cunning drunk. His father had wanted the money from whatever he was doing to spend on his liquor, and that last day he'd waited for him to come home with a club in his big, meaty hands. If his mother hadn't called out a warning when he opened the door...

Cole curled his fingers and thumbs, studied his large fists and remembered the satisfaction of burying them in his father's distended gut, of landing them in strong jabs on his father's belligerent chin, then picking that club up off the floor and walking out of the cabin and back into the woods. He should have taken the beating.

I'm sorry, Ma. I'm so sorry. Guilt washed over him, soured his stomach and burned like acid on his tongue. He rubbed his eyes, trying to erase the image that never went away. He'd found her in a huddle on the floor, holding her stomach, her face swollen and bleeding from being battered by his father. It wasn't the first time he'd come home and found her bruised and beaten— but it was the first time it was his fault. He'd wanted to wake his father from his drunken stupor and beat him senseless, but his mother had stopped him, told him to take the shakes downriver and sell them as they'd planned and then come back for her. She'd said she would be all right, that the beatings would stop when he was gone.

God help him, he'd believed her. He threw his legs over the side of the bed and sat up, propped his elbows on his knees and buried his face in his hands. He'd believed her—and he'd been so afraid the fury in him would surpass his ability to control it and he'd kill his father, he'd done as she said. He'd kissed her goodbye and spent the night packing those shingles on one of the log rafts scheduled to begin their journey downriver the next morning.

If only he'd stayed home.

He straightened and blew out a breath to quell the memories roiling around in his head and knotting his stomach. He'd thought he'd buried them deep enough not to trouble him. But the fear in Sadie's eyes when he came close to her was so like his mother's when she'd looked at his father....

Did Sadie see something in his face he couldn't? He lunged to his feet, crossed to the washstand and leaned close, studied his image in the mirror. The dark gray eyes looking back at him from under straight, black brows darkened. The mouth, with its full lower lip, pressed into a thin line surrounded by a black beard. Curling black hair hung wild around his face. The bile churning in his stomach surged into his throat. It might have been Payne looking back at him. Or his father. No wonder Sadie refused to look at his face.

He jerked back, shoved his hand in his pocket and pulled out his jackknife, opened it and felt the edge with his thumb. It was good and sharp. He leaned toward the mirror again, grabbed hold of his black beard and lopped off a chunk.

Sadie gathered her long skirts and settled herself at the desk, opened the first book and read the words written at the top of the first page in her grandfather's flowing hand. *Camp One. Lower quadrant (120 acres) of Owings purchase.* She lowered her gaze and scanned the column headings. *Timber, Wages, Expenses, Sundries, Profit.* The timber cut was sold to her grandfather's sawmill. That could provide an avenue for theft.

She turned over the pages to reach the last entries and gazed at the writing that had changed to a bold slant. It looked like Cole, assertive and certain. There was a sureness about him that was comforting, if unnerving. It made her want to trust him. If only she dared.

She frowned and yanked her thoughts back to her quest. This wasn't about Cole or the image he conveyed or how he made her feel. It was about truth. And protecting her grandparents.

She looked down at the figures on the page and pursed her lips. How could she prove if Cole was altering the numbers? She had no way of knowing the amount of timber cut off the land. Unless…

She flipped backward through the pages, checking the amount of timber logged and delivered to the sawmill in the past weeks after Cole had taken over management of the businesses against the totals on her grandfather's pages. If Cole's amounts were consistently less— *More?* That didn't seem right....

Her brow creased. She checked the amounts again. The board feet of timber delivered from the logging camps had increased since Cole had taken over. Profits were higher in every camp.

How could that profit Cole? No answer occurred to her. Perhaps when she had more information she would understand.

She set the logging ledger aside and opened the one for the sawmill, glancing at the totals as she thumbed through the first pages. If Cole was stealing from her grandfather, the proof would most likely be found in this book.

If? The word stiffened her spine. When had she started doubting? She mustn't let that happen simply because Cole was kind to her grandparents—and to her. Whatever his purpose for returning early from wherever he had been, he *had* rescued her from Sweetpea.

The image of him standing there in the stable, holding Sweetpea's reins and pulling the mare away from her, swarmed into her head, and the odd sort of tingling warmth she'd felt that day returned. She shook her head to rid herself of the memory, blinked a film of tears from her eyes and bent over the ledger. She couldn't allow Cole's actions to undermine her determination. She must remember his motives were selfish ones and that she was her grandparents' only protection from him. "Lord, please help me to find the answers I seek."

She took a deep breath, skipped to the last page and looked at the balances. Everything inside her went still. She was right. Cole was stealing her Poppa's money.

The proof was there on the page. There was barely a profit. Embezzlement was the only explanation.

Her stomach churned. She rose from the chair, smoothed the front of her long skirt with her palms, then crossed to the window and stared out at the moonlit night. She had expected to feel vindicated, *elated,* not…well…not the way she felt. Though it was likely natural to be disappointed when you learned a person's kindness wasn't kindness at all but rather self-serving obfuscation.

She tucked a wisp of hair that had fallen onto her forehead when she bent over the books into the thick roll at her crown and turned back to the desk. She had asked for the truth, and she had found it. Now she had to figure out how Cole had worked his scheme so she could discuss it with her grandfather. Heaviness weighed on her spirit. She resumed her seat and thumbed backward through the pages to where Cole's accounting began, stared at the totals. A *loss?*

Her face drew taut. He'd stolen all the profits from the sawmill. Anger joined her snarled emotions. How *dare* he steal from her helpless poppa! Well, that would stop right now.

She squared her shoulders, pulled the oil lamp closer and leaned over the ledger to learn how he had worked his theft. The totals of the various columns matched those in the book every time she figured them. Her brow creased. She tapped her foot, turned to her grandfather's last entries and jerked back. A loss?

She held the page close to the light and examined the numbers for alterations, found nothing and turned back another page and then another and another. They all told the same story. The sawmill had been failing.

Business had been falling off and the profits steadily dwindling for the past year. It had operated at a loss for the three months prior to Cole's management. How could that be? Had her grandfather not been feeling well before his seizure? Had he been distracted by her grandmother's failing mind? Poor Poppa. She had not been here when he needed her.

Tears stung her eyes. She swallowed hard and closed the ledgers, trying to absorb the facts. Cole hadn't been stealing. He'd done the very opposite. He had increased business and brought her grandfather's sawmill back to being a profitable venture.

I had intended to give them to you after supper.... Her—not her grandfather. Now she understood why he had brought her the ledgers. He knew she thought him a thief and thus had brought her the proof of his innocence. He had correctly assumed she would never have believed any explanation he might have offered. And, had he given them to her grandfather, she would have thought her grandfather's assessment swayed by his need and Poppa's pride would have suffered.

Shame washed over her. Willa was right. She had let Payne's attack color her estimation of Cole, at least as far as him having a scheme to steal her grandfather's money. Was she wrong to doubt his sincerity as well? Were his kindnesses truly that? How could she know? There were still those unanswered questions about the strange horse.

She wrapped her arms about herself and rubbed her left arm, her fingertips massaging the hidden lump. The sale of two wagonloads of clapboard to Dibble's Livery were duly recorded in the ledger, one on the day he'd told them about the sale and one on the day after.

It was delivering the clapboards himself he had lied about. And you couldn't trust a liar. No matter how much you wanted to.

Chapter Fifteen

It was getting dark. Cole tugged off his dusty red work shirt, brushed the sawdust from his pants and hurried to the washstand. He was late again. But Manning's chair was finished. He'd taken time to attach the gears even after the long afternoon spent ironing out the resulting effects of the accident with the jobber at camp two. And that was worth the tardiness. Manning wouldn't mind a bit.

The water was lukewarm. He scrubbed his soapy hands over his skin, felt the slight cleft in his chin and frowned. His face felt strange without the beard—like it belonged to someone else. He leaned close over the washbowl, dipped his cupped hands in the water and splashed it on his face and neck. Water slid down his forearms and dripped off his elbows.

He toweled off and opened his eyes, looked askance at his reflection in the mirror. No hair fell against his neck, and his face looked naked. And pale. At least the lower half did. His forehead and cheekbones were as brown as the leather on Manning's chair.

Thankfully, the collar on his new blue shirt would

hide his bare neck. He picked up the pair of gentleman's grooming brushes he'd bought from Joe Fabrizio that morning after getting his hair cut and his hacked-up beard shaved off, hefted them and frowned. They felt light, smooth, foreign. He was used to wielding tools with hard, thick wood handles attached to jagged teeth or sharp edges. And he was a sight more comfortable handling them.

A grin slanted across his lips, erased the frown creases from his forehead. It had been years since he'd seen his ears. They'd been buried under his wild, curly black hair for as long as he could remember. Now there was just a short cap of wavy black hair and some long sideburns around them. It was a good thing they didn't stick out like Charley Whitewater's did.

He swiped the brushes over the hair at his temples and above his ears the way the barber had that morning. Another stroke down the back of his head smoothed the hair waving at the nape of his neck and grazing his collar. Done.

Satisfaction surged. There was nothing of Payne looking back at him now—except the dark gray eyes, and there wasn't anything he could do to change them.

He put the brushes on the wash table, opened a bottle and splashed a bit of witch hazel into his palm, rubbing his hands together, then swiping them over his bare face. Would the haircut and lack of beard enable Sadie to look at him? To *see* him for who he was? Not that that mattered so much. He just didn't want to see that fear in her eyes any longer. He wanted to put the memory of Payne's deed and his father's cruelty behind him.

If he could.

* * *

Sadie roamed around the sitting room, stopped in front of the mantel and fussed with the vase of tansy, moon wort and sweet william her grandmother had brought in from her garden that afternoon. She slid the pewter candlesticks sitting at the ends of the mantel closer to the vase, then moved them back again and stepped over to look out the window. Dusk had given way to nightfall. It was close to her grandparents' time to retire. Where was Cole?

The nervous tension that had taken up residence in her stomach increased. He'd arrived early that morning and had left before she'd come downstairs. And he'd sent a mill worker to care for Poppa at dinner and supper. Had her suspicious, ungrateful behavior caused him to stay away? Was it a message that he was tired of the way she treated him and would no longer care for her grandfather or manage the businesses? Perhaps that was the real reason he had brought back the ledgers—because he was through helping them. If so, it would be her fault. What if the sawmill failed and the logging camps closed? What if Cole didn't come?

Her stomach contracted in a painful spasm. She lifted her hands and rubbed at the ache in her temples, straining to hear the click of the back door opening and closing over her grandfather's voice. If she talked to Cole before he came to the sitting room, perhaps she could undo the damage she'd wreaked. *Please help me, Lord. Poppa needs Cole.* That truth had settled deep. Cole was much more to her grandfather than a strong back and a pair of strong arms. How glibly she had spoken of hiring someone to take his place!

Where *was* he? The moon and stars were out. How

would she get her grandfather to bed? Surely Cole wouldn't leave him helpless… No. He was conscientious about that. Oh, she couldn't simply stand here stewing about things a moment longer! She had to *do* something.

She whirled away from the window and walked over to where her grandfather sat reading aloud to her grandmother, touched his shoulder and forced a smile when he looked up. "It's a lovely evening. I'm going outside for a breath of air."

"It's dark, Sadie."

"I know, Nanna." She rested her other hand on her grandmother's plump shoulder and leaned down to kiss the frown from her forehead. "I'll be all right."

"Very well. But don't stay out long."

Her heart squeezed with thanksgiving at the bright awareness in her grandmother's eyes. "I won't, Nanna." She avoided her grandfather's gaze. He was too good at reading her state of mind.

The kitchen was empty and Gertrude's bedroom door was closed. She took the old straw hat her grandmother wore when she worked in the garden off its peg, settled the hat over the thick roll of hair at her crown, tugged it down as far as she could for protection against any bats that might be flying around and stepped out onto the porch. Balmy evening air caressed her face and her arms left bare below the softly puffed short sleeves of her blue-and-white-striped cotton gown.

How lovely if her life could be as serene and calm as the night seemed. But there was nothing serene about trying to find out the truth. The facts contradicted one another. There was no denying the figures in those ledgers. Cole had saved her grandfather's business. And he was not stealing money. But there was also the horse. Cole had lied about delivering that load of clapboard. If only she could find the answer to that horse!

Her long skirts swished quietly as she walked to the steps, the sound blending with the chirping of crickets, the rustle of some small creature in the flowerbeds and the whir of an owl's wings as it swooped low to the ground, then soared off into the night.

She moved down the steps to the moonlight-dappled stone path and walked to the garden bench, took hold of the back and looked toward the fence and the wooded, hard-trod path beyond the security of the weathered pickets. Where was he? He was supposed to be here. Cole might be a liar and an…an opportunist, but he had never forgotten her grandfather. Had something prevented him from coming?

Worry sprouted, took root. Perhaps he was hurt or injured. The workers at the sawmill had gone home long ago. There would be no one to help him. With those saws… He could be bleeding….

She caught her breath, glanced over her shoulder at the oil lamp left burning in the dining room window to light Cole's way to the house, then looked back at the path. No. She couldn't do it. She hadn't the courage. And there was no reason. She was being foolish to let her imagination carry her thoughts along that way.

A chill prickled the flesh on her upper arms. *Let him come, Lord. Let Cole be all right. Please let him be all right.*

The moon slipped behind a cloud, and darkness settled around her. The night creatures stilled. She tipped her head back and looked up at the stars, trying to shake the image of Cole lying bleeding on the sawmill deck from her mind, but it refused to be dislodged.

Please, Lord...I can't walk that path. Tears stung her eyes. She glanced again at the lamp, drew a shuddering breath and turned toward the house. Cole mustn't suffer or bleed to death because of her cowardice. She would tell Poppa of her concern, get some clean towels and then ride Sweetpea down the road to the mill. She wouldn't go on the path. And she would not dismount if Cole were well.

An odd sort of whispery rumble came from the woods. She paused. It sounded like...*wheels.* Yes, rather like buggy wheels rolling over hard-packed dirt, only quieter. Now what could—

A man in a blue shirt, pushing a barrow in front of him, stepped out from the trees.

She gasped and whirled to run.

"Sadie?"

Cole? He was all right. *Thank You, Lord.* She took a breath to calm her racing pulse and turned. "You're wearing a blue shirt." An inane thing to say. It sounded like an accusation. But he always wore red shirts. Loggers did. "And you've no lamp." More silliness. Heat climbed her neck, spread warmth across her cheeks.

"I couldn't manage one with the chair. I'm sorry I frightened you. I'd have whistled had I known you were outside." He rolled the strange-looking barrow through the gate and onto the garden path, the wheels bumping against the stones.

"I came out to—" *Chair?* "You were late..." She stared at what she'd thought a barrow of some sort. It *was* a chair. With *wheels* on it. She looked up to ask about the strange thing and promptly lost her train of thought. Where was his long hair?

"I'm sorry for that. I lost track of time while I was finishing this." He stopped in front of her. "I hope Manning isn't too uncomfortable?"

And his beard was gone. No wonder she hadn't recognized him. "What? Oh. No…" She shook her head and looked down at the odd chair to keep from staring. "Poppa's reading to Nanna." Her gaze slid back to his clean-shaven face of its own accord. "When did you—" The heat climbed into her cheeks again at the slip of her tongue. "—I mean, what's this strange object?" She gave a flustered little wave toward the thing between them, thankful for the darkness that hid her blush at her rudeness.

"It's a surprise for Manning."

"A chair with wheels?"

"Yes."

"But what—" She bit off the question, annoyed by her runaway tongue.

"You'll find out when I get it inside."

"Yes, of course. I didn't mean to pry." She spun about and started up the path to the house. "Perhaps I can open the door for you?"

He replied, but his low voice blended into the rumble of the wheels on the path behind her and she was too discomposed to ask him to repeat his answer. She hurried up the steps and across the porch to open the dining room door and stole a glance at Cole as he carried the strange-looking chair inside. She barely recognized him without his wild, curly hair and black beard. He looked younger and…handsome. Of course, it was hard to see him well outside in the dark, or here in the dim light given by the lamp in the window.

She closed the door, tossed the straw hat on the server and smoothed back her hair as she walked to the hallway, Cole following behind with the chair. And what did his appearance matter anyway? Nothing. It was only that the change was so stark and surprising. She frowned and kept her gaze fastened straight ahead as they passed the stairway. She'd been rude enough with her staring.

The wheels of the chair whispered against the floor and Cole's boots thudded in rhythm behind her. Why had he brought that odd chair for Poppa? Of what use was the ugly thing? She circled around the center table in the entrance to give him room, glanced down at the rolling chair as they came back together and jerked to a halt.

He stopped beside her. "What's wrong?"

"Nothing. It's—" She swallowed hard against the sudden lump in her throat and rubbed her hand over a swelling tightness in her chest. "—it's just…I understand now. The chair, I mean." She reached out and touched a wheel. "Poppa will be able to—" Tears welled. She gulped them back, shook her head and ran her fingertips over the smooth, waxed wood. The chair was beautiful. *Beautiful.*

"It's an experiment, Sadie. Don't expect too much. I don't know if it will even work." Cole's voice was pitched low, his tone cautionary.

She drew in a breath and lifted her chin. She'd caught hold of his vision and she wouldn't let him rob her of the hope of it. "Of course it will. It's a perfectly *wonderful* idea."

She walked to the sitting room doorway, smiled when her grandparents looked her way. *Oh, Poppa, wait until you see...* Her smile wobbled. "Cole is here."

There was movement behind her. She stepped aside, watched her grandfather's eyes shift from her to Cole, then narrow in bafflement when he glanced at the chair.

"Why, Cole!" Her grandmother huffed and rose from the settee. "What is that...*thing?* I don't want that in my sitting room." She made shooing motions with her small hands. "Take it outside."

Her grandfather leaned forward and caught hold of one of her grandmother's hands. "Let...be, Rachel. I want to...see it." The starch went out of her grandmother's spine.

"Oh, very well, Manning. But then Cole must take the ugly thing away. I can't imagine what Mother would say if she saw it in here." Her grandmother gave another huff, resumed her seat and picked up her needlepoint.

Her grandfather looked at her, a silent message in his eyes that moved her to stand beside her grandmother while he turned his attention back to Cole.

"What...sort of...con...traption is...that?"

"The sort that will work, I hope."

Please grant it, Lord. She watched her grandfather's face as Cole pushed the chair across the room, swallowed hard when his eyes widened and brightened with understanding. Her heart thudded as he lifted his big, work-worn hand and touched one of the wheels.

"You...made this...Cole?"

The gruffness in his voice brought the lump back to her throat.

"Nate Turner made the wheels. And David Dibble made the braces."

"But you…planned it…and…made the…rest." It was a statement, not a question. Her grandfather cleared his throat and slapped his palm on the rim of the wheel. "How's it…work?"

"Let's get you in it, and I'll show you."

She held her breath as Cole lifted her grandfather into the chair and settled his flaccid foot on the board between the front legs, then tapped his finger beside it. "You put your other foot here. Good. Now…" He stepped to the side and rested his hand on the wooden handle sticking up beside the right arm. "This lever works the gears that propel the chair. You pull it to go forward and push it to go backward. Take hold and give it a try."

Her grandfather leaned over the chair arm and examined the gears, then grasped the lever with his good hand.

I don't know if it will even work.

She couldn't watch. She closed her eyes. *Please, Lord…*

There was a clicking sound, then another and another that settled into a rhythm.

"Well, *gracious!*"

Her grandmother's shocked voice mixed with her grandfather's happy chortle and a deep chuckle. Cole was laughing. The chair must be working. She opened her eyes. Poppa was propelling himself across the room in the rolling chair, his face a picture of pure joy. Tears gushed. A sob caught in her throat. Her poppa could move around by himself again. He no longer had to sit in one place and wait for someone to carry him where he needed to go, and Cole had made it possible.

She blinked the tears from her eyes and looked over

at Cole, standing straight and tall and watching her grandfather move around in the rolling chair. His expression was almost as joyous as Poppa's, except there was a bit of cautiousness in it. And he *was* truly handsome. In that blue shirt, with his hair cut and his beard gone, he didn't look at all like— His gaze shifted. He'd caught her staring at him again! She mouthed "Thank you" and looked away, hoping he'd think the heat spreading across her cheeks was from excitement.

Her grandfather stopped the chair in front of the wall and looked over the arm at the mechanism that worked it. "How…turn it?"

"The pin." Cole strode across the room and crouched down beside the chair, then tapped something.

She rose on tiptoe to see over his broad shoulders and watched the movement of his hands. He had hardworking, helpful hands, not cruel, hurtful ones like his brother. Something hard and tight inside her released. She pressed her hands against her abdomen, caught her breath. She'd been so wrong.…

"This pin holds the axle so the wheels turn together. When you pull out the pin, only the right wheel turns and the chair moves in a circle."

"Ah." Her grandfather nodded, smiled. "Cle…ver." He yanked the pin and pulled the lever. The chair turned. He put the pin back in place, swiped his hand across his eyes and held it out to Cole. "Thank…you, son."

"My pleasure, sir."

Her grandmother rose, bustled across the room and tugged Cole's sleeve, kissed his cheek when he bent down. "Thank you, Cole."

He straightened, touched his cheek and smiled. "Thank *you,* Mrs. Townsend."

Her grandmother's face creased into a smile. She patted Cole's arm, then ran her pudgy hand over one of the chair's wheels, her over-bright eyes twinkling. "And lest there be any doubt, you may leave the chair."

Oh, Nanna, you understand. Sadie's heart swelled, and her throat closed. She caught her lower lip between her teeth and looked down at the floor, fighting for control.

"I'm…tired, Cole. Too much…excitement. Go to… bed…now." The chair clicked. Her grandmother's skirts swished as they headed toward the hall. Cole followed.

"Good…night, Sa…die."

She swallowed hard and smiled, afraid to run and hug her grandfather as she longed to do lest she start bawling. "Good night, Poppa. Good night, Nanna."

She held her place until the room was empty, then buried her face in her hands and let the tears come. When she gained control, she took a breath to steady herself and walked across the hall to the library.

Cole closed Manning's bedroom door and grinned. The chair had worked better than he had dared to hope. Manning was reveling in his new freedom. He'd even refused—

"May I have a word with you, Cole?"

His pulse leaped at the sound of Sadie's soft voice, and he frowned at the unwanted reaction. He had no business being interested in any woman, especially Sadie. "Yes, of course."

"Thank you." Her long skirts rustled.

He turned and followed her toward the sitting room

trying to ignore the graceful way she moved, remembering how her long hair had come free of its restraints and tumbled down her back that day in the stable. He glanced at her waist, so small he could span it with his hands, and stopped walking. It was best to keep space between them. Sadie Spencer drew him in a powerful way.

She stopped, turned and looked at him—straight up into his eyes, just the way he'd wanted. His heart slammed against his chest wall so hard it made him cough. He looked into the depths of her beautiful brown eyes and hated himself for his thudding heart and thundering pulse, for cutting his hair and shaving off his beard, for ever following her into the room. He clenched his hands, hard put to keep from reaching out and drawing her into his arms to taste her full, rose-colored lips.

"I want to apologize, Cole. I've been judgmental and inhospitable in the face of your considerate kindness to Poppa and Nanna, and that was wrong of me. Very wrong…"

Did she have to look so contrite? So beautiful? His hands flexed. He shoved them into his pockets. "But understandable in the face of my brother's actions."

She stiffened, looked down and expelled a breath.

That had come out far from the way he'd intended it. Where was his considerate kindness now? He looked at the way she'd wrapped her arms around herself like a shield, at her delicate hand rubbing her upper left arm and wished he could take back the words—wished he had been in Pinewood four years ago to protect her from Payne. "What I meant to say was—I've never blamed you for distrusting me, Sadie."

His words drew her gaze back up to meet his, and

his heart slammed against his ribs again. His gut tightened, twisted into a knot at the cloud that shadowed her eyes. She looked so vulnerable.

"Nonetheless, I was wrong to judge you by your brother's…behavior. And I'm sorry for doing so."

She stepped to the lamp stand at the end of the settee, picked up something and came back to stand in front of him. He glanced down at the green ledgers in her hands.

"Thank you for helping Poppa, Cole. I know, now, that you saved his sawmill business and prospered the logging camps as well." She held the ledgers out to him. "You'll be needing these. Please take them back to the mill. And please, take adequate compensation for the work you do. I noticed that you have taken no wages thus far."

"I want no wages." His voice was gruff, the words more brusque than he intended, but she'd touched a sore spot.

"I don't understand." A tiny vertical frown line formed between her delicately arched brows. "It's only fair. I'm certain Poppa would insist."

He shook his head. "My compensation is in making up, in a small measure, for the pain my brother caused you and your grandparents. I wish I could change what Payne did, Sadie, but I cannot. *This* is all I can do." He took hold of the ledgers, careful not to touch her hands, and turned to leave before he said more than he ought.

"Cole…"

"Yes?" He tucked the ledgers under his right arm, sucked in air and looked back at her. There were tears in her eyes. They might as well have been knives the way they pierced his heart.

"What Payne…did—" Her throat worked, her hand

rubbed her arm, and everything in him wanted to hold her, to comfort her, to take away the hurt of the past four years. "—it's not your fault." She blinked her eyes and smiled, but her lips trembled. "Thank you for your kindness, and for making the rolling chair for Poppa."

He clenched his jaw and nodded, then looked away from the temptation she presented and headed for the door.

The curtains fluttered, flapped and snapped in the rising wind. The flame in the oil lamp flickered. Sadie settled her nightgown on her shoulders, shook out the long skirt, then slid the lamp out of the direct draft and glanced toward the window. The stars had disappeared. A storm was brewing.

She snatched the ribbon off the spindle that held the tilting mirror to the frame attached to the washstand, slipped it beneath the hair at the back of her neck and tied it. A rainstorm fit her unsettled state perfectly. Clouds roiled around in the sky. Wind bowed the trees, their leafy branches quivering at its approach.

How happy Poppa had looked tonight, propelling himself around the room. Her throat tightened at the mere thought of his new freedom. And it was all due to Cole's kindness and ingenuity. How had he ever thought of such a thing as a rolling chair?

She walked to her bed, propped a pillow against the headboard and stepped out of her slippers. She'd meant to ask Cole about that after Poppa had settled in bed for the night, but she'd been…nervous.

Nervous. Yes. Her stomach had quivered like those leafy branches.

She sat on the edge of the bed, then leaned back

against the pillow, pulled the other pillow into her arms and hugged it against her chest. She hadn't been frightened tonight. Not even outside in the dark, *after* she'd learned it was Cole who'd come out of the woods. Of course, she'd been distracted by the chair and by his appearance. The way the corners of his mouth turned up was surprising. He looked pleasant, not at all cruel. And his eyes…

I wish I could change what Payne did, Sadie.

The way he had *looked* at her. Her stomach fluttered as it had then. She patted the pillows into place, blew out the lamp, then stretched out and drew the folded-down sheet up over her. It was when she looked into his eyes she'd become nervous. They were dark gray, though not at all like…like his brother's. Payne's eyes were hard and glittery, almost black. She'd never forget the cold, cruel look of them.

She shuddered, rolled onto her side and curled into a ball, drawing her thoughts back to Cole. His eyes were softer, and warmer…and kind…and…caring… and…

She sighed and snuggled deeper beneath the sheet.

Small, dark objects struck her head and shoulders with soft patting sounds. Bats! She couldn't move. The horse wouldn't let her move! She covered her head with her arms, felt the bats' small, bony bodies strike her flesh and screamed.

A green ledger flew open. Cole rode out of it astride a golden chestnut horse with flaxen mane and tail. He dropped his raincoat over her and pulled away the mare that had her trapped.

The patting grew louder against the rubber cloth of his coat that covered her….

* * *

Sadie opened her eyes and stared into the darkness, became aware of a real pattering sound and yanked the sheet up over her head. This was not a dream. And there was no Cole to save her. "Lord, *please* make the bats go away!"

The sound grew louder. She burrowed deeper beneath the sheet, tensed and listened. It was *raining*.

Laughter bubbled up. She lowered the sheet, turned on her side and listened to the raindrops dancing on the porch roof outside her open window, thinking about Cole rescuing her from the bat and Sweetpea. If only he hadn't been riding that chestnut horse...

Chapter Sixteen

Dinner felt wrong. Sadie put down her fork and glanced at the empty chair across the table. She'd become accustomed to Cole sitting there—to the sound of his deep voice as he engaged in conversation with Poppa and Nanna. Not with her, of course. She'd been cold and terse in any response she'd made to him when he'd tried. Guilt reared, an unwelcome addition to the meal sitting in her stomach.

I've never blamed you for distrusting me, Sadie.

He'd been so kind when she apologized last night. But he wasn't here today. Of course, there was no need. Her grandfather sat at the head of the table in his rolling chair, a glimmer of his old self shining in his eyes. Cole had given him back at least a measure of his independence—and had gained back a portion of his own in doing so.

She folded her napkin and placed it on the table, looked to her grandmother and smiled. "Gertrude baked maids of honor for our dessert, Nanna. Would you like me to serve them now?"

"I believe we'll wait and have them later with Pastor Calvert and Willa, Sadie. He'll be paying his Sunday call soon."

"Oh, no! I forgot I promised Willa white cookies!" She shot to her feet and started gathering up the dishes.

Her grandmother stood and grasped her wrist. "You go start the cookies, Sadie. I'll bring the dishes along."

"But Poppa—"

He shook his head and smiled. "Don't need…help. I'm going to…sitting room and…read my…Bible." He placed his palm against the table edge and pushed his chair backward, then grasped the lever and propelled himself toward the door.

Poppa didn't need help, and Nanna had remembered about the pastor's visit. *Thank You, Lord.* She cleared the lump from her throat. "I'll carry these in with me, Nanna." She picked up the plates she'd stacked and hurried for the kitchen.

Sadie placed the last of the cooled cookies into the tin and turned to survey the clean kitchen. Nanna had washed, dried and put away the dishes—once. Had whatever been vexing her mind healed? *Please, Lord, let it be so. Let it be more than simply a good day.*

She sighed and removed her apron, hung it on its peg and rubbed cream into her hands. The fresh, warm breeze coming in the window beckoned. She smoothed her hair back, tugged the waist of her gold-on-gold embroidered cotton gown into place, then crumbled a dry piece of bread in her palm and went out onto the porch.

Chickadees called to one another and flitted from tree to tree. She stepped to the railing and held out her hand. "Chicka-dee-dee-dee. Chicka-dee-dee-dee." One of the tiny, black-capped birds flew to a branch of the lilac bush beside the porch and looked at her. She smiled at the curious tilt of its head, held perfectly still and spoke in a low, quiet voice. "Come along, now. You know you want to." The friendly little bird hopped to the end of the branch, then spread its wings and flew to her hand, took a crumb into its beak and flew back to the branch.

She laughed and strewed the rest of the crumbs along the top of the railing, brushed off her hand, then hurried to the steps at the sound of a horse and buggy turning into the gravel way.

"Good afternoon!" She returned Willa's smile and wave as the carriage rolled to a halt, then watched Matthew Calvert leap lightly to the ground, tie the horse and lift his wife out of the phaeton. The happiness and contentment in her friend's eyes brought a hollow feeling to her heart. She smiled a welcome as they came up the stone walk.

"Let me guess…you've been feeding the birds."

She looked from Willa's smiling face to the chickadees, nuthatches and titmice flying from the trees and bushes to the railing and gave a soft laugh. "That's not much of a guess."

"I know." Willa took Matthew's offered arm, lifted her hems with her other hand and started up the steps. "Did you have them eating out of your hand as you used to do?"

"One of them." She glanced at Willa's hand holding so comfortably to her husband's arm, as if it was meant to be there, and wondered, for a brief instant, what it would be like to be able to have that sort of trust in a man. She veered her thoughts from that direction. There was no profit in thinking about things that would never be. "I thought your children would be with you. I was looking forward to meeting them."

"Not today. There is a new foal and a new litter of kittens at the Finsters'. Kurt asked Joshua and Sally to come see them." Willa shrugged and smiled. "I hadn't the heart to deny them the chance."

"I should say not." She laughed and stepped back. "I would like to see that foal myself. And the kittens."

"Actually, I'm fearful of the outcome of the children's visit."

"Is there danger?" She glanced at Matthew and saw the look he gave Willa.

"Taking Sally to see kittens can have consequences. Sometimes, lovely, life-changing ones."

There was a teasing note in Matthew Calvert's voice, but even so, there was a fullness to it that made her think of pews and soft light coming through stained-glass windows. It was obvious from the loving look on Willa's face she was thinking of something else.

"Well, perhaps Joshua and Sally will come next time. For now, Poppa and Nanna are waiting for you, Reverend Calvert." A smile tugged at her lips. "Poppa has something to show you."

"Indeed? Well, then, I must hurry inside."

"And you, Willa. You must come and see also." She turned and led the way through the door Matthew held open for them.

"What is it, Sadie?"

Willa had caught her excitement. "You'll see." She laughed and crossed the dining room. Willa caught up and walked at her side with Matthew close behind as they went down the hall to the sitting room.

"Wait here." She motioned them to stand by the door

and stepped into the room. "Poppa, Reverend Calvert and Willa are here. I've told them you have something to show them."

"Indeed I…do! Step…in…folks."

She turned to face the door as her grandfather grabbed the handle on his chair and pulled. Willa's eyes widened with every click. Matthew's lips slanted in a lopsided grin.

Her grandfather stopped the chair, pulled the pin to turn it around, put the pin back in place and grinned. "What…do you think…of…that?"

"Well, I—I don't know what to think. Praise the Lord! A rolling chair!" Matthew laughed and raised his hands palms up in front of himself in a gesture that bespoke disbelief and wonderment.

"Well, I do. I think it's wonderful, Grandfather Townsend!" Willa hurried forward, leaned down and hugged him.

"Wherever did you find such a chair, Manning?" Matthew rubbed the back of his neck, shook his head. "I've never seen anything like it. Not even in the city."

"Cole…made it…for me." Her grandfather patted the mechanism. "Come see…how it…works."

Nanna smiled and rose from the settee to accept Willa's hug as Matthew strode across the room and knelt by the chair. "I'll just get the refreshments. I believe this will take some time."

Sadie looked at her poppa, happily explaining how the chair worked to Matthew, and nodded. "Willa and I will be out on the porch visiting, if you wish to join us, Nanna."

"Thank you, dear. But I'll stay in here and listen to Reverend Calvert's message." Her grandmother glanced at the two men, looked back up at her and smiled. "If there is to be one, that is."

"*Cole* made that rolling chair for your grandfather?" The words popped out of Willa's mouth as soon as the kitchen door closed behind them. And the way she said Cole's name made it clear that she was remembering their last conversation.

"Yes. Isn't it *marvelous?*" Sadie carried the refreshment tray to the table. "You were right about Cole, Willa. He made Poppa the chair. And he saved Poppa's businesses, too."

"Oh?"

The single little word held a plethora of questions— and the tiniest bit of smugness. She stuck out her tongue at Willa.

Willa laughed and lifted the glasses of tea punch off the tray, placing them on the table.

"Cole brought Poppa's ledgers to me." She handed the small plates to Willa, put the plate of white cookies and maids of honor in the center of the table and set the tray aside.

"And?"

"And when I looked over the books, I discovered that Poppa's sawmill and logging camps had been failing the past few months before Cole began managing them."

"*Failing?*" The plate Willa was placing in front of her clattered to the table. She looked up, her eyes wide with shock. "Why?"

Sadie shook her head, smoothed her skirts and slipped onto her chair. "I don't know why. I've thought that perhaps Poppa was unwell before he had the seizure. Or perhaps he was distracted by Nanna's illness of the mind…" She looked down at the brown liquid in her glass. "Whatever the reason, I should have been here."

Willa reached across the table and took hold of her hand. "That wouldn't have changed anything, Sadie. What could you have done?"

She sighed and dredged up a weak smile. "I don't know. Perhaps nothing. But I still feel guilty."

Willa nodded and withdrew her hand, picked up a cookie. "What will you do about the ledgers?"

She took a breath and squared her shoulders. "I've already apologized to Cole and returned them to him."

"Oh, Sadie, I'm so relieved! I felt terrible when he caught us sneaking—"

"We were not sneaking!"

"It felt like we were."

"Not to me. I had a perfect right to go after Poppa's ledgers."

Willa's brows rose. "Without telling him?"

Heat crawled into her cheeks. "I didn't know what I would find. And I didn't want to give Cole a chance to alter the ledgers or prepare a story to cover the truth."

"Which turned out to not be necessary."

"It *could* have been." She snapped a cookie in two and put it on her plate. "And there is still the matter of the clapboard delivery to Dibble's. The sale is recorded, but Cole lied about delivering it."

"How can you be so certain, Sadie?" Willa broke off a bite of cookie. "And don't jut your chin at me."

The sound of the breath she huffed out reminded her of her grandmother. She frowned and reached for her glass. "I told you he was riding a *horse* that day. You can't deliver lumber on horseback." The words left a sour taste in her mouth. She took a sip of her tea punch, looked up and found Willa staring at her, a speculative glint in her blue-green eyes. "What?"

"Nothing." Willa popped another piece of cookie in her mouth. "Mmm, these are as good as I remember. Mine never taste quite the same."

"It's souring the milk first."

"You never told me that!"

"You never asked." She took another sip of her drink and tried to forget about that horse. And the bank note. And the way the day seemed so long.

The dusky light cast its warm glow on the pond. A willow growing along the bank hung the tips of its drooping branches in the still water. Cole picked up a handful of the small stones strewn along the dirt path and threw them one by one into the water, watching the ripples and listening to the birds twittering their night songs. He never should have accepted that supper invitation from the Conklins—even if it was to thank him for stopping that runaway mare. Chloe was too…friendly.

He scowled, brushed the dirt from his hands and made his way back along the path to the log yard. He'd caught Chloe glancing at him several times with an appreciative, interested look. And a few young ladies in church had done the same that morning. And the other night Sadie had, at last, looked at him…*really* looked at him. His heart jolted at the memory. Maybe he shouldn't have shaved his beard after all.

He threaded his way through the piles of logs waiting to be sawn into rough lumber, made note of the quantity, then climbed the steps to the mill deck and leaned against a support beam. The rough grained wood pressed into the skin on his back as he looked out over the pond to the forested hills. The last rays of light outlined the feathery tops of the pines standing tall and proud along the ridges. There was a loud click as a June bug threw itself against the globe of the oil lamp dangling from the bracket that hung out over the water. Crickets chirped.

He glanced up at the darkening sky, shifted his back to a more comfortable position, stretched out his legs and crossed his ankles. It was still too early to go to the Townsends'. Another half hour or so and he'd get ready. His pulse quickened, proof that he should stay away. If Sadie looked at him the way she had last night…

A mosquito flew around the lamp, dipped low and hovered over his bare hand. He swatted it away and picked up a sliver of wood, shredded it with his thumbnail and threw the pieces in the water to float away, glanced again at the sky. His gut tightened.

Another thirty minutes…

Chapter Seventeen

There were weeds mixed in with the flowers.

*Oh, Nanna...*Sadie stared at the dark triangle on the heartweed leaves, the limp squaw plum vines dangling down the side of the vase her grandmother had set on the mantel, and that awful feeling took her by the throat again. It still happened like that when she came on something unexpected—something that showed so clearly that her nanna's mind was slipping away.

She took a deep breath and blinked the film of moisture from her eyes, spread her dusting rag on the mantel and glanced over her shoulder. Her grandmother was busy fluffing the pillows on the settee. *Please don't let her look this way, Lord. She would be so hurt if she knew what she'd done.* She pulled the weeds from the vase and rolled them in the rag to dispose of them later. Done. And her grandmother hadn't noticed. *Thank You, Lord.* She expelled her held breath and turned.

"I'm finished with my morning's tasks, Nanna, and it's so fresh and lovely outside after last night's rain I thought I would go into the village this afternoon." She held the wrapped weeds out of sight behind her long skirt and started for the entrance hall. "Would you like to ride into town with me after dinner? I'm sure Gertrude has a list of things she needs."

"Not today, dear. I'm a little tired." Her grandmother held a pillow against her thick middle and batted at it to fluff the feathers, then placed it back on the settee. "I think I'll lie down and rest for a while after we've eaten."

Alarm shot through her. "Are you feeling unwell, Nanna? Perhaps you should lie down now."

"No." Her grandmother gave her a fond, though somewhat annoyed, look. "There's no need to fuss, Sadie. I'm only a bit tired. The rain last night kept me awake. After dinner will be time enough for me to rest."

That horrible helplessness swept over her again. "Very well, Nanna. I'll go see if Gertrude has dinner ready."

"Sa...die..."

She took a breath and turned. "Yes, Poppa?"

"Set place for...Cole. I asked him...come and...eat."

She nodded and hurried out of the room. Her emotions were all in a turmoil again, and she wasn't at all certain of what her grandfather would read in her expression save one thing—relief. It was hard to fathom, but she missed Cole. Somehow, some way, his kindness and thoughtful care of her grandparents had made everything seem more...manageable. She hadn't realized that until he was gone.

"I have all the information on the clapboard machine now, Manning." Cole crossed his knife and fork on his empty plate and reminded himself not to look at Sadie. "I'll leave Mr. Eastman's letter with you and you can read it over."

"No…need. Can't afford…one."

He looked at Manning's set face, decided to try once more to convince him. "You're right. The sawmill hasn't enough money to purchase one. But with a bank note—"

"Don't want…debt."

"I wish you would reconsider your position on taking out that bank note, Manning." He placed his napkin on the table and rose. "Why don't I leave you the letter anyway? I think you'll find the information about the machine interesting."

"No…need."

"Very well." He turned and smiled at Rachel Townsend. "Thank you for the meal, Mrs. Townsend. It was delicious as always." He turned to leave.

"Wait!"

He stopped, looked down at Manning. "Yes?"

"Sadie going…to town. I want to…go. You…put me…in buggy?"

"Why, Poppa, you didn't tell me! How lovely."

The thickness in Sadie's voice broke his self-control. Cole looked across the table, saw the shimmer of tears in her eyes and wished he hadn't. "Would you like me to hitch Sweetpea to the buggy for you, Sadie? Or—" She blinked and looked up at him, a half smile on her lips, the memory of the last time he had offered in her eyes. The rest of the words stuck in his throat.

"If you would please, Cole. It will give me time to gather my things."

Her smile stole the little breath he had left. He nodded and strode from the room.

* * *

"Cole…"

His heart slammed against his ribs. He coughed, frowned. His heart had better stop doing that every time Sadie sought him out or it was going to break—though he was fairly certain that would happen anyway.

"Is Manning ready for me?" He wiped the frown from his face and looked toward the stable door. His heart jolted again. The sunlight behind Sadie made a silhouette of her neat, trim figure, brushed gold over her brown hair and the green gown she wore, caused the tiny pinpoints of amber in her brown eyes to shine. She looked far too appealing.

"Yes. But I wanted to talk to you before you go in to carry him out."

Sweetpea snorted, tugged. He loosened the death grip he'd taken on the reins and led the mare toward the door. "What can I do for you?" *Anything. You ask and I'll do it or die in the effort.*

"I wondered if you would leave Mr. Eastman's letter with me?" She turned and stepped back outside.

So she still didn't trust him. "If you wish." What more could he do to convince her—

"I thought perhaps if I read the letter tonight after supper and asked Poppa questions about it…"

Her voice faltered. Her cheeks turned a deep rose, and he realized he had stopped and was staring down at her.

"I know that is a little…devious. But Poppa can be stubborn at times, and I learned—"

He grinned. He couldn't help it. She looked so *guilty*—like a child caught doing something she'd been told not to. The color in her cheeks deepened, and she lifted her hand to finger the silk edging on her dress's collar.

"Never mind. It's not a very good idea. I'll—"

"It sounds good to me." He smiled to hide his shock that she was offering to help him and continued walking Sweetpea to the hitching post. "Does it work—this… er…sidewise approach?"

Her eyes sparkled with a mischievous look. "Most of the time."

Her smile set his pulse to thundering. She must have looked like that before— He yanked his thoughts away from that path. He'd face what Payne had done to her later, when he was alone and had more control over his emotions. For now he simply wanted to enjoy this Sadie he was meeting for the first time. He pulled the letter from his pocket and handed it to her. "I take it this method has been tested in the past?"

She laughed, a soft rippling sound that picked up his heart and carried it away. "It has." She tugged on the drawstring and tucked the letter in the purse dangling from her wrist. "Usually when Nanna objected to my going off on an adventure with Daniel."

Daniel? His pulse stuttered down to normal speed.

"And Willa and Callie and Ellen, of course. We had wonderful adventures together." She tipped her head and looked a challenge at him. "How many times can you make a rock skip across the pond?"

He pulled his gaze away from her eyes and made a manful effort to catch up to her conversation. "I'm not sure—four or five, I suppose."

"Seven, for me. I hold the record." She laughed and looked at the house. "I'm sorry, I shouldn't keep you.

Poppa is waiting, and you've got to get back to the sawmill."

He nodded, dragging his mind away from wondering what her hand would feel like in his if he handed her into the carriage—not that she would let him. "Stop by the mill when you return, and I'll come along to carry Manning into the house."

He headed for the porch and fought back disappointment he'd no business feeling as he listened to her climb into the carriage the minute he turned his back. Obviously, her new friendly attitude toward him extended only so far. And that was good. It was very good. And maybe if he kept telling himself that he'd stop wanting more.

"Good crop...of...hay...this year. Stock will...fare well this...winter."

Sadie looked across the seat at her grandfather grasping the hold strap with his good hand and leaning out to survey the countryside. "I'm sorry I didn't bring you to town before now, Poppa. I've been...preoccupied with...things. It was selfish of me."

He looked at her. "Not selfish...Sa...die. I under... stand. Is it...getting...better?"

"Yes, Poppa, it is." She urged Sweetpea to pick up speed when they entered Brook Street. "Though there are some things I don't believe will ever go away."

"Night...mares?"

She glanced at him, saw the concern and love in his eyes. "How do you know about the nightmares?"

"Heard you...scream. Couldn't...come—" His voice broke. He cleared his throat. "Wanted to...comfort... you. Rachel...can't."

"Oh, Poppa." She dropped the reins and leaned over to hug him. "You do give me comfort—every day. I never could have come back home without your strength to lean on."

He patted her back and gave her a little push. "Sweet…pea."

She jerked around and grabbed the reins, pulling Sweetpea away from the bush she'd stopped to nibble, and urging her around the corner onto Main Street. The buggy lurched onto the planks of the Stony Creek Bridge.

"Want to…see…Dibble's new…build…ing."

"So that's why you wanted to come to town." She smiled and reined Sweetpea off the street to the hitching post beside the livery so he could see the new addition. She eyed the clapboard that now covered the building and remembered Cole's lie. The knowledge of it settled like a stone in the pit of her stomach.

"Manning. It's good to see you out and about." David Dibble strolled up to the carriage and extended a hard, callused hand to her grandfather, nodding in her direction. "Miss Sadie. You here to visit Willa's ma?"

"Good afternoon, Mr. Dibble. No. Another time, perhaps. I stopped because Poppa wanted to see your new addition. I have errands to run." She glanced at her grandfather. "Do you want to stay here or go on to the stores with me?"

"Stay, Manning. It's been a while since we had time to jaw about things."

She smiled at her grandfather's nod to David Dibble, snatched up the basket at her feet and climbed from the carriage. "I'll be back shortly, Poppa."

She lifted her hems above the hard-packed dirt yard,

hurried out to Main Street, crossed to the block of stores and climbed the steps to the raised walkway. The bell above the door at Barley's announced her entrance.

The storekeeper's wife paused in filling an order and looked her way. "Good afternoon, Sadie. What can I do for you?"

"I need some groceries." She smiled and took a piece of paper from her purse, placed it in the basket, then set it on the counter. "Gertrude made a list. If you would be so kind as to fill the order, I'll be back to pick it up. I have some other shopping to do."

"Of course, Sadie. I'll get to it as soon as I finish up here."

"Thank you. Please tell Ada I send my greetings." She left the store and hurried to Cargrave's, stepped into the recessed entrance and halted as the door was pulled open and the bells tinkled their greeting.

"Good afternoon, Miss Spencer." The man stepped back to let her pass. "How is your grandfather faring?"

"Poppa is doing fine, Mr. Finster." She smiled and stepped into the store's cool interior. "He rode to town with me. He's waiting in the carriage at Dibble's livery."

"Why, I'll have to go over and greet him. Good day." The man doffed his hat and walked outside.

"That's good news about your grandfather, Miss Spencer. It's been a while since he's been out and about."

"Yes. I don't want to tire him." She smiled to take any rudeness from her words and stepped to the counter. "I came to check on the book I ordered for Poppa, Mr. Cargrave. Has it arrived yet?"

"It came in yesterday." The proprietor bent and

pulled the leather-covered book from the shelf beneath the counter. "Will there be anything else, today?"

"No, only the book, thank you. I want to get back to Poppa." She took the volume in her hand and crossed to the post office, her long skirts whispering across the well-trod plank floor.

"Is there any mail, Mr. Hubble?"

The postmaster looked at her over the top of his wire-rim glasses and smiled. "Cole already came by and picked it up. There's a letter for you from Miss Ellen."

"Oh, lovely! Good afternoon, Mr. Hubble." She turned and hurried out the door, debated dropping in on Willa for a quick visit but decided she shouldn't leave her grandfather waiting any longer. She would pick up her basket of groceries at Barley's after she got the buggy.

She hurried down the wooden walk to the livery, started across the dirt yard to the buggy and froze. *The horse!* She stared at the golden chestnut with the flaxen mane and tail being held by a man she'd never seen. It was the same horse. The one Cole had been riding the day he rescued her from Sweetpea. She was sure of it. But who was the man? And what had he to do with Cole?

She started forward, then stopped again as the man handed the reins over to David Dibble.

"That's a fine animal, sir. Too fine to be a livery mount, if I may say. If I weren't a traveling man I would buy him for my own." The man turned and walked her way.

A livery mount. Why would Cole be riding a horse from the livery stable? She returned the man's polite nod and hurried to the buggy. "What a lovely horse, Mr. Dibble. I believe I've seen it before."

"Possible you're right, Miss Sadie. Cole was in an almighty hurry to get back to your place the day he brought the first wagonload of clapboard, so he left the wagon here for my men to unload and borrowed Goldie." David Dibble tugged on the reins and turned the horse toward the stable. "I'd best get back to work. It was good to see you again, Manning. Don't forget to tell Cole I need another load of clapboard, soon's he can get it here."

He hadn't lied.

"Something wrong…Sa…die?"

"What? Oh, no, Poppa. I was only admiring the horse." She placed the book on the seat, loosed Sweetpea's reins from the hitching post and climbed into the buggy.

Cole was in an almighty hurry to get back to your place…

A warm, lovely feeling, absent from her life for four years, swelled and spread. Cole had come back to rescue her from Sweetpea. Absurd that that should make her so happy. She took a long, deep breath, gave the reins a snap to get Sweetpea moving, then reined her around and headed for Barley's to pick up her basket of groceries.

Chapter Eighteen

Sadie glanced at her grandfather, rattled the paper in her hand and heaved a loud sigh. No response. He was too involved in reading his new book to notice. She gave the paper another shake, rose and paced about the room. "Hmm…"

"What is making you so restless tonight, Sadie?" Her grandmother looked up from the apron she was hemming. "Is there bad news in that letter you're reading?"

Her grandfather lifted his head. "What…let…ter?"

Bless you, Nanna! She stepped closer to her grandfather's chair. "The letter Cole received from Mr. Eastman, Poppa." She looked away from his frown. "And I'm quite certain it is good news, Nanna, though I don't understand all of it."

"That's foolishness, Sadie. If you don't understand it, how can you be certain it's good news?"

Her grandmother shook her head and went back to her sewing, but she'd inadvertently given her the opportunity she needed. She leaped at it. "Well, Mr. Eastman writes, 'the machinery, though simple, is so constructed that it will cut two clapboards in a minute, regulate itself without any manual labor, and cut from a block, two feet in diameter, one hundred and twenty clapboards. These are found much superior to rifted clapboards.'"

"Two…clapboards…a min…ute?"

"That's what he says, Poppa." She'd caught his interest! She pulled her brows together in a frown. "That is good, isn't it?"

He nodded and laid his book on his lap. "Fast. How… many from…block?"

She held back a smile and glanced down at the letter. "One hundred and twenty clapboards."

He stared off into the distance, his eyes narrowed, his brow furrowed.

She pressed on lest he go back to his reading. "There's more, but I don't understand this part. It says, 'The novel feature of the clapboard machine is the method of converting the bolt log into feather-edged clapboards of uniform thickness. The saw cuts from the exterior or circumference toward the center of the log. The bolt is made to revolve between iron centers, and the self-regulating machinery saws a series of clapboards all around the log.'"

"Hmm…"

She looked from his face to his fingers drumming on his book and smiled. He was thinking about how the machine worked. She wiped her smile off as he looked back at her.

"Does he…say…cost of…machine?"

"Yes. Forty dollars."

His eyes clouded. He took a breath then shook his head. "Can't…do it." He looked back down at his book.

But it was obvious he wanted to, so why was he

standing stubborn? She studied his face, caught her breath. If he thought— "Poppa, have you seen your business ledgers since Cole became your manager?"

His head jerked up, his gaze locked on hers. "You've…seen them?"

There were so many emotions in his eyes…shame… anger… With Cole? She hadn't thought of that. She cleared her throat and nodded. "I—Cole knew I wanted to see them, so he brought them to me."

His eyes narrowed on her the way they'd done when he was displeased with her as a child. "How…did he… know?"

The conversation had taken an uncomfortable turn she hadn't expected. She squared her shoulders. "I noticed the ledgers were missing and I went to the sawmill to look for them."

"Why…"

The look in his eyes made her want to fidget. And Nanna was peering up at her now. She lifted her chin. "Because I thought Cole was stealing from you."

"Stealing!" Her grandmother gasped out the word. "Why, Sadie Spencer! Whatever gave you such an idea? Cole is a wonderful young man. He would never steal from us."

"I know that now, Nanna. But, then, I thought— He *is* Payne's brother." She wrapped her arms about herself, and the letter crinkled in her hand. "I couldn't imagine why Cole was in our home, of all places, after…what happened."

"Sa…die…" Her grandfather reached up and tugged her arm free, took hold of her hand, a fierce look of love in his eyes. "Cole is…good man. He…hunted…

for Payne. Still looks…for him. Cole would…never hurt…you."

I wish I could change what Payne did, Sadie, but I cannot. This is all I can do.

Cole's words filled her head—and her heart. "I know that now, Poppa. And I knew then you would never have Cole in your home if you thought…" She drew a breath and shook her head. "I don't want to talk about the past, Poppa. It's over—and someday I will forget. What I wanted to tell you is that the sawmill is making a profit. And the logging camps as well. Not as much as when you were running them, of course, but some. Enough that you might consider signing a bank note to buy that clapboard machine as Cole recommends."

Breath gusted from him. He sat straighter in his chair.

She'd saved his pride. And she hadn't lied. The mill and camps *had* made more profit under him—until the decline began. "Why don't you read Mr. Eastman's letter, Poppa? I'm sure you'll find it interesting." She placed the letter in his lap and straightened. "Now, if you will excuse me, I'm going to the library to write Ellen a letter."

She hurried from the room before he could tell her to take the letter away.

Sadie closed the door and leaned against it, taking a deep breath to settle the emotions stirred by talking about the past. "Almighty God, please let my words be true. Please let me forget someday."

Would she? *Could* she? It didn't seem possible. But perhaps there would come a day when Payne's attack would only be a memory in the back of her mind she seldom thought about. She was already much better since coming home.

She breathed in the scent of Poppa's room, frowned and took a deeper sniff. Her lips curved. Joy bubbled up. He'd been in here. The smells of wood smoke and leather were still faint, but those of candle wax and bayberry were stronger. Poppa could enjoy his room again—thanks to his rolling chair.

Tears stung her eyes as a fresh set of emotions rose. How she wished things could be as they were, with her grandparents healthy and strong. But time could not turn backward. She wiped the tears from her cheeks and pushed away from the door. She must be thankful Poppa was improving a bit, and grateful for her nanna's love. That had not changed. That would never change, even if Nanna forgot.

She opened the desk and took the writing supplies from their cubicles, pulled Ellen's letter from her pocket and placed it in front of her as she penned her answer.

Dearest Ellen,

How lovely to receive your letter. I do apologize for not writing you of my move home to Pinewood. I left Rochester immediately upon learning of Poppa's illness, and I have been occupied in caring for him and Nanna since my return. To answer your question, they are doing as well as can be expected. Poppa grows a bit stronger with each passing day. Alas, I cannot say the same for Nanna. She remains confused but as loving as always. Thank you for your concern.

I must say, Ellen, that your social life, with

all the teas and soirees, theater engagements and balls you write of, sounds a bit overwhelming to me after my reclusive life. I am happy you are enjoying your time in Buffalo with all of your many suitors. However do you keep from confusing them? Were I you, I should live in fear of calling one by the wrong name, or—

"Oh!" She jerked at the knock on the door, frowned at the line her pen had made when she jumped, blotted it and went to open the door. "Yes, Nan— Cole! Does Nanna or Poppa want—"

"They've retired."

"Is it that late?" She glanced at the dark outside the window, returned her gaze to him and resisted the urge to press her hand against her stomach to stop its fluttering. "You wanted something?"

"Yes. To thank you for helping me."

"Poppa talked to you about the letter?"

He nodded and moved back. She followed him out into the entrance, grateful to be out of the confines of the small library. His commanding appearance was still unsettling.

"Manning told me to arrange for a bank note and send for the clapboard machine."

"That's wonderful. I'm so glad, Cole." She led the way into the sitting room, then turned to look at him. "I'm certain, after reading Mr. Eastman's letter, that the machine will increase profits as you said." She looked away from his eyes. Something in them made her nervous. She focused on the hint of a dent in his chin, wishing it were permissible for her to touch it. He grinned. "Your 'sidewise' approach worked."

"Perhaps a little." She gave in and pressed her hand against her stomach to stop another surge of fluttering. "But it was when I told Poppa the sawmill and lumber camps were making a profit that he considered buying the machine." She picked up her grandmother's sewing and started snipping out the oversize stitches instead of being polite and waiting until he was gone. It gave her an excuse not to look at him. "Why haven't you shown him the ledgers?"

"For the same reason you're taking out those stitches. I wanted to spare his feelings."

His soft-spoken words landed square in her heart. She looked up, caught her breath. She tried to think of something to say to break the feeling that rose and stretched between them, but her mind refused to cooperate. All she could think of was the look in his eyes.

"Good evening, Sadie."

His voice felt like a touch. She watched him turn and stride from the room, leaving her breathless, wordless, helpless to understand what was happening to her. It felt as if her entire insides were coming undone.

She sank onto the settee cushion and stared down at the sewing in her trembling hands.

He had to stop going there. Cole stooped and scooped up a handful of wood chips, leaned against the support beam and tossed them one by one into the pond. They floated aimlessly a moment, then were caught and pulled by the unseen current toward the runoff downstream—the same as everything in him was pulled toward Sadie.

He straightened, shoved his hands in his pockets and hunched his shoulders. Tonight, for the first time, he had seen a tentative response in Sadie's eyes—an innocent questioning, confusion and vulnerability. It made him ache to hold her. He sucked in air and scowled down at the water. If he kept spending time with her, his strength to resist would be eroded. He had to be strong enough to deny himself for her sake. If he ever hurt her...

He dragged his hands from his pockets and stared at them, thought about their power and strength, about what could happen if the monstrous violence that flowed in his father's blood and had surfaced again in Payne rose in him and he used those hands to abuse the woman he loved. His stomach soured.

If he only knew what had happened to change Payne there might be a chance— No. That was useless speculation. He'd had no responses to the letters of inquiry he'd sent. Not one. He might never know what had happened and that meant he had no right to woo Sadie, or even think of marrying her. He had nothing to offer her but a tainted name and the possibility he could someday harm her due to some heinous lack of self-control.

He shrugged out of his shirt, twisted around and dove for the pond, his well-muscled body arcing through the moonlight, cleaving the water with barely a ripple. There would be no sleep for him tonight unless he drove away the thoughts that haunted him. He stroked for the far bank and began the circles of the pond he would continue until he hadn't strength left to drag his arms through the water.

Sadie folded and sealed the letter, directed it to Ellen's aunt's home in Buffalo and set it aside to wait for her next trip to town. The thoughts she'd been holding at bay swarmed while she put the desk to rights.

She rose and went to the settle, kicked off her slippers and curled up in the corner the way she used to do. The old, worn pillow she pulled into her arms and hugged against her chest was a poor substitute for Nanna's shoulder. She blinked her eyes and burrowed her chin into the feathery softness. "I need you, Nanna. I don't understand what's happening to me. I need you to help me to know what to do...."

Her whispered words bounced around the library and came back to her as empty as the room. She sighed and closed her eyes. One thing was certain; the fear that had ruled her life had somehow become less dominant since her return home. She hadn't shivered once when she saw men in town today. And tonight, when she'd looked into Cole's eyes...

She heaved another sigh and hugged the pillow tighter. What had made his dark gray eyes go all smoky that way? Whatever it was, it unnerved her. Her insides had coiled as tight as rope around a well arm, but it didn't frighten her. That was the odd thing. She was no longer afraid of Cole. Cautious, yes—but not afraid. "Thank You, Lord, for taking that fear from me."

She leaned her head back against the settle, thought about Cole chasing away the bat and rescuing her from the stubborn mare. He hadn't lied that day. He'd been telling the truth when he said he'd come back to help her in case Sweetpea had her cornered. A delicious feeling, rather like a warm, cozy blanket, spread through her. It had been a long time since she'd felt protected.

Chapter Nineteen

"I believe we have enough for supper, Nanna." Sadie picked up the overflowing bowl of green beans, held it against her hip and smiled at her grandmother. "Why don't we go sit on the porch and snap them for Gertrude."

"Gertrude?" Her grandmother frowned and tugged another handful of beans off the vines climbing the tripod of sturdy branches that supported them. "The cook's name is Martha, Ivy. And, I'm sure I don't know why you persist in calling me Nanna. You are to call me Miss Rachel." Her grandmother sighed, tossed the beans she held on the ground and picked another handful. "Truly, I don't know why Mama keeps you on. You are so forgetful."

Sadie watched her grandmother throw the second handful of beans to the ground and swallowed against the tightness in her throat. "Poppa is calling for you."

"Well, why didn't you say so?" Her grandmother threw down the beans she held, wiped her hands on her apron and hurried toward the house, her long skirts swishing back and forth with the sway of her ample hips.

She took a tighter grip on the bowl and followed. Her grandmother always responded to the mention of her grandfather. The connection between them seemed to penetrate the fog of confusion that came over her as nothing else could.

The kitchen door clicked shut. Sadie sighed, dumped the beans on the porch table, set the empty bowl beside them to hold the scraps. The clean bowl waiting there, she placed it on her lap. Poppa would take care of Nanna now. He was so gentle and patient with her. He always had been.

She grabbed a handful of beans, pulled the stems and leaves from some her grandmother had picked, tossed them into the bowl on the table then snapped the beans into the bowl on her lap. She couldn't remember ever hearing Poppa and Nanna speak harshly to one another, though she'd caught them snuggling and whispering to each other a few times. A smile curved her lips. Poppa's voice had a special tone when he spoke to Nanna that he never used with others, not even her. And when he looked at Nanna—

Her hands stilled. She stared into the distance, remembering how her grandfather looked into her grandmother's eyes as he handed her in and out of the carriage, how he smiled the special smile he gave to Nanna alone when she entered a room.

She shook her head and grabbed another handful of beans. How could she have forgotten how Poppa's eyes looked when— Her breath caught. The pieces of bean she'd snapped fell from her hand into the bowl. That was the way Cole—

She jerked to her feet. The bowl crashed to the floor and pieces of beans scattered everywhere. That couldn't be. It *couldn't*. Poppa loved Nanna. Her imagination was running away with her.

She dropped to her knees, batted her puffed-up long skirts out of the way and righted the bowl, snatched up pieces of beans and tossed them into it to erase the image of the way Cole had looked at her last night. She was wrong. She had to be wrong. But her fluttering stomach said otherwise.

Her stomach. Last night, when Cole had looked at her that way, her stomach—no, her whole insides—had quivered.

The whistling streaked through her like lightning. *Cole.*

She jerked her head toward the wooded path, listening. He was close, almost to the yard. She couldn't face him now! She had to sort this out first. She lurched to her feet, yanked open the kitchen door, leaped inside and ran past Gertrude into the hallway.

"Why, Sadie, what— Where's the beans?"

"On the porch!" The slap of the soles of her slippers on the stairs drowned out her reply. She grabbed the railing, whirled around the landing and sped up the last few steps and down the hall to the safety of her room.

Cole stepped out of the woods and looked toward the house, caught the flash of a blue skirt at the kitchen door and heard the slam as it closed.

Sadie. It had to be. Rachel couldn't move that fast. His gut tightened at the thought of seeing her. He forced himself to stroll up the path but couldn't stop from watching the kitchen door, hoping she'd come back outside.

He climbed the porch steps and frowned. Fresh-picked green beans were piled on the table. A bowl sat on the porch floor, pieces of snapped beans scattered around it. Had she hurt herself? Or had she heard his whistle and dashed inside to avoid him? He'd revealed more of what he felt for her than he intended last night. He'd probably either frightened or disgusted her. Either way it seemed he'd undone the progress he'd made in gaining her trust. *Fool!*

He scowled, picked up the bowl and set it on the table, scooped the pieces of beans into his hands, then threw them over the railing.

Birds flew from the nearby trees and bushes and hopped along the ground, pecking at the unexpected bounty. He watched them for a minute, then turned and strode to the dining-room door. He had business to discuss with Manning, and he'd do well to keep his mind fixed on that. His heart was a different matter.

Sadie climbed from the buggy, wrapped Sweetpea's reins around the hitching post and started toward the parsonage, stopped and ran her palms down the sides of her skirt. Perhaps this spontaneous visit was a bad idea. Willa was even better than Poppa at sensing her moods, and— Yes, it would be better to wait until the confusion of emotions roiling around inside her calmed. She'd been foolish to panic like this. She'd come back tomorrow, after she'd given things more thought. She blew out a breath, turned and reached for the reins.

"Sadie!"

She whipped around, stared at the young woman with a mass of black curls atop her head running down the porch steps. Who...Callie? *"Callie!"*

She broke into a run and was caught up in a fierce

hug. She clung to her childhood friend, laughing and crying, gulping out words. "It's so good—to see you. I thought—" She cleared her throat, stepped back and wiped her cheeks. "I thought you were in New York City."

"We returned last night." Callie's dark-violet eyes, bright with tears, sparkled at her, her full red lips curved in a tremulous smile. "Oh, Sadie, I can't believe you're here. Willa told me you had moved back to town. We were going to come visit—" Callie gave her another hug. "Are you all right?"

Her tone gave the words their meaning. Callie was honoring the promise she'd given never to speak of what had happened four years ago. "Not yet, but I'm getting better." She was. She wasn't even trembling at thinking about it. She blinked her vision clear and stared at her friend. "Callie...You're so beau—"

"Don't say it, Sadie! She hates to hear that—except from Ezra." Willa laughed, braced her hands on the porch railing and leaned toward them. "Tell her she's a wonderful cook. She likes that."

"Oh, hush, Willa Jean." Callie laughed and looked toward the porch. "Sadie can say anything she likes to me. And we all have so much to catch up on. I know—let's go to the gazebo and talk the way we used to." Callie's black curls bobbed as she looked back at her. "Shall we?"

Sadie nodded and grinned. "I say yes. We're too big to fit under your aunt Sophia's porch."

"Too bad. That was fun." Callie blinked, giggled. "You still have that impish grin, Sadie. You look ten years old!"

"She can still run, too." Willa trotted down the porch steps.

"Then I'm not racing!"

She laughed, feeling like a kid again. "That's what you always said, Callie. But you always did."

"And I always *lost*."

Willa giggled. "Well, your running has improved somewhat, Callie. You certainly led Ezra a merry chase when he was trying to court you."

"As you did Matthew!"

The mention of their husbands brought Sadie's dilemma back to the forefront. She could feel their happiness. Would the peace and release from fear she sought be enough for a lifetime? She'd thought so, but now... She gathered her skirts and started across the park toward the gazebo. "If I correctly remember what you wrote me in your letters, *both* of you gave your husbands-to-be a merry chase—all the way to Buffalo." She forced lightness into her voice and kept her face averted.

"That's true." Willa and Callie chorused the answer, laughed and took up places, one on each side of her.

"And, Callie, not only are you stunningly beautiful, but you look radiant with happiness." She glanced to her left. "As do you, Willa." She faced front again, lest they read envy in her eyes. "I'm so glad for both of you."

"I am happy, Sadie." Callie gave her a sober look. "I never knew marriage could be this wonderful. Of course, you have to marry the right man."

It was the perfect opportunity to ask the questions burning in her mind. How did they know their husbands were the right ones? And once they knew, how did they get beyond the fear and doubt and— She took a breath and let the moment go. The questions had no true purpose. The very idea of falling in love…

"I can't believe you're here in Pinewood, Sadie… that after all these years, we're together again." Callie shook her head. "Isn't it strange to see each other as we are now? All this while I've pictured you as a bigger version of the young girl you were when we moved away. And while your features are the same, they're so delicate and refined now. You're much lovelier than I imagined."

She pulled a face.

"Now, that's the Sadie I remember!" Callie laughed and linked arms with her. "Anyway, it's good we're all together again."

"Except for Ellen." She looked from Callie to Willa. "Do you think she will return to Pinewood?"

"Only on occasion to visit her parents." Willa frowned and led them up the gazebo steps. "Ellen fancies herself too good for our small village."

She shot a surprised look at her friend. "I've never heard you sound so disapproving, Willa."

"With reason, Sadie." Callie smoothed out her skirts and sat on one of the benches. "We love Ellen, but she has become exceedingly vain and *grasping*—to put it kindly."

"Truly?"

Willa nodded and sank down on the bench beside her. "We're very concerned about Ellen and her plans, Sadie."

"What plans?" She glanced from one to the other. "She only writes me of her social life."

"That's part of it." Callie shook her head and sighed. "Remember how I wrote you that the socially elite men in Buffalo are all determined to have the best, the shiniest, the biggest or the prettiest of whatever they are seeking?"

"Yes, but that was about them seeking to outbid one another for your hand."

Callie's face tightened. "Well, now it is Ellen. And unlike me, she is determined to take advantage of their competitive ways and trade her beauty for their lavish lifestyle. She is using one suitor against the other to achieve her goal, and I must say, she is quite artful at it."

"Callie and I have tried to talk to her, to tell her that the most important things to seek in a marriage are respect and trust and love. But she refuses to listen." Willa sighed and brushed at her skirt. "We're dreadfully afraid she will make an unhappy choice."

"Enough about Ellen." Callie twisted toward her on the bench. "I want to know about you, Sadie. How are you doing since you came home? And how are Grandmother and Grandfather Townsend?"

She looked away from Callie's concerned gaze and skirted around her unspoken question about coming back to the place where Payne had attacked her. "It was very difficult when I first came home, but as I said, that is better now." She took a breath and forced out the truth she didn't want to acknowledge. "Nanna is as you wrote me. And Dr. Palmer can offer no hope for her recovery. He simply doesn't know what causes her mind to slip away as it does. And that is dismaying and heartbreaking." She blinked away the tears that sprang to her eyes and looked down at her friends' hands holding hers. "But Poppa is improving." She raised her head and smiled. "He's getting stronger, especially since Cole made him his rolling chair. It gives him much more independence."

"A rolling *chair?* What is *that?*"

Callie looked dumbfounded. Sadie launched into an explanation, grateful to be off the hurtful subject of her grandmother's health. "Exactly as you might suppose. Cole attached wheels and gears to a chair, and now Poppa pulls this lever and propels himself all about."

"Cole?" Callie's brows furrowed, then arched in surprise. "Cole *Aylward?*"

"Yes." A twinge of irritation shot through her at the way Callie spoke his name. Yet who was she to judge? She'd done the same until she'd come to know Cole for himself and not as an extension of his brother. Now she respected—

"Cole has been caring for Grandfather Townsend since he returned home after his seizure."

Callie gaped at Willa. "*Truly?* My, a lot has happened since we left for New York City. Oh, Sadie…" Callie looked back at her, sympathy and concern darkening her eyes. "To have Cole Aylward around Butternut Hill has to be…hard…for you."

Warmth stole into her cheeks at the thought of him and how he had looked at her. She dipped her head to hide her face and framed her answer carefully. "It was at first. But I've become accustomed to his presence." *More than you know.* "And he's very kind to Poppa and Nanna. And helpful—he manages Poppa's businesses. And as I said, he made Poppa that rolling chair, and now Poppa is able to do more for himself. Of course, that means Cole does not have to come around as often as he did. He only comes mornings and evenings now to help Poppa in and out of bed—or when he has business to discuss."

She was prattling. She stopped, feeling Willa *looking* at her. She took a breath and rose. "I'd love to visit more, but I'm afraid I must get back. I don't like to leave Nanna and Poppa for too long." She leaned down and gave them both a hug. "Please come to Butternut Hill for a visit soon. It's so wonderful to talk with you instead of writing letters."

She hurried down the steps accompanied by their called farewells, then angled across the park to her buggy, well aware that she had lacked the courage to ask the questions that had prompted her visit. Nonetheless, she had come away with at least a partial answer.

Respect…trust…love… Respect…trust… love… The three words whispered through her mind in a rhythm that blended with the rumble of the buggy wheels as she drove away.

Chapter Twenty

Sadie creamed her freshly washed face and neck, rubbed more cream on her arms and hands, then slipped her ecru poplin dress on and shook the long skirt into place over her petticoats.

Outside birds twittered and sang their morning songs. Sunlight glowed in the east, slanted in the window and pooled on the floor at her stocking-clad feet. She tugged the bodice of the dress into place at her narrow waist, secured the joining hook then fastened the small horn buttons that marched single file up to the high collar.

A rising breeze riffled the hems of the curtains. She glanced out at the brightening sky, then looked down at the garden path. Cole would be coming soon. Her stomach quivered at the thought of facing him. She'd hidden here in her room again last night when he'd come to help her grandfather into his bed, but that couldn't continue. Poppa and Nanna would start to wonder, though they couldn't become any more confused than she. If she were right…Oh, she had to be wrong. Otherwise the situation would be…would be…*untenable*.

She turned back to the mirror, stared at her image and frowned. She looked like a *wren*. Everything about her was brown…colorless. Brown hair, brown eyes, brown eyebrows…flat, dull *brown*. Like a piece of wood. Why couldn't she have curly black hair like Callie? Or blue-green eyes like Willa?

And her *dress*. The kindest way to describe it was plain. And brown. Well, not quite, but it was *tan*—like the underside of a wren's body. She eyed the high collar and tugged at the elbow-length sleeves. Her teaching position at the seminary had not lent itself to fashionable displays and her gowns were all unadorned and serviceable. Today, she wanted something more. Something flattering like Willa's yellow gown. Or stylish like the red dress Callie had worn.

She stepped to the wardrobe and scanned the contents as if she didn't already know perfectly well what was there. She pulled the pale green gown off its peg, held it out in front of her and studied it. Perhaps if she added a lace collar? And a bit of trim on the sleeves…

The sound of boot heels striking the porch steps floated in her open window. She glanced at the sky, still dark in the west. Cole was early again. And she was unready to go downstairs. Was that by design? And what did that matter? Either way, it showed clearly that she had been wrong in her interpretation of the way he'd looked at her. Obviously, her nerves had gotten in the way of her common sense that evening. She'd been concerned over nothing. She'd no need to hide from him—except from embarrassment. *That* was a relief.

She hung the gown back on its peg, closed the wardrobe and walked back to the washstand. She'd been concerned that—if she had been right—Cole would no longer come around when Poppa needed his help. And, of course, Nanna enjoyed his company. She didn't want to deprive her of it. That was what had been upsetting her. Through no fault of her own—had she been right—she would have been the cause of more hurt for them.

She blew out a breath, held her arms above her head and twirled. Finally, she had figured out what had been disturbing her. It was liberating. And she'd no business envying her friends either. Didn't it say something in the Bible about not comparing yourself to others lest you become dissatisfied? God had made her the way He chose. If that was like a wren, she would be content. She yanked off the ribbon confining her hair, shook it loose, then grabbed her brush and stroked through the long, thick mass.

The low rumble of Cole's deep voice came up the stairs. She stopped brushing and listened. Had he noticed her absence? Was he asking after her? No matter. She looked back to the mirror and wound her hair into a thick coil on the crown of her head, jabbing in hairpins to hold it in place.

She turned away, then turned back. Why shouldn't she indulge her own vanity? She selected a tan ribbon that matched her gown and wound it around the base of the coil, tied it into a bow and let the ends dangle down to her neck. Nice. But not enough. She stared at her reflection and sighed. If only she had a brooch. As if wishing would help! She snatched up a narrow dark-brown ribbon and fastened it around her neck with a neat bow at the front of the collar, just where her pulse had throbbed when Cole—

She whirled from the mirror and headed for the chair to put on her shoes. One was missing. She went down on her knees and found it under the bed. The distinct clicking of her grandfather's rolling chair sounded as she put on her shoes. She was ready.

The back door opened and closed, and the sound of boot heels thumped down the porch steps and faded away. So Cole was not staying for breakfast today either. That was good. Her grandparents were becoming too dependent on him. Someday he would meet a young woman, start his own family and no longer come around.

She rose, stepped to the window and looked out toward the woods. Perhaps that was why he'd accepted the Conklins' supper invitation instead of dining with them as usual the other night. And Chloe Conklin was probably the reason he had cut his hair and shaved off his beard. Yes, that made sense. He had made that change to his appearance after he'd stopped the Conklins' runaway carriage, and Chloe was a very pretty young woman.

Anger knotted her stomach. So much she had once wanted from life had been stolen from her. She reached up and removed the ribbon at her throat, tossed it onto the nightstand and headed for the stairs to join her grandparents in the dining room.

"Come in, Mr. Aylward."

Cole stepped into the bank president's office and scanned a knowing gaze over the wood-paneled walls and bookshelves. All of the wood in the American Founders Bank of Pinewood had come from Manning Townsend's sawmill. The door closed behind him and he made a quick assessment of the man who stepped to his side. He'd seen him around the village, but never this close up. Ezra Ryder was near to his age, an inch or so shorter, and he'd guess fit under that gray suit.

The man offered his hand. "Ezra Ryder, Mr. Aylward." A grin slanted his lips. "In case you're the only resident of Pinewood who doesn't know who everyone else in town is."

He liked the direct look in the banker's blue eyes. "Cole Aylward." He matched Ezra Ryder's grin and grip.

"Have a chair, Mr. Aylward." The banker motioned toward two chairs and walked around to seat himself behind his desk. "Now, tell me what brings you to see me?"

Friendly, but straight to business. He liked that, too. It let you know where you stood. He sat in the chair closest to the desk. "I want to make arrangements to take out a bank note for Manning Townsend. I manage his businesses since he took ill."

"Yes, I'm aware of that. What is the amount you wish to borrow?"

"Forty dollars."

"And when do you want it?"

"As soon as I can get Manning in here to sign for it."

"That's not necessary. I know you by reputation, Mr. Aylward. Your signature is all that will be required." Ezra Ryder opened a drawer in his desk, pulled out a paper and began writing.

Cole maintained the polite expression on his face, but it took an effort. *I know you by reputation. Your signature is all that will be required.* He felt like shouting. He'd worked so hard to overcome the stigma attached to the Aylward name and he'd succeeded. At least as far as business was concerned. He sat a little taller, listened to the scratch of the nib over the paper.

Ezra Ryder applied the blotter and turned the paper toward him. "These are the terms of repayment." He dipped the pen in the ink bottle and held it out. "If they are agreeable, you will sign here, Mr. Aylward." He indicated the place.

Cole leaned forward and took the pen, offering a silent *thank you* for the old Jewish storekeeper who had taken an interest in him and taught him to read and write and cipher as a kid. He read the agreement, signed his name and handed back the pen. "Would it be possible for me to get a forty-dollar draft made out to a Mr. Robert Eastman in Brunswick, New Hampshire right now? I'll pay the fee."

"Of course." Ezra Ryder blotted his signature and set the note aside, pulled another paper from another drawer and began to write. "I was going to take a ride out to the Townsend place later in the hopes of seeing you, Mr. Aylward."

"Me?" The response was startled out of him. He frowned. "Mind if I ask what for?"

Ezra Ryder blew on the paper, handed it to him, then leaned back in his chair and fixed his gaze on him. "I wanted to talk with you about this rolling chair you made for Manning Townsend."

"The rolling chair? How do you know about that?"

The banker laughed and leaned forward. "Mrs. Ryder is a childhood friend of Sadie Spencer. The subject came up when they were visiting the other day."

"I see." He frowned and scrubbed his hand across the back of his neck to stall for time, but couldn't figure where the conversation was headed. "What did you want to know about the chair?"

"Everything." Ezra Ryder rose and came around his desk, turned the other chair to face him, sat down and leaned forward. "Look, Cole—do you mind if I call you Cole?"

"No." He looked straight in the banker's eyes, saw interest and subdued excitement and waited.

"Then I'm Ezra. Now, as I was saying…Miss Spencer told Mrs. Ryder this tale about you making a chair with wheels and gears and a lever that Manning Townsend pulls to propel himself about. Is that true?"

"It's a little more complicated than that, but yes."

Ezra shot to his feet and paced around the small office. "So Manning Townsend, who has no use of an arm and a leg, can move himself around by using your chair?"

"Yes."

Ezra dropped back into the chair and leaned toward him. "Can you make another?"

There was no sewing for her to repair tonight. Nanna had enjoyed a good day. Sadie gathered the checkers off the game table and put them in the drawer, eyeing the candle in the pewter candlestick sitting on the game table's pull-out shelf. It had started guttering and needed to be replaced. But the candles were in the butler's pantry, and that meant she had to walk down the hallway past Poppa's bedroom. Past Cole.

She stepped to the doorway and listened, then turned back into the sitting room. He was still with her grandfather. There was no mistaking his deep voice. She would get the new candle tomorrow.

A quick glance around the tidied room showed there was nothing to do now but wait. She crossed to the chest under the front window, snuffed the oil lamp, then moved to the table at the end of the settee and did the same. Darkness settled into the room, broken only by the golden pools of light from the candles on either end of the mantel. She would snuff them and go upstairs as soon as Cole left.

She brushed a tendril of hair back off her forehead and wandered about the room, stopping by the window beside the fireplace and gazing out into the dark night. How mighty was the hand that hung that sliver of moon and the stars.

The melancholy she'd been fighting all day washed over her. "Almighty God, thank You for blessing Willa and Callie with love and happiness. I'm truly happy for them." Her throat squeezed, choking her words. "I know I'm only a mortal and should not concern myself with things above my understanding...But, Lord, why have I been denied my dream? Why have I been given fear in place of love, and turmoil in place of happiness and contentment? What—"

"Sadie."

Cole. Had he overheard her? Must she continually embarrass herself in front of him? She blinked her eyes clear of moisture and turned, thankful she'd snuffed the lamps. "Yes?"

He started into the room, then stopped. "I've come to thank you—again."

"Thank me?" She lifted her chin and stepped away from the window. "I've done nothing."

"But you have. You told your friend Mrs. Ryder about the rolling chair I made for your grandfather."

It was so unexpected she forgot and looked at him. His dark gray eyes were fastened on her. The nervous quivering took her. She swallowed and wiped her palms down the sides of her long skirt, averting her gaze. "I don't understand. What has my talking to Callie to do with anything?"

"I went to the bank today to take out the note and send for the clapboard machine."

She looked back at him, the question in her eyes.

"Yes, I was given the note—and the bank draft. It's on its way to Mr. Eastman."

His smile quickened her pulse. She turned and moved back by the fireplace. "I'm so glad. But what—"

"Ezra questioned me about the chair."

His boot heel thumped against the floor. *He was coming into the room.* She concentrated on what he'd said. There was more—and it was good. She could hear it in his voice.

His boot heel thumped against the wood again. She took a breath.

"He asked me if I could make another one." His boot brushed over the carpet.

He was getting close.... "Why?" The word came out a whisper.

"He said he'd never seen or heard of such a chair and he wants to take it to New York City to show to some businessmen he knows. He's certain they'll be interested in selling the rolling chairs in their stores."

"Cole! That's *wonderful*. I'm so—" She spun around, looked up. The lamplight shone on his face, made a tiny shadow of the dent in his chin, brightened his eyes. His eyes... She tried to swallow, to speak, but her mouth was dry. She grabbed a handful of her long skirt to keep from raising her hand to cover the wild, breath-stealing dance of her heart. "—happy for you."

"Thank you, Sadie."

His low, husky voice stole the strength from her knees. She braced her hand on a chair back and nodded. The silence that stretched between them felt like forever. At last he turned away.

She watched him walk from the room, his back straight, his shoulders squared. His footsteps faded away down the hall, and the back door opened and closed.

Her knees gave way and she sank to the floor, moving her head slowly from side to side, denying what her heart whispered.

Chapter Twenty-One

Cole pushed down on the handle that closed the flume gate, straightened and looked through the dusky light at the pond. The saws behind him chattered to a halt, helpless without their source of power. The rush of creek water beneath the deck under his feet grew loud in the sudden quiet. He was beginning to hate this moment when the workers had gone home, the saws were silenced and he had nothing but his thoughts for company.

He turned and walked over to the workbench, picked up a rasp and began smoothing the axle he'd made. The days weren't bad. His mind was occupied and his energy and strength spent solving the problems or emergencies that cropped up in one business or another every day. It was the quiet nights that were hard to get through. Try as he had to dislodge thoughts of Sadie, they filled his head the way the sawdust permeated every nook and cranny of the mill.

He tugged the lamp hanging from a swinging hook overhead closer and bent over his work. At least the hours between the mill's shutting down and nightfall were now filled with making the wheelchairs for Ezra to take to New York City. He'd have to find something else to do when the chairs were finished.

He cleaned the fuzziness from one of the cuts where the axle squared off to accept the wheel, turned the axle and cleaned the cut on the other end. He checked for any burrs or rough spots.

Birds twittered their night songs. Bats swooped around the oil lamp hanging over the water, their shadows large on the deck floor. Bats. He scowled at the bony creatures. That's when it had started. He'd been attracted to Sadie from the start, but he'd managed to stay aloof until that night the bat had scared her.

He pitched a piece of wood at the bats and glared down at the bench. She'd lifted his jacket off her head and stood there looking all mussed and flustered and embarrassed... He'd been hard-pressed not to kiss her. He'd resisted, but the damage had been done.

His fingers found a section of rough grain on the axle and he picked up the rasp to smooth it away. And that day in the stable when her hair came free of its pins and fell down her back and she'd stood there trying to be all unperturbed and dignified with that blush on her face... His breath stuck in his throat. He'd had to turn away to keep from pulling her into his arms. And then the other night...

His hands stilled. He took a deep breath and lifted his head to stare out at the dark hills. She'd been happy for him. Her eyes had been sparkling at his news about the chairs when she turned toward him. And then—

He shook his head and rubbed at the tight muscles at the back of his neck. It had been almost a week, yet he could still see the way her eyes had warmed as their gazes met, the way her mouth had softened and her lips had trembled when he'd moved closer. It had been an unexpected moment of clarity and truth when what *was* had not been hidden behind what had been. A moment. If only…

His face tightened. He glanced at the sun still hanging above the hill and reached for the oil to rub into the axle before he attached the wheels, forcing himself to concentrate on the work. This chair was different than Manning's. It was for a person with two good arms who could propel it by simply gripping the wheels and pushing or pulling. The idea had come to him while taking hold of the wheels on Manning's chair to help him over a doorsill. The only mechanism needed for this chair was a brake, and that was easily made. He should have it finished before it was time to go and help Manning to bed.

Sadie would be there.

He shot another look at the sky and set his jaw. And that's all he would do, help Manning. He would not seek Sadie out, no matter how he ached to see her. It was too dangerous. Something warm and wonderful had replaced the fear in her eyes. And he didn't know if he had the strength to resist.

Nanna was humming. Sadie smiled and turned onto her side, grabbed for the cloth that slipped off her forehead and opened her eyes. The pinkish-gray light of dusk filled the room. She'd fallen asleep. And she'd dreamed about her grandmother picking flowers in the garden.

The throbbing pain in her temples was gone. She pushed herself to a sitting position, leaned back against the headboard and let out a sigh. She must have needed the rest. Sleep had evaded her for the past week, ever since Cole had stopped coming to Butternut Hill except for brief visits in the early morning and late evening to care for her grandfather. Visits when he only politely acknowledged her—if she happened to be in the room.

The sick feeling she'd been suffering for days settled in the pit of her stomach again. Had she said or done something to anger Cole that night he'd told her about Ezra wanting him to make another rolling chair? Was he too busy making the chair to come around? She frowned, folded the damp cloth into a square, then folded it again. Or was it that he had new interests elsewhere? At the Conklins' perhaps?

Her stomach churned and she pressed her hand against it, regretting the supper she had eaten before coming upstairs to lie down. Not much supper. Her appetite had disappeared. The dining table seemed empty without Cole sitting across from her. She missed the sound of his deep, quiet voice when he was conversing with her grandfather, his rumbling chuckle when something amused him. And the way he always seemed to know what to say to bring her grandmother back to the present when her mind slipped into the past. She missed him. He'd become her friend.

Tears welled. Why hadn't she realized that when he was still coming around throughout the day to care for her grandfather? While he was still a part of her life? By extension, to be sure, but still...

A soft humming floated in the window.

Nanna? She dabbed her eyes with the square of cloth, scooted off the bed and stepped to the window. It hadn't been a dream. Her grandmother was kneeling on the walkway pulling weeds, the old straw hat on her head, the folded blanket she spread to keep her skirts clean beneath her.

She glanced up at the setting sun, then looked back at her grandmother, who showed no signs of quitting her gardening. Was she aware of night approaching? Where was her grandfather? They'd been together in the sitting room when she came upstairs.

She hurried to pull on her shoes, then ran out of her room and down the stairs to the sitting room. Her grandfather was sleeping in his rolling chair, *The Pathfinder*'s adventures open in his lap.

The kitchen was clean, dimly lit and empty. Lamplight flowed out from the crack beneath Gertrude's door. Her heart squeezed. No one had been watching over Nanna. Soft, warm evening air caressed her face and arms as she stepped out on the porch, her head full of what could happen to her grandmother if night fell and she got confused and wandered into the woods.

Worry followed her down the steps and up the path. She slowed to a walk and caught her breath. *Oh, Nanna...*Flowers and weeds, soil clinging to their roots, were strewn helter-skelter on the stone walk. Her grandmother was humming softly and pulling a handful of the few remaining flowers in the garden bed in front of her.

Tears gushed from her eyes. A sob clawed its way up her throat. She swallowed hard, brushed the tears from her face and stepped closer. "My, you've been hard at work."

"Yes." Her grandmother looked up and smiled. "I'm weeding my moon pennies."

"I see that, but it's getting late and Poppa would like

you to come inside. Perhaps I could help you finish your weeding tomorrow?" She pasted on a smile and reached her hands down.

"Oh, very well. If Manning sent you to fetch me, I'd best go in." Her grandmother brushed the soil from her small, pudgy hands, placed them in Sadie's and rose. "Bring along the blanket, Ivy. But see you give it a good shaking first. I don't want any bugs left on it."

She snatched up the blanket, gave it a quick shake, tossed it over the back of the garden bench and took her grandmother's elbow. "Why don't I walk you to the house and then come back for the blanket? It's getting dark."

The throbbing was still in her temples. The cold cloth hadn't helped this time. Sadie reached up and slid the cloth off her forehead, opened her eyes and stared into the moonlit room. If only she had someone to talk to. She was afraid it would burden her grandfather's heart overmuch to tell him about the things Nanna did when he was not there to witness them. And Cole—well, Cole wasn't here to talk to. By the time she'd gotten cleaned up after making certain her grandmother was safe with her grandfather, Cole had come and gone, and her grandparents were abed.

She tossed off the quilt she'd pulled over her, rose, crossed to the washstand and dropped the cloth into the washbowl then pulled the pins from her coiled hair. The thick, wavy mass tumbled over her shoulders and down her back in a brown cascade. She arched her neck backward, ran her fingers through the silky strands to bring them under control and gathered them in her hands. A ribbon, wrapped once around and loosely tied, restrained her hair at the nape of her neck but allowed the length to flow free.

She eyed her nightgown but chose her shoes instead. She was too upset to sleep. Perhaps a cup of tea would help.

Quiet accompanied her down the stairs. She tiptoed by her grandparents' bedroom and made her way to the kitchen. Moonlight flooded the room. Its cool, silvery gleam fit her mood. She left the oil lamp trimmed and crossed to the stove. The damper scraped quietly against the inside of the stovepipe as she opened the draft. The coiled metal handle of the lifter was cool to her touch. She fitted it into the slot and lifted a front plate on the stove, placed a few small pieces of wood from the wood box on top of the shimmering coals and replaced the plate. A quick twist of her wrist adjusted the draft on the firebox door.

The iron teapot was half-full of water. She set it on the front plate over the fire and lifted the china teapot down from the shelf, grabbed a crock of dried peppermint leaves and carried them to the work table.

The keen aroma of peppermint when she opened the crock brought back memories of helping her grandmother harvest the leaves for winter use. She would have to remember to do that with Nanna this fall.

Tears blurred her vision as she spooned some of the astringent herb into the china teapot then replaced the crock on the shelf. There was no point in denying the truth to herself any longer. Nanna was not getting better. She would have to be the one to run the household now.

A sigh escaped her. Nanna had lists. She'd seen her

bring them out and go over them at different seasons. She'd ask her about them tomorrow.

Steam whispered from the spout of the iron teapot. She grabbed a towel and lifted it from the stove, filled the china teapot, set the iron one at the back of the stove and shut down the dampers to preserve the embers for morning.

The flowers... Her temples throbbed. This was nothing as simple as removing wrongly placed stitches. How could she ever make this right? Flowers died. She draped the towel over the steeping tea, wrapped her arms about her ribs and leaned against the table, her stomach knotted and tense. If Nanna had a good day tomorrow and saw what she had done to her flowers, she would know something was happening. How could she keep that truth from her, to keep her happy as long as possible...

She closed her eyes, trying to think of a solution. Perhaps if she tossed the flowers and weeds piled on the stone walk back into the garden bed, Nanna would think some animal had uprooted them. She glanced at the window. Had she courage enough to go outside into the night? She took a breath and pushed away from the table.

"Please let this work, Lord. Please don't let Nanna realize what she's done." The whispered prayer hung on the silence of the room. She opened the door and stepped out onto the porch.

The moonlight threw slanted shadows of the posts and railing across the porch floor and played hide-and-seek among the swaying folds of the long skirt of her rust-colored gown as she walked to the steps and moved down them to the path, her breath coming short and shallow.

Soft, rustling sounds of small night creatures accompanied her steps. And then another quiet sound in front of her, beyond the farewell bush by the bench, stopped her cold. Her heart pounded. Scraping? Was it possible an animal really was digging in the bed her grandmother had disturbed? A polecat looking for grubs?

She held her breath and eased forward, peeked around the bush. *"Cole!"*

"Sadie!" He jerked to his feet and stared down at her, his expression of shock a mirror of her own.

"What are you doing here?" The question was automatic, unnecessary. She looked down at the wilted flowers leaning every which way in the garden bed, at the pile of weeds beside where he'd been kneeling. "You're replanting Nanna's flowers." Her voice wobbled, and the words were barely audible. She blinked, gulped and blinked again.

He cleared his throat and took a step back. "Is that why you came out—to replant your grandmother's flowers? I figured, when I saw them earlier, that's what you would want to do, but I wasn't sure you cou—*would* come out here at night."

His voice was gruff, so unlike him. She looked up into his dark gray eyes, smoky in the moonlight, and her heart stopped, her lungs froze, not out of fear, but out of something just as frightening—if she had the courage to acknowledge it. *Help me, Lord....*

He turned away, knelt on the walk and cleared his throat again. "Anyway, I thought I'd lend a hand. She's ripped up quite a few flowers and they would be pretty well wilted by morning." He tugged a stem free from the tangled heap of foliage on the walk beside him, pulled the weed twined around the flower off, then leaned forward and stuck the roots in the hole he had ready for it.

Her breath and courage returned. She sank to her knees and reached toward the pile. He did the same, and his hand covered hers. She caught her breath and braced herself for a rush of fear. There was nothing but the feel of his hard palm and strong fingers, the grit of clinging soil and a tingling warmth that somehow connected to the quivering in her stomach.

"Sorry." He jerked his hand back. "I didn't know your hand was there."

She pulled a moon penny free and held it out to him. "I'll untangle the flowers and you plant them. The work will go faster that way."

He nodded, took the daisy and planted it, the silence of the night stretching between them. She separated another flower and held it while he dug another hole. The moonlight shone on his face and she studied his features from beneath her lowered lashes, choking on the flutter that leapt from her stomach to her throat when he glanced her way.

She waited for his touch, but he took the flower by the root and turned back to his work.

She untangled the last flowers, rose and picked up the bundle of weeds, carried them to the fence and threw them into the woods on the other side, disposing of the evidence of her grandmother's indiscriminate weeding.

A loose strand of hair tickled her cheek. She brushed it off her face with the back of her hand, felt the dirt clinging to her fingers and palms and brushed them together then looked up. Cole's gaze was fastened on her. Warmth stole into her cheeks, and more sneaked into her heart. She lifted her chin. "I must look a sight."

He shook his head, motioned with his hand. "You've a smudge of dirt on your cheek is all."

The gruffness was back in his voice. She nodded, examined her hand for remaining dirt, then wiped at her cheek.

His Adam's apple slid up and down his throat. He strode to the well and pumped a bucketful of water.

An owl hooted. A coyote howled and was answered by another. She shivered and looked toward the woods.

"They're only hunting food. There's no danger from them."

She looked back at him, so strong and sure and capable, and a sense of safety she hadn't felt in a very long time swept through her. The shock of it held her silent.

He carried the water to the flowerbed. "This should have them standing up like soldiers by morning."

"Cole…" He looked at her and it was a moment before she found her voice again. "When the coyotes howled…I was thinking of Nanna." Her throat tightened. "I was ill and fell asleep earlier. When I woke it was dusk and Nanna was here in the garden weeding. Poppa had fallen asleep and Gertrude was in her room. No one was watching Nanna, and I keep thinking about what could happen if she…wandered off." Tears flowed into her eyes, spilled over and clung to her lashes. She took a deep breath and wiped them away. "Would you…that is, I hate to impose, but…the gate swings free and…"

"I'll put a latch on it tomorrow. One with a lock."

The warmth and caring in his voice undid what remained of her control. A sob broke from her throat. He strode toward her but stopped short. His jaw clenched.

"Thank you, Cole." Her voice broke. She lifted her gaze from his jaw to his eyes, cleared her throat and tried again. "I can't express how much I appreciate what you do for Poppa and Nanna."

He looked at her so long she went weak in the knees. He pulled in a breath she could hear from where she stood and looked away.

"Your grandmother is a special lady. She invited me for supper when the other residents of Pinewood had nothing but scorn and suspicion about me."

As she had. How could she have been so wrong about him? "Cole—"

"I'll see you safe to your door."

The interruption was deliberate. She looked at the set of his jaw and nodded. "Yes, of course. Thank you again for what you've done." She walked up the path and climbed the steps. He stood like a rock at the bottom. She pulled open the door, nodded good evening and went inside.

Chapter Twenty-Two

If he could find Payne, he'd beat him to a pulp! Of course that would only prove the violence he was capable of, the very thing he feared. Cole scowled down at his fisted hands pumping at his sides in rhythm with his pounding feet and sucked in a breath to satisfy his straining lungs.

Swimming the pond was too easy for tonight. He'd needed something hard enough to exhaust him beyond the point where he could stay awake, something to deaden his mind to thoughts of Sadie Spencer! The woman was a thorn in his side for sure. A temptation that was growing harder and harder for him to resist. He loved her heart and soul—and he couldn't have her.

A growl tore from his throat, ripped from his heart by frustration and pain. It had been hard enough when her disgust and distrust of him stood between them, when the fear Payne had instilled in her with his depraved attack formed a wall she hid behind. But now...

His mouth went dry; his heart thudded. He staggered, caught his footing and picked up his pace, but the vision of Sadie standing so still and looking up at him with love and trust and wonder in her eyes stayed with him. He never should have broken down those walls.

A coyote howled somewhere up ahead, and something big moved through the woods at the side of the road. A bear? Good. He was of a mind to wrestle one. It would be a lot easier than trying to wrestle his heart.

He raced into the curve of the road, his legs flashing through the tree shadows that fell across the hard-packed dirt, his gaze scanning the area ahead for any danger.

Moonlight filtered through the towering trees and splashed pools of silver on the road. Deer snorted and bounded into the woods, fleeing his presence. A fox darted out from the trees and ran for cover on the other side.

He drove himself on, in the opposite direction of Butternut Hill, leaving behind the woman who drew him as no other, trying to outdistance the ache in his heart that cried out for her.

She was wrong. That was all. Cole's behavior tonight proved that. Sadie lowered the cold cloth from her red, puffy eyes and paced around her bedroom. She had drawn the wrong conclusion. And that was not surprising. Her isolated existence behind the brick walls of the seminary in Rochester had left her ill-prepared to interpret the…the *glances*…of men. But not their actions. And Cole's actions were very clear this evening.

Oh, it was all so confusing! Cole had always been thoughtful and kind and…and *nice*. And then there were those *moments*…and she'd thought…but then, somehow, everything changed. And she didn't know how or why or even when, but now Cole didn't want to be around her, and she wanted…well, she wanted *Cole.*

The tears flowed again. "Oh, Nanna, I *need* you." She swiped the tears from her cheeks and took a calming breath. There was no help available. She would simply have to solve this herself. Or perhaps there was nothing to solve. It had seemed as if Cole had looked at her the way her grandfather looked at her grandmother, but she was obviously wrong.

The curtains fluttered on the current of warm air flowing in the window. She turned her back, unable to bear the sight of her grandmother's moonlit garden while her memory of the night was so raw.

She could remember how her grandfather had always squeezed her grandmother's hand when he helped her in and out of the carriage, and Cole didn't even want to *touch* her hand. He had done so accidentally tonight, and he'd withdrawn his hand very quickly and apologized. And after that he was careful not to touch her hand again, though he had many opportunities to do so.

She tied the fastening on her dressing gown and walked down the stairs, the hem whispering softly from step to step, her slippers tapping against the polished oak. She hadn't been afraid tonight. At least, not in the way she had been before. God had answered her prayer and taken that terrible, debilitating fear from her. And the nightmare. She was now able to go to bed without fear of being awakened in a state of terror. She would be content in that.

But the way she had felt with Cole's hand covering hers… He hadn't been holding it, he'd never closed his fingers around her hand, though she'd thought he was going to once when his fingers twitched. Her breath had caught…and then he had withdrawn his hand and apologized for touching her. But, oh, she had wanted him to. She had wanted him to take her hand in his. And then later, when he had stood looking at her, she'd held so still, waiting…hoping.…

She turned at the bottom of the stairs and walked toward the kitchen. The tea she'd made was still sitting in the teapot covered with a towel. She'd clean it up, make more tea and think about other things. Her responsibilities were going to increase and she had to be prepared.

Silence wrapped itself around her, and she stood there in the dark hallway filled with an ache she couldn't deny or understand. She crossed into the dining room instead, opened the door and stepped out onto the porch.

The moon had risen high overhead. The porch was in darkness, the moonlight sliding off its slanted roof to brush the garden at its feet with silver. A gentle breeze stirred the ends of her long hair, slipped beneath the edges of her dressing gown and billowed it softly as she moved to stand at the top of the steps. She plucked a rose from the climbing bush, twirled it between her fingers and breathed in its sweet fragrance.

Respect…trust…love… Cole had garnered them so quietly she hadn't realized it was happening. But it had. She'd known it tonight when she'd found him replanting her grandmother's flowers.

She closed her eyes and leaned her forehead against the post beside her, struggling to accept what she now knew was true. Cole had touched something deep inside her that had been closed away ever since Payne's attack, and tonight it had opened fully to him. It had been rejected. Regret swelled the ache in her heart and brought a painful tightness to her throat.

"'I opened to my beloved; but my beloved had withdrawn himself and was gone: my soul failed when he spake: I sought him, but I could not find him; I called him, but he gave no answer.'"

She whispered the beautiful words from the Bible's Song of Solomon into the darkness. Tears slipped down her cheeks. She tossed the rose away and went into the house.

"Hey, Quick Stuff!"

"Daniel!" Sadie smiled and stepped out of Cargrave's entrance onto the wood walkway. "What are you doing in town?"

"There was some shifting in the teams of workers and I finally got my days off. Things happen quick at a logging camp, and there's no way of getting word out lest someone happens to be coming to town for some reason."

"I understand." She wrinkled her nose at him when he took her elbow to help her down the steps. "And I wasn't complaining."

"I was." He grinned and reached for her package, his long fingers covering hers. "I'll carry that for you."

She looked down at their hands. There was no tingling warmth like she'd felt with Cole last night. She sighed at the loss of her childhood dream. Daniel was, and would always be, only a dear friend. "I was going to put it in the buggy and do some more shopping. I'm waiting for my grocery order to be filled."

He placed her package on the seat and smiled down at her. "Meeting you here has spared me some time.

I was planning to run out to Butternut Hill to call for you."

She laughed and turned back toward the stores. "You mean like when you hid out behind the barn and pretended to be an owl?"

He chuckled and took her elbow as they climbed the steps to the walkway. "That was so your grandmother wouldn't come out and throw me off the place."

"I know." She tried, but the sadness crept into her voice.

He shot a look at her. "I'm sorry about your grandma's illness, Quick Stuff. That's got to be hard for you."

"It is. But there are good days. How is your mother?"

"Ma's the same as always, chatting and cooking and praying." He tossed another grin her way. "Mostly chatting."

"Daniel." She gave him a sidelong look.

His grin widened at her reproving tone. "Just speaking the truth. Ma does like to pass news around." He pulled her to a halt. "How about you forget the shopping and I take you to the restaurant for dinner while you're waiting for Ina to get around to your groceries?"

There was the warmth of a long friendship in his eyes. She pulled the comfort of it around her and nodded. "I'd like that."

"I'll have you know it's big doings to eat at the Sheffield House restaurant. A bit different than in a big town like Rochester, I suppose."

"I wouldn't know." She gave his arm a tug. "Slow down. I'm a young lady now."

"I noticed. I'd have to be blind not to." He waggled his eyebrows at her and grinned. "You've grown up a lot prettier than you promised back when you were all skinny arms and legs."

"Daniel!"

"And you're cute as a new fawn with your cheeks all pink like that." He laughed and took her arm to start her walking again. "So you didn't eat in fancy restaurants in Rochester?"

"I didn't leave the seminary." She was so discomposed the truth slipped out.

He stopped and looked down at her, his face tight, his green eyes shadowed. "I wish I'd found Payne Aylward, Sadie. I looked for him for weeks. We all did. Even Cole."

Her pulse quickened at his name. She started walking again lest Daniel notice a change in her expression. "That had to be difficult for him."

"It was—as much as we could make it."

"What do you mean?" She asked the question, but she was afraid, from what Cole had said the other night, she already knew the answer.

"I mean he came into town a couple of days after... what happened, and none of us were in the mood to be friendly to an Aylward. He didn't quit, though. He said he wanted Payne brought to justice, and he was out there prowling through the woods every day looking for his brother. We know because we watched him to be sure he brought Payne in if he found him." His boots crunched across the gravel way beside the Sheffield House. He helped her up the steps to the porch and ushered her inside.

"Sadie! Daniel!" Sophia Sheffield hurried to them and gave them each a hug. "How good to see you.

Though it's a bit odd to see you here in the hotel instead of in my kitchen."

Daniel grinned down at the proprietress. "I can't very well ask my best girl to dinner in your kitchen, Mrs. Sheffield."

"Your best girl?" Sophia faked shock. "Why, Daniel Braynard, I thought Callie was your best girl."

"I lost your niece to Ezra Ryder." He put on a mock-sad face.

"*And* you lost Willa to Matthew Calvert, Daniel." Sadie laughed, held up her hand and extended a finger. "Callie—" and another finger "—Willa—" she frowned and extended another "—And me. Hmm, I believe that makes me best girl number three."

Sophia laughed. "Unless you count Ellen."

"Oh, of course, how could I forget?" She extended her fourth finger. "Ellen."

"She doesn't count. She's in Buffalo."

Daniel folded her pinky finger back down, but his grin looked a little sour.

"No. She's in the dining room, with her parents."

She looked at Sophia's smiling face. "Truly?"

"Yes. And I know it's been…a while since you've seen one another, so I'll stop chatting and you two can go on in to the dining room. There's a table free since the Haggers just left."

"Thank you, Sophia." She gave Callie's aunt a quick hug and hurried down the hall to the dining room, jerking to a halt when Daniel grabbed her hand.

"I've got to treat my best girl right." He smiled, tucked her hand through his arm and stepped into the dining room.

The hum of conversation stopped. Diners glanced their way, nodded, smiled, raised a hand in greeting.

"Sadie?"

She glanced at the beautiful, blonde, exquisitely gowned young woman rising from her chair. "Ellen?"

"That's her."

The words were a low-pitched growl behind her as she rushed forward into a mutual hug. "It's so good to see you, Ellen!"

"And you, Sadie." Ellen squeezed her, then stepped back, adjusted her small, flowered hat into its forward tilt over the blond curls dangling on her forehead and glanced beyond her. "Good afternoon, Daniel."

"Hey, Musquash. You in town hiding out from all those rich squires of yours?"

Two spots of red sprang into Ellen's cheeks. "Stop calling me that!"

"You like Muskrat better?" Daniel's voice matched his grin.

"You're perfectly *hateful,* Daniel Braynard." Ellen fairly hissed the words. Daniel's lips tightened at the edge of his grin.

"Are you two still fussing at one another?" She glanced from one to the other and shook her head. "You sound the same as when we were kids."

"That's because some people never learn their manners!" Ellen tossed her head and turned her back toward Daniel.

"And others never grow up."

She glanced toward Daniel, shocked by the bitterness in the under-his-breath remark, then leaned down to give Ellen's mother a quick hug. "Good afternoon, Mrs. Hall…Mr. Hall." She nodded to Ellen's father, who was standing politely by his chair. "It's so nice to see you both again."

"It's a shame we were just leaving." Ellen grabbed the drawstrings on the purse sitting at her place at the table, turned and gave her another quick hug. "Please come to call on me, Sadie—when you're *alone.* I'd love to visit with you." She stepped back and lifted her chin. "I'm ready now, Father. Mother, shall we stop at the shop before we go home?"

"Yes, of course, Ellen." Mrs. Hall rose and gave her a warm smile. "So nice to see you again, Sadie. Please remember me to your grandmother."

"Thank you, I shall." She stared after Ellen as she flounced out of the dining room with her parents in her wake, shocked by her friend's display of bad manners. "Daniel, what—?"

He shook his head. "She's above the likes of me now, Sadie. Has been for quite a while." He smiled and placed his hand at her back to urge her forward. "We'd best take our seats. Your groceries will be ready soon."

She nodded and walked with him to the empty table.

She strolled along the wooded path, smiled at the birds flitting from branch to branch. The curve ahead was dim in the dusky light of the fading day. Boots thudded on the hard-packed soil and she stopped, peering ahead.

A tall, broad-shouldered man came striding around the curve. Her heart swelled at the love in his eyes. She smiled and started toward him.

He pivoted and walked back the way he'd come, leaving her alone on the forest path.

* * *

"Cole!" Sadie jerked to a sitting position, blinked her eyes and gazed around her bedroom. It was a dream. A very real one.

She shivered, sank back onto her pillow and tugged the covers over her shoulders, thankful it hadn't been a return of the nightmare, though there were similarities. Both started the same way, with her walking on the wooded path, but in the dream it was dusk, not daylight. And a man appeared in both, but the similarities ended there. The man in the dream was Cole, and she'd been happy to see him.

I called him, but he gave no answer. Her stomach flopped. She turned onto her side and stared at the dark outside the window. Why would Cole, who was so kind and thoughtful of others, turn and walk away at the sight of her, leaving her alone and unprotected on that path?

Your grandmother is a special lady. She invited me for supper when the other residents of Pinewood had nothing but scorn and suspicion about me.

The memory made her feel ill. She took a breath and slipped her legs over the side of the bed. Was the dream about Cole being angry with her for the way she had treated him? He'd interrupted her when she'd started to apologize.

...none of us were in the mood to be friendly to an Aylward...

Daniel's words struck her with the force of a blow. How selfish she'd been, thinking only of herself. Cole, too, had suffered because of Payne's actions. She had to apologize, to let him know she understood.

She rose and went to look out into the dark night.

"Oh, Lord, forgive me please. I was wrong to judge Cole because of Payne. I've been wrong about so many things. And selfish in my hurt. Please help me to undo any hurt I may have caused Cole. And thank You, Lord, for taking away my fear and showing me the truth."

Chapter Twenty-Three

Nanna was getting close to the gate. Sadie edged toward the steps and rested her hand on the railing. Her grandmother had been having a good day, but that could change in an instant. And if she went through the gate and got on the wooded path… A shiver slid down her spine. She would have to go after her. There was no one else. *Almighty God, please—*

"Something…wrong, Sa…die?"

"No, Poppa." She couldn't tell him. It would only burden him with worry and guilt and frustration because he wouldn't be able to do anything to protect Nanna. She glanced at him, then leaned over the railing and picked a rose so she didn't have to turn from watching her grandmother. "Why do you ask?"

"You've been…quiet…tonight."

She turned sideways so she could see him and still keep watch, and pulled up a smile. "Are you saying I'm a chatterbox?"

He peered up at her, but there was no answering smile.

Hers faded. "I'm sorry, Poppa. I didn't mean to

sound flippant." She sighed and sniffed the rose. "I've been thinking…and remembering. I was away from home for so long, and though I knew better, of course, in my mind things and people remained the same. The changes are a little…off-putting at times."

"Nanna…and…me?"

He was referring to their illnesses. Sadness clutched at her heart. He would know she was lying if she denied it. She nodded and searched for a way to explain her melancholy. "And me. I've changed, too." She raised her hand and sniffed, glanced at her grandmother over top of the rose. "I was remembering how, when I was young, Nanna would tell me when it was time for you to come home—probably to keep me out of her way when she was busy cooking supper." A wry smile touched her lips. His eyes smiled agreement at her. "And I would come out here on the porch and watch for you to come walking out of the woods. That was one of the best times of my day."

Thank You, Lord, for the lovely memories. She blinked her eyes and gave a little laugh. "Do you remember how I ran to meet you at the gate when I was small?"

He nodded, and his gaze shifted from her to the garden path and back again. "You wanted… piggyback…ride."

She wrinkled her nose at him. "I liked the way I bounced when you ran." Her heart lifted at his chuckle. She tossed the rose away and looked into the distance, seeing those long-ago days. "You smelled like sawdust. Sometimes I could see it on your hair." Her throat clogged. He'd been so big and strong, her poppa. And she'd felt so safe when he held her… She cleared away the lump.

"And I liked standing on a chair and helping Nanna make pudding and cookies—especially the brown ones. And the way she tucked the covers around me and kissed me good-night after I said my prayers." The tender ache in her heart was becoming too strong. She took a breath and veered away from those memories. "And, of course, later on, when I was older, going off on adventures with Willa and Callie and Ellen and Daniel. My, some of the things we did!"

"Worried…Nanna." He cleared his throat. "She blamed…Daniel."

"I know." She shook her head and smiled, then took a lighter tone. "Don't tell Nanna, but the truth is, we hounded poor Daniel. He tried to go off on adventures by himself, but we would run after him." She laughed and leaned back against the post. "I was the fastest runner, and I could follow him if he didn't have too much of a head start."

Nanna was coming to the house. She stepped back away from the railing, grinned and put her finger to her puckered lips.

Her grandfather chuckled and nodded.

She moved over to the table. "And now we're all adults and everything is different." The scene in the restaurant between Ellen and Daniel flashed into her head. "Except Daniel still teases Ellen, and Ellen still gets in a huff about it."

"Who gets in a huff about what?" Her grandmother climbed the steps, let go of the railing and gripped the basket of herbs she was carrying with both hands.

She watched her grandfather's eyes. He always exchanged a look with Nanna when they'd been separated, as if they were somehow reconnecting. Her breath caught. It *was* the same look. Well, not quite the same. There was something less intense, more…*comfortable* in her grandfather's eyes. Still—

"Sadie?"

"What? Oh. I'm sorry, Nanna." She jerked her thoughts back to the conversation. "I was speaking of Ellen. She gets in a huff when Daniel teases her."

"Well, it doesn't surprise me. Daniel needs manners, and Ellen needs to be less pouty. Her mother spoils her. I warned Frieda about that when you children were young, but she didn't listen." Her grandmother gave a small huff of annoyance and headed for the kitchen door, the brim of the old straw hat bobbing in time with her swaying skirts.

"Daniel…good man. Rachel…knows it." Her grandfather patted her hand. "It's…getting late. Help me… go inside…Sa…die."

"Of course, Poppa." It *was* getting late. She looked up at the setting sun, then glanced toward the garden gate. Cole must have forgotten about putting a latch on it. She would have to watch until Nanna went to bed.

Her grandfather's chair clicked. She propped open the dining room door, then grasped the wheels of his chair and rolled it over the raised sill.

"I'll see you in the morning, Manning." Cole closed the bedroom door and glanced toward the sitting room. Sadie would be there. Sadie—forbidden fruit. He set his jaw, turned his back and strode down the hall to the dining room, yanked the door open and stepped out into the night.

The lantern he'd left on the railing threw a circle of gold onto the porch floor. He grabbed its handle and trotted down the steps. It wouldn't take him long to affix the latch on the gate, and then he could leave, putting distance between himself and the one he wanted to be with more than any other.

He squatted, set the lamp on the ground and upended a small leather pouch he'd left there. His hammer, nails and the pieces of the iron latch clanged against the slate of the path. A rustle of fabric came from behind him.

"I came to help—if I'm able."

Sadie's soft voice set his pulse racing. He glanced over his shoulder at her slender form in the darkness and shook his head. "That's thoughtful of you, but there's nothing you can do." He pulled his lamp close and began lining up the various pieces of the latch in the small circle of light.

The hems of her long skirts whispered against the stone, and the fabric brushed against his arm as she stepped forward and lifted the lantern. The circle of light widened, spreading over the ground. "I can hold the lamp for you."

He nodded, stuck the broad heads of the specially cut nails in his mouth, selected one of the pieces of iron and snatched up his hammer. He rose and fitted the piece against the frame of the gate, hammered it in place. A narrow piece of iron bar dangled from it, held in place by a nail with a flattened head.

"What is that?" Her arm brushed against his as she moved the lantern closer.

He sucked in a breath and snatched the nails from his mouth before he choked on them. "It's a bar lock."

He grabbed the other piece, swung the gate closed

to line them up, then shoved the gate back open and nailed the second piece to the end post of the fence.

"How does it work?" She leaned close to see.

He jerked his head back, flipped the bar over to drop behind the bent-up pieces of iron on the lock and tugged on the gate. It didn't budge.

"That works perfectly." She straightened and looked up at him, the lamplight gilding her hair, spreading across her fine cheekbones and caressing the clean line of her small, square chin, shadowing the slender column of her neck. "Thank you, Cole. I'll feel much better about Nanna working in her garden now."

His heart pounded so hard he could feel it in his hands. He dropped his gaze from the soft warmth in her eyes to the small half smile on her lips. All he had to do was lean forward and... He gritted his teeth and turned away, stooped to put his hammer and the few leftover nails back in the leather pouch. "Don't count too much on the latch lock, Sadie. Your grandmother will soon learn how to open it."

"I know." The light wavered as she lowered the lantern to shine on the nails on the stone. "But at least she won't simply wander through the open gate and go... onto that path." The light flickered.

He reached to steady the shaking lantern, felt her hand trembling and closed his over it. His heart thundered. He rose and looked down into her eyes. "Sadie..."

"Yes?"

Her name was a gruff plea from his constricted throat—her answer a barely heard whisper. Time was lost in his need to comfort her, to protect her, to love her forever. He sucked in a breath, fighting his heart with every bit of strength he possessed and hating himself for winning the battle. "I'll see you safe to the house."

He took the lantern from her hand, holding it so she could see the path, acutely aware of her beside him, of the golden light warming the pale flesh of her arm and hand. He stopped at the foot of the steps and held the light for her to see. "The window lamp will light your way across the porch."

She turned toward him, taking a breath he could hear.

"Before I go inside, I have something to say. I trust you will listen." Her gaze sought and held his. "I didn't come outside only to help you while you worked, Cole. I am troubled because the other night you would not let me apologize for treating you so shabbily when you were being nothing but kind and generous and thoughtful to Nanna and Poppa."

Her soft, quiet words settled deep in his heart. "Sadie—"

"No. You'll not stop me from speaking this time, Cole. Please."

He bit back the words he'd been about to say and nodded. "All right, I'll listen."

"Thank you." She took another breath. "I had a disquieting dream the other night. It started the same as the…nightmare I've suffered the past four years." Her voice quavered. She wrapped her arms about herself.

He clenched his jaw, set the lantern on the steps and shoved his hands in his pockets to keep from reaching for her.

"But in this dream, I am walking along the path to Poppa's sawmill, and you come around the bend walking toward me. At the very place—"

"Sadie, don't—"

She shook her head.

He clenched his teeth and held his silence.

"We stop and…look…at one another, then you turn and walk back the way you had come. I call to you, but you keep walking."

She looked at him, and the hurt in her eyes took his breath.

"You are a kind, thoughtful and caring man, Cole. Yet you walk away and leave me alone and unprotected on that path. The only reason I can see for your behavior is anger." Her head bowed. "I am so very sorry for judging you according to Payne's deed, and not for yourself. I was wrong. And I ask you to forgive me. I—" her head lifted "—I don't want you angry with me any longer."

Lord, give me strength…. "I've never been angry with you, Sadie."

"But—I know it's only a dream, Cole. But why else would you walk away and leave me unprotected on that path?"

Lord, help me. I love her. And the only way I can protect her is to tell her the truth. "I *am* protecting you, Sadie—by walking away." He picked up the lantern and started down the path.

"Cole, wait!"

Her footsteps sounded behind him. He stopped and turned to face her.

"You're not talking about the dream, are you?"

"No."

"I don't understand."

He looked straight into her eyes. "My father was a drunk. He beat my mother to death." He winced at her gasp but pressed on, sparing himself nothing. "You, better than anyone, know the depravity and violence that lives in Payne." He took a breath and forced out the words. "Who knows if or when that same violence will rise in me?"

"Oh, Cole, *no*. That can't be."

"Denying it doesn't make it so, Sadie."

"Actions do." Her chin lifted. "You're kind, and—"

"So was Payne. At least, the Payne *I* knew was. I don't know what happened to change him, and that's what's troubling. He's my brother—and our father's blood runs in both our veins. Who knows what I might be capable of doing someday? You're right to be frightened of me, Sadie."

He pivoted on his heel and strode down the path. Opening the gate, he picked up his leather pouch and walked into the woods.

"Cole!"

The despair in her cry, the sound of her running after him seared his heart. His nails dug into the leather pouch, and the force of his clench bent the lantern handle in the curl of his fingers.

He stared straight ahead and kept walking. It would be all right. She would stop at the gate. She would never come onto the path. Rage at what had happened to her, at Payne for attacking her, at the injustice of his being unable to have her, choked off his breath, darkened his vision. He stumbled, caught himself and kept on, every step driving the pain of losing her deeper into his heart.

Chapter Twenty-Four

It was too much. It was simply too much. She felt as if she were breaking into little pieces. Sadie gripped the broom handle and attacked the corners of the step, swept them clean and turned her fury on the next one. Dust flew.

She closed her eyes and wiped her face, wincing at the feel of grit clinging to the tear tracks on her cheeks. No doubt she looked a sight. Poppa and Nanna would notice. She propped the broom against the wall, took the hem of her long apron in her hands and scrubbed at her face. What could she do? How could she convince Cole what he feared was untrue? Surely it was untrue!

A sob broke from her throat. She twisted around and collapsed onto a step, buried her face in the apron and fought to control her crying. If Poppa or Nanna heard...

Tears slipped from beneath her lashes and wet the apron pressed against her eyes. Cole was Payne's brother, but she knew now he was not like him. She had looked into Payne's eyes. She had seen the cruelty glittering there, and there was nothing of cruelty in Cole. His eyes were... were— Oh, what if he went away...?

"What's wrong, sweeting?"

Sweeting?

She lifted her head and lowered the apron. Her grandmother stood on the landing, her eyes full of love and concern. Sadie gulped back a sob and shook her head, but she couldn't stop her mouth from quivering.

"Oh, Sadie, sweeting…"

Her grandmother climbed to the step and sat beside her, pulled her into her arms and tugged her head down against her soft shoulder.

The sobs broke free at her nanna's touch. Tears streamed from her eyes. Her grandmother's small hands patted her back and smoothed her hair as she struggled to get control. Bittersweet pain squeezed her throat.

"Shh, Sadie. It will be better. I promise it will be better. Tell me what's hurting your heart, sweeting. Tell me what's troubling you."

She shouldn't. She didn't want to worry her grandmother, but the temptation to have the comfort and wisdom she'd known all her life was too great to resist. "I—I think C-Cole's—" she gulped back a sob "—going away."

"Nonsense."

"Wh-what?" She lifted her head and blinked away the watery blur, looked into her grandmother's clear, focused gaze.

"I said that's nonsense, Sadie. Wherever did you get such an idea? Cole isn't going anywhere."

She sounded so *certain.* "Cole told me, Nanna. He said he was…'walking away.'"

"Well, he won't."

She stared at her grandmother. She seemed so positive. Did she understand? She looked as if she was having a good day, but… "Why do you say that, Nanna?"

"Because Cole is in love with you. And love is stronger than any spat the two of you might have had." Her grandmother smiled, reached over and patted her hand.

Shock froze her tongue. She shook her head, drew a breath and blew it out again. "H-how do you know that?"

"Because of the way he looks at you, dear—when he thinks Poppa and I aren't watching, of course." Her grandmother laughed softly and wiped her cheeks. "And, if I may say so, I think these tears mean you are beginning to return Cole's affections. Now why don't you go to your room and put a cold cloth on your red, puffy eyes? If you've had a spat, you'll want to look your prettiest when Cole comes tonight."

If he came tonight. She shoved the thought away and gave her grandmother a fierce hug. "I love you, Nanna."

"I love you, too, sweeting. Now run along and do as I say. I'll finish the stairs."

She nodded and headed to her room, the swish of the broom accompanying her steps and the heavy, aching beat of her heart. Cole would come, but not to see her. He would help Poppa into his bed and then he would go away. Unless she could think of some way to change his mind.

Because of the way he looks at you, dear.

Her pulse skipped. She'd been right about his eyes. But it was too late. No! She wouldn't accept that. She wouldn't let it be too late. There had to be something…

And ye shall know the truth, and the truth shall make you free.

The Scripture verse flowed into her heart. She stood

frozen in the quiet of her room, feeling the power in the words, knowing that, somehow, it was the answer she sought. She took a breath and closed her eyes.

"Thank You, dear God, for the promise of Your word. I know there is no cruelty or depravity in Cole. Please show me how to convince him of that truth. Please set him free of his fears. Amen."

She crossed to her washstand, washed her face and stared at her reflection in the mirror, amazed at the change that had been wrought in her. Love had taken the place of fear, and she hadn't even realized it was happening.

Cole slipped from the saddle and looped Cloud's reins over the hitching post. His stomach had knots the size of his fist, but it was the best way. He crossed the wood walk and climbed the stone steps, opened the door onto the coolness of the bank's interior. No jangling store bells greeted him. That was taking some getting used to.

He closed the door, looked across the room and caught the busy clerk's eye.

"Good afternoon, Cole. I'll be with you in a minute."

"No need, Tom. I only want to talk with Ezra, if he's free."

"He is. Go on in."

He nodded his thanks, rapped his knuckles on Ezra's office door and opened it.

Ezra looked up from the paper on his desk and smiled a welcome. "Come in, Cole. How are the rolling chairs coming along?"

"That's what I came to talk with you about."

"I see." Ezra's gaze narrowed on his face. He rose

and came around his desk, leaned a hip on it and sat, his one leg dangling free. "Is there a problem?"

"Not with making them." He blew out a breath and scrubbed his hand across the back of his neck. "I was thinking that it might be a good thing if I went along with you to New York City to explain how the chairs work to these store owners you were talking about. I could answer any questions they might have."

Ezra studied him for a moment, then nodded. "That sounds like a good idea. We can work that out. Is there anything else?"

"A couple of things." He took a breath and said the words that drove a knife into his heart. "First, the chairs should be finished in another week, but I'd like to delay the trip until I have a chance to install the clapboard machine I've sent for at the sawmill and train men to run it."

"All right. There's no hurry about our trip."

"Good, because I also want time to find a good man to take over managing the sawmill and logging camps for Manning."

Ezra's brow rose. "Is there trouble between you and Manning Townsend, Cole?"

"No." He held his face calm, his voice steady and businesslike. "That's the second thing. I'm hoping to sell my business to him. But—"

"You're going to sell your shingle mill?"

He nodded and worked to keep his hands from clenching. "I'm planning on it. I figure if the store owners feel the chairs will sell well, it would be best to buy a shop and make them right there in the city."

"I see." Ezra frowned and rubbed his forefinger over his chin. "That makes good business sense."

The knots in his stomach twisted tighter. "The problem is, I know Manning doesn't have money enough to buy the shingle mill outright, so I thought, if he's interested, I would let him pay me as he could."

"That's generous of you."

"He's a friend. And his business is gaining."

"Under your management."

The praise of his skills helped a little. At least he wouldn't leave Pinewood under a cloud. "I'll find a good, honest man to take over."

He drew his thoughts away from that pain and focused on his business. "That's where you come in. I've got some money set aside, but I doubt it's enough to secure a property in the city. So, before I start talking to Manning, I need to know if the bank will give me a note for what I'll need—against the sale of my business. Should that fail, I'll stand good for it."

Ezra rose and came to stand in front of him. "If that's what you want to do, Cole, there's no need to involve the bank. I will personally lend you whatever you need. I told you I'd back you in getting this rolling chair business started for a small percentage of the first five years' profits, and this will be part of the deal."

He should have felt relief instead of a crushing disappointment. "That's it then." He dredged up a smile and shook Ezra's hand. "I'll talk to Manning as soon as the clapboard machine comes and his profits increase. Meanwhile, I'll get those chairs finished, and I'll start looking for a man to take over as manager of the Townsend businesses."

"I deal with a lot of business men from the nearby towns, Cole. If I hear of anyone with managing skills looking for work, I'll let you know."

"I'd appreciate it, Ezra. Thank you." *Liar.* He pulled his shoulders back and walked from the office.

The door. Sadie glanced at her grandfather nodding over the book in his lap. He was too tired to want to visit or discuss business. Was that Cole's plan? Is that why he was so late?

"Good evening."

Her breath caught at the sight of him in the doorway. "Good evening."

His gaze skimmed over her, then rested on her grandmother.

"I'm sorry I'm late, Mrs. Townsend. I was detained by work."

"No matter. You're here now." Her grandmother wove her needle in the backing of her needlepoint, set the frame aside and rose. "I'd best go turn back the bed." She came and gave her a hug, patted her hand, then headed for the hallway.

"Good night…Sa…die." Her grandfather pulled the lever on his chair, propelling himself toward the doorway.

"Good night, Poppa." She bit back her disappointment as he reached Cole's side.

"Problem…at the…mill…Cole?"

"No." Cole turned and walked beside her grandfather's chair as he clicked his way into the hall. "I was working on one of the rolling chairs I'm making, trying to fit one of the gears…" The bedroom door closed on his words.

She gazed at the empty spot where he'd been standing and clenched her hands as tears stung her eyes. He'd paid her no more mind than one of the moths flitting around the candles on the mantel.

She moved over to the settee, checked the stitches on her grandmother's needlepoint piece. They were as neat as ever they had been. There was no need to re-work them tonight. Her heart swelled. *Thank You, Lord, for Nanna's good day.*

Her grandfather's book lay open on the lamp table. She placed a yarn marker in the pages and closed its cover and snuffed the lamp. The quiet snick of the latch on her grandfather's bedroom door made her heart skip.

Please, Lord... She stood in the quiet room, waited. His boot heels clicked against the wood, his footsteps faded away down the hall. The back door opened and closed.

I am protecting you, Sadie—by walking away.

Determination stirred. She clenched her hands and marched to the fireplace to snuff the candles. Cole may have ignored her tonight, but he wouldn't do so for long. Until God told her how to help him, she would fight with what she knew. Tomorrow she would go to Frieda Hall's shop and spend some of her savings on a new gown.

Chapter Twenty-Five

Of all the days for the weather to suddenly turn nasty. Sadie shivered and ducked into Cargrave's recessed entrance, opened the door and stepped inside. The bell jingled news of her arrival.

"You got here in the nick of time, Miss Sadie. It's working up to a good storm out there."

She smiled at the tall, lanky miller standing by the counter. "I hope you're wrong, Mr. Karcher."

He shook his head and pointed to the window behind her. "The rain's starting."

She turned to look. Her heart sank at the sight of the rain pelting down out of the sky to dance on the hard-packed dirt of Main Street. It would be a mire in no time.

The miller stepped around her to the door, tugged the collar of his shirt up and looked back at her. "There's not much protection in that bit of a jacket you're wearing. I hope you have a blanket in your buggy or you're going to have a cold drive home. Leastways until you turn up Butternut Hill. The storm's coming out of the west, and, judging by that sky, it's going to get worse as the day wears on." He pulled the door open and hurried outside, letting it bang shut behind him.

"He's right, Sadie." She spun around to see Callie hurrying her way from the dry-goods section. "Why don't you come home with me and wait the storm out?"

She glanced down at the flowered chintz spencer she'd worn over her blue cotton gown and frowned. The rain would soak through it in no time. She sighed and shook her head. She wouldn't be shopping for a new gown today. "I can't, Callie. With the storm it will take me longer to get home, and I don't want to leave Poppa and Nanna alone. It's hard for Gertrude to cook and care for them, too."

Her heart squeezed. What if Nanna wandered out in the storm? She had to leave. "I'll get the things I came for and then start home. I never would have come to town had I realized a storm was brewing." She moved to the notions shelf, picked up spools of magenta and dark-blue needlepoint yarn, fingered a length of lace. Perhaps a collar instead of a new dress. She could make it this afternoon.

"I understand." Callie's voice softened with concern. "It must be difficult for you to care for your grandparents, even with help. What will you do when Cole is gone to New York City?"

Her breath froze in her lungs. She drew her hand back from the lace. "I didn't know he was going to the city."

"Hmm, he and Ezra discussed it yesterday. Oh, look at this lovely trim."

As if the green-and-gold braid Callie held mattered. "It's very nice. What did they decide?"

"It seems Cole thought it would be good if he sold his shingle mill here and bought a shop in New York City so he could make the rolling chairs there where the large stores are. If the proprietors decide to sell them, that is."

Her stomach churned. She put her hand against it and pressed hard. "Cole is going to sell his shingle mill and move to the city?"

"Yes, Ezra agrees with Cole that it's a wise thing to do. And it does make sense, don't you think?" Callie put down the packet of buttons she held and looked over at her.

She nodded and forced words from her constricted throat. "Yes, I suppose it does."

Callie's eyes narrowed on her. "Are you feeling well, Sadie? You're very pale."

"I'm fine. It's likely the dim light from the storm." She glanced at the window, then returned the spools of yarn to their place on the shelf. "The storm is getting worse. I'll get these another time. I must get home. Come for a visit soon, Callie."

It took forever to reach the door. She tried to hurry, but her feet moved as if she were dragging herself through thick mud. *Cole was leaving Pinewood.* Rain dribbled down her neck and soaked the shoulders and back of her dress as she made her way to the buggy, loosed Sweetpea's reins and climbed inside. The gray deluge blew in under the hood and wetted the skirt over her knees as she urged the mare forward.

I am protecting you, Sadie—by walking away.

Did Cole care that much for her, that he was willing to give up the life he'd built over the past four years and leave town because he thought he was a danger to her? Shivering and shaking took her. Tears flowed from her eyes and mingled with the raindrops pelting her face. She had to stop him. Somehow, she had to convince Cole that she needed him. That her happiness and safety were in the strength and security of his love.

Cole stopped in the recessed entrance, slapped his hat against his thigh, then jammed it back on his head and opened the door. The jangle of the bell was lost in the drumming of the rain on the walkway.

"Beastly weather out there."

He looked at Allan Cargrave and nodded. "I'll say."

The proprietor grinned. "Seems as though a smart man would stay indoors."

He chuckled in agreement. "It does seem that way."

"Where'd the storm catch you?"

"On my way back from Olville." He stomped water from his boots, moved to the table holding baskets of hand tools and picked up a small whetstone.

"You must have passed him, then."

"Passed who?"

"A fellow by the name of Frank Trent. He stopped in a short while ago. Said he was passing through town and left this letter for me to give you." The proprietor held out a folded piece of paper.

Frank Trent? The name meant nothing to him. He crossed to the counter, blew on his hands to dry them, then took the letter, broke the wax seal and unfolded it. The light was too dim to read the writing. He raised the paper toward the lamp hanging from a hook overhead.

Mr. Cole Aylward
Sir:

I am writing with information you seek, however, I must tell you I am the bearer of bad news.

It is my sad duty to inform you that a logger
answering to the description you set forth for your
brother in the letter received by the mayor's office in Warren, Pennsylvania, is in trouble with
the law.

This logger, believed to be your brother, committed a most heinous act upon a young lady of
our town last evening and is now fleeing from the
authorities and townspeople. He is believed to be
in the surrounding hills.

This information is true and useful. Please
present my recompense of ten dollars to the may-
or's office in Warren.

Respectfully,
Frank Trent

Cole sucked in a breath through clenched teeth,
folded the letter into his palm and looked at Allan Cargrave. "Thank you for holding this for me. I'll be back
for the whetstone."

He turned his back on the curious light in the proprietor's eyes and left the store, swiped his saddle clear
of rainwater, mounted and rode up Main Street to the
parsonage.

The letter crushed as he fisted his hand and knocked
at the front door.

This logger, believed to be your brother, has committed a most heinous act upon a young lady...

His stomach heaved and bile rose into his throat. Payne had done it again. He'd attacked another young woman. He stepped back as footsteps sounded inside and the latch lifted.

"Cole! Come in." Matthew Calvert smiled and pulled the door wide.

"I'd rather talk out here, Reverend. I won't be staying and there's no need to mess up your floor."

Matthew gazed at him a moment, then nodded, stepped out onto the stoop and closed the door. "What can I do for you, Cole?"

"It's not for me—it's for Manning. I believe I've had news of my brother." He opened his fist, showed him the crushed letter on his palm. "If the logger this man writes of is Payne, he's in Warren, Pennsylvania, and he attacked another woman."

He swallowed hard against the burning sourness in his throat, took a deep breath and continued. "They're searching the hills for him now. I've got to go and help. Would you see to Manning while I'm gone?" The muscle along his jaw jumped. "I can't say how long that will be. I'm planning to stay until we find him."

Matthew nodded. "Of course I'll see to Manning for as long as necessary. There's no need for you to be concerned over that. But why don't you come in and warm yourself before you leave? Willa can pack you some food to take along and—"

He shook his head, opened his rain jacket, shoved the letter into his pocket and turned to go. "Thank you, kindly, Reverend, but there's no time. If I start now, I'll make Warren by nightfall. I know Payne's habits in the woods and can track him better than those other men. He won't get away this time."

The weather was horrible, the wind and rain relentless. Would Cole come tonight? Yes, he had to come—he had to take care of Poppa. Sadie tightened her arms about herself and worried the corner of her lip with her teeth. Tonight might be her last chance. What should she say to him?

"Sa…die…"

Should she confess her feelings for him? Would that conv—

"Sa…die!"

"Oh!" She turned from the window, dragging her thoughts from Cole. "I'm sorry, Poppa, what is it?"

"Someone is…at the…door."

"In this weather?"

She hurried out into the entrance and down the hall to open the door. "Willa!" She stared at her friend, then shifted her gaze to the man behind her. "And Reverend. What—" A gust of wind blew rain across the porch, spattering her face with the cold drops. "I'm sorry, come in. Let me take your wet coats. I'll hang them in the kitchen."

She moved to the lamp on the serving table and twisted the knob to raise the wick and give more light. "There, that's better. Now give me—" She stared at Willa's face. "What is it? What's wrong?"

"Nothing, Sadie. It's only…there's been news about Payne Aylward."

The name was like a blow. She stepped backward, pressed a hand to her throat. "He's here?"

"No! Oh, no, Sadie, I didn't mean that. Payne is in Warren, Pennsylvania." Willa unfastened the button at the neck of her cape and stepped out from under its damp folds as Matthew lifted it from her shoulders. "At least, the man who wrote the letter to Cole *thinks* the logger there is Payne. And Cole has gone to—"

"What letter?"

Matthew moved toward the hallway. "Cole has never stopped looking for Payne. He was riding to nearby towns to question people, but since your grandfather's seizure, he's not been free to do that. Instead he's written letters to the authorities in the towns. This letter is an answer to one of his queries."

She listened to Matthew's factual tone and relaxed, felt the fear waning.

"So Cole has gone to Warren to find out if this man is Payne?" *Oh, grant it, Lord, I pray. Let Cole find Payne and learn the truth about the difference in them. Let him come back to me, Lord. Please let him come back to me.*

"Yes. He left this afternoon. But he came to me first, to make sure your grandfather would be taken care of while he is gone."

Yes. That is like him. "I see. Well, thank you for coming out on this awful night." She took their coats and led the way into the hall. "Why don't you go on in to Poppa and Nanna while I hang these coats and fix some hot tea to warm you after your cold ride."

She went into the kitchen and hung the coats on a peg, added wood to the fire and filled the teakettle. What did it all mean? Would Cole find the answers he sought? Would he come back and stay in Pinewood?

Or would he still sell his shingle mill and go to New York City to make chairs?

There were so many questions. But one mattered more than all the others. Did Cole love her? Or were his feelings based on his guilt for what Payne had done?

She sighed and looked out at the rain sheeting off the porch roof. No matter what Cole felt for her, she would tell him the truth. She would convince him that she loved and trusted him and that she no longer feared him. But how?

Chapter Twenty-Six

Dawn was no more than a promise behind the heavy, overcast sky as Cole joined the loggers gathered at the foot of the hill. A short, burly man with a scar that started at the corner of his left eye and ran over his prominent cheekbone to disappear into a curly red beard stepped out in front of the small group.

"You men know why you were chosen to come here this morning. This is the hardest, most dangerous climb in the area, and you're the best climbers we've got. It's not likely Allyson—or whatever his name is—would've come here, but it's the only place left to search, and we've got to find him, lest he escape and hurt another woman."

A low growling sound rose from the bearded faces of the assembled loggers.

Allyson. Aylward. Cole's face tightened. The man was wrong. If this was the most dangerous hill to climb, it's exactly where Payne would choose. His brother was as sure-footed as a mountain goat.

He stared at the steep, forested face of the hill, tugged up his collar and hunched his shoulders against the cold mist that seemed to sink right through his clothes and skin to his bones. Payne would have made a nest of old leaves or pine boughs to sleep in through the storm last night, and though he would have broken the nest down and strewn the leaves and boughs around, there would be signs. He intended to find them and follow them straight to Payne. His brother had almost killed that poor woman. His own brother. *God, what has happened to Payne? I have to know!* Could it ever happen to him? The knots in his stomach twisted tighter.

"…split into pairs. Taylor, you and Morgan take the creek. Foster, you and Benson take Stony Bend—" the burly man's hamlike hand waved through the air, his thick finger pointing in various directions "—Clemons, you and North take Dead Man Spring. Aylward, you say you're a climber?"

He dipped his head, holding the man's steely gaze with his own. "I'll get to wherever I need to go." *Lead me to him, Lord.*

"All right, then, you come with me along Devil's Drop. The rest of you, spread out and search along the bottom of the hill. And keep a sharp eye out. Allyson's a woodsman, and we don't want him doubling back and slipping away."

The crowd of men broke up, fanning out along the bottom of the hill and starting into the woods.

"This way, Aylward." The burly man turned and plowed into the woods.

Cole looked ahead as far as he could see through the thick trees and detected a faint, narrow trail that led straight up the left side of a steep-sided cut on the right that appeared to sever the hill. No need to keep watch that way. Not even Payne could cling to those smooth walls of stone.

He scanned the area to his left, studying the trail and the man ahead. He was setting a good pace. "Have you got a name, in case I have to call you?"

"Kelly."

The word was curt, cold. Obviously, Kelly had reservations about him as Payne's brother. He'd probably told him to come along with him so he could keep watch on him. His mind flashed back to Pinewood four years ago, to the cold, suspicious treatment he'd received from the village men as they'd searched the hills. And he thought of Sadie. Beautiful, warm—

He shoved her image out of his head, timed his breaths, rolled his shoulders to relax them and bent his knees as he hit his climbing stride. Thinking of Sadie wouldn't find Payne, but it might get him injured or killed if he made a misstep because of lack of attention.

Sadie swished the soapy cloth in and around the chimney globe, then dipped the globe in the pan of hot rinse water and set it to drain with the others on the towel.

She cast a quick glance at her grandmother taking all of the clean flatware out of the cupboard drawer again and snatched up a towel to dry the globes and carry them to the butler's pantry before she came and put them back in the water.

Her temples throbbed. She placed the globes on the clean, trimmed bases, took two of the lamps into the dining room and set them on the mantel, turning them so the knobs were on the inside facing each other as Nanna liked before returning to the pantry.

The cold off the small glass panes of the window chilled her face, neck and hands. She glanced at the relentless drizzle falling from the gray sky and shivered. Where was Cole? Was he out in the wet and the cold? Was he in danger?

A ripple quivered through her already upset stomach. *Please keep Cole safe, Almighty God. And please let him find the truth that will set him free of his fears.*

The tears that were so ready to fall stung the backs of her eyes. She blinked them away and took another hold on her emotions that were too raw to stay controlled, picked up two more lamps and carried them into the sitting room.

She had suffered physical fear for four years, and Cole's kindness and consideration of her grandparents had broken the grip of that fear. Now there was a new fear inside her—the fear of losing Cole. How had her love for him grown so strong when she hadn't even realized it was happening?

She gazed around the room, searching for something to do. There was no more work to be done. Her cleaning frenzy had taken care of that. She picked up the book she'd been reading, thumbed the pages and put it down again. She was too restless to play checkers. And she couldn't walk in the garden in the rain. There was only one thing she wanted…one thing that would satisfy her—to be with Cole.

How she longed to hear the back door open and his boot heels thump against the hall floor. But not tonight. Tonight it would be Matthew who came to help her grandfather.

Poppa. She hadn't checked on him since dinner. He'd become quite independent thanks to his rolling chair—

and Cole. She lifted her hands and rubbed at her temples, closed her eyes and breathed deep to stop the roll of nausea. Everything she thought of brought her back to Cole. Her heart swelled, ached.

She walked to the partially open library door and peeked into the room. Her grandfather was sitting by the hearth in his rolling chair, cracking hickory nuts on the flat stone he'd lifted onto his lap, the book she had given him open on the butterfly table. Cole had restored some of Poppa's independence. It was a precious gift. How wonderful that he might also be able to do the same for others.

Her pulse pounded, increasing the pain in her temples. Would he truly sell his shingle mill and move to New York City to begin a new business making the chairs there? Could she begrudge him that success? Not if she truly loved him.

She caught back a sob, whirled and hurried down the hall to the kitchen. Nanna and Gertrude were busy with a pudding. She grabbed an old cape off a peg by the door, swirled it around her shoulders and went out on the porch to pray.

The path had grown treacherous, slick with clay. Cole pushed a tree limb out of his way, shivered as water from the leaves dripped down his neck. His shirt was dry for the most part, thanks to his rain jacket, but his pants were soaked from brushing against low-hanging branches and his boots were heavy with clinging mud.

He stopped and looked around, checked his back trail. He had no desire to be lost in a strange woods with nightfall approaching. And he didn't wholly trust

Kelly's goodwill toward him. The stigma of him being Payne's brother colored the man's opinion. He was tolerant…but that was all.

Frustration gnawed at him. He swiped the moisture from his brow and blinked his eyes. He'd seen no signs of human passage on this narrow game path. And it was exactly the sort of place Payne would choose, difficult and dangerous enough to make anyone who was trailing him give up the chase.

"You thinking about quitting?"

Kelly's question grated against his strained patience. "No." He looked upward through the trees, putting himself in Payne's position. "Where does this game path lead? How would it benefit him in getting away? He can only stay in the hills so long."

Kelly studied him a minute, then scratched at his beard. "The path leads clear to the top of the hill and down the other side, but that's got more bare area." He waved his meaty hand through the air crosswise. "If he veers off near the top and walks the ridge, he goes clean into hills of thick forest—still lots of Indians hunt there—with the Allegheny flowing around their feet. He could come down any place he chose, make himself a raft and float on downriver to Pittsburgh."

He nodded and looked toward the ridge. "If I were trying to get away from someone without being seen, that's what I would do." He drew his gaze back to Kelly. "What are our chances of catching him?"

"They're middling here on the path. That's the reason we been pushing so hard. If he reaches those forests ahead of us, our chances fall to next to nothing. There wouldn't be any point in going in there after him." He scratched at his beard again. "Best thing then would be to watch the water."

"All right then, we'd better pick up the pace if we're going to overtake him on this path."

Kelly nodded and started off up the trail, looking back over his shoulder. "You mind if I ask what's between you and your brother that you want to catch him so bad?"

"The answer to a question." His voice sounded grim, even to himself. He pointed to a small cut with big rocks and boulders shoving out of the earth a short distance ahead and off to the right. "Is that where the path veers onto the ridge?"

"No. That cut goes along for a bit, then ends in a sheer drop-off."

"Any way out of there?"

"Not 'less you're a mountain goat."

His instincts reared. His gut tightened. "Let's take a look at that cut."

Kelly shrugged his massive shoulders and veered right.

He followed the logger until they reached the cut, then stepped up beside him. "I'll lead now, Kelly. It's my idea to follow along here. If there's danger I'm the one who should face it."

The older man nodded, looked at him with a flash of respect in his eyes. "If that's what you want, but be careful—them stones ain't always fixed as solid in the ground as they look. You don't want to start this whole side hill to sliding."

"I'll watch." He turned and climbed over a couple of large rocks, slipped around a boulder and out onto a narrow ledge. The ground fell away in a series of slate shelves. He started along the top shelf, stopped and stared down at a scraped area in the dirt at the edge of the shale. His heart thudded. No animal had made that mark. It looked as if a boot had slipped. He slid his gaze along the shelf until he spotted another, smaller scrape. A scrape made by a grasping hand?

His pulse jolted, raced. He knelt and looked over the edge of the shelf. Bile rose, burning his throat.

"He down there?"

Sorrow gripped him. And anger. Now, he'd never know. He nodded and took a breath. If he had ever had a chance for a life with Sadie by his side, it was gone.

"Looks like he slipped, then grabbed hold trying to save hisself."

"Yes." He pushed to his feet, remembering all their forays into the woods as boys. "Something must have happened. Payne never slipped or stumbled." An image of a young, grinning Payne looking at him over his shoulder and calling to him to come on flashed into his head. "He was very sure-footed."

"Not when he was drunk."

The words wiped away the image and landed like stones in his stomach. He turned his head and stared at Kelly. "What did you say?"

"I said Allyson wasn't sure-footed when he was drunk. He staggered around same as any other man when he'd had too much of the hard stuff."

"Payne didn't drink." His words were quiet, measured.

Kelly stared up at him. "He did if he's Allyson. And a shame it was. He was a good worker and a friendly sort when he was sober, but he turned ugly mean when he was drinking."

Like our father. Cole fisted his hands, sucked in air and found himself hoping in the excuse. "Was he drinking the night he attacked the young woman?"

Kelly nodded, looked around. "He was in town drinking and got in a fight with a couple of loggers. He attacked the woman on his way back to camp. Course, then he run off—and us after him soon's we learned what he'd done. Ah, there it is."

Kelly bent down and reached under one of the stubby pine trees fighting for life on the rock shelf and picked up a pewter flask. "See for yourself."

Cole took the flask into his hand and uncorked it, jerked his head back at the hated smell. Memories surged. His father beating his mother, turning his fists on Payne and on him. Payne swearing he'd never be a drunk like their father… His fingertips touched an engraving on the smooth metal. He turned the flask over and stared at the initials *P.A.* etched into the pewter. "What did my brother—or Allyson—say his given name was?"

"Paul." Kelly motioned below. "You sure that's your brother?"

"Yes. That's Payne."

Kelly stepped closer and went to his knees. "Guess there's only one more thing to do, then." He braced himself and looked over the edge of the shelf, rose and brushed the dirt from his hands. "That's Allyson. Guess they're the same man. I'm sorry, Aylward."

So am I. He nodded, stared down at the flask in his hand. *Thank You, Lord, for answering my question.*

"There's no way we can get him up from there, you know."

Kelly's words brought a hollow ache to his chest. "I

know." He stepped close to the edge and closed his eyes, his heart hurting at the ruin and loss of his brother's life. He cleared his throat and looked up. There was nothing below him but the empty shell of the man who might have been. "Almighty God, may You have mercy on Payne. He was a good brother when we were young. I pray he rests in peace. Amen."

He uncorked the flask again as his words died away, held it out beyond the ledge and poured out the contents, then corked it and put it in his pocket. "I'll keep this to remember."

He turned to retrace their steps, his boots scraping against the shale as he led the way over the rocks and out of the cut that was his brother's grave.

Chapter Twenty-Seven

Cole scooped grain into the bucket on the stall floor and forked some fresh hay into the manger, burdened and weary with sorrow and regret for Payne and for his mother and father. The loss of his older brother was enervating—the waste of his life infuriating.

Anger shook him. He stepped out into the warm, dusky night, barred the stable door and walked to the sawmill. Payne had known the devastation and horror liquor could cause. He'd seen their mother being beaten, and he'd been the recipient of the blows from their drunken father's abusing fists. He'd sworn he would never be like him. So why had Payne ever taken that first drink?

He shoved aside the question he'd never know the answer to and climbed the steps, walked by the silent saws and on through the office to his private quarters. His entire family was gone, their lives wasted, cut short by the liquor that killed them all.

The pewter flask bulged in his pocket. He pulled it out, ran his thumb over his brother's initials, then set the flask on the shelf over his makeshift washstand. It was all he had left from his family. It was also the answer that set him free to have a family of his own someday. He hated liquor, couldn't bear the sight or smell of it.

He removed his mud-caked boots, flopped down on the bed and closed his eyes. What Matthew had said when he'd stopped to let the pastor know he was back in town had helped set him free, too—that God was not a dictator, that He allowed men to make their own choices.

Payne had chosen to take that first drink. *He* had chosen not to. He didn't have to be afraid he might someday follow his father's and Payne's path and abuse a woman—especially a woman he loved. He was free to woo Sadie and try to win her for his bride.

Sadie… Warmth swelled in his heart. A smile touched on his lips. Beautiful, sweet, Sadie… He'd see her…tonight…

Dusk was deepening. Sadie looked up at the last remnant of daylight clinging to the sky above the hills in the west. It would soon be full night, and Matthew wasn't here. Did that mean Cole was back? She wrapped her arms about herself to hold the hope glimmering to life in her heart.

What had he learned about Payne? Would it change his decision to sell out and move to the city? What would she say to him? No matter what his plans—whether he moved or stayed—she wanted him to know she believed in him and trusted him. She wanted him to know that no matter how he felt, she *knew* he could never be like his father and Payne. *How can I convince him, Lord? What can I do or—*

Was that a light? She leaned toward the window, focused on the wooded path. There it was again. A flicker of lamplight through the branches. She froze, stared. That was it! *Thank You, Lord!*

She whirled from the window, ran across her bedroom into the hall and raced down the stairs, her heart pounding.

"Sadie, what—"

"Cole's home!" She ran by her startled grandmother, down the hall and out the dining room door, racing toward the garden path. *Please, Lord, let me be on time!*

She threw over the latch, thrust open the gate and ran onto the wooded path. Trees shadowed the way. Darkness closed around her. She slowed her steps, blinked to see better and ran on. She had to reach the bend....

The path curved. Moonlight shone through a space in the overhead branches, puddling on the hard-trod dirt. She stopped to catch her breath. A light flickered through the trees ahead. He was coming. *Please, Lord...*

She stepped into the pool of moonlight, listened to his approaching footsteps, watched the lantern light growing and breathed out one more prayer. *Let him know, Lord. Make him know.*

Cole clamped down on his emotions, held himself from running. He'd scare Sadie if she were in the garden and he came bursting out of the woods like some man made crazy by love for her.

He grinned at the truth of the thought, puckered his lips and began to whistle. The lantern threw yellow light against the thick tree trunks and bobbed its glow over the path as he strode around the curve, wobbled as he came to a dead halt.

"Sadie!" Her name burst from his throat. He stared

at her, standing in the middle of the path, moonlight outlining her slender form, shining on her beautiful face. His heart clutched. She would never be on this path if something weren't horribly wrong. Manning! He stepped forward. "What's wrong? Why are you here? Is Manning—"

"I came to meet you."

He froze at the softness in her voice, swallowed hard as she walked toward him.

"I wanted you to know that I'm not afraid of you, Cole. Not now, not ever."

Her voice broke. He set down the lantern, straightened and jammed his hands in his pockets. His breath caught as she stopped in front of him and looked up. *Her eyes!* Could it be true? His heart lurched, thundered. His hands jerked out of his pockets.

"You are the kindest, gentlest, most caring and loving man I have ever known. Oh, Cole, don't you see?" Her voice choked to a whisper. "There is nothing for me to fear in you. I love you. You are my safety, my—"

He closed his arms around her waist, lowered his mouth to cover hers and tasted her sweetness. Her lips parted beneath his and her hands slid up from his chest to circle his neck. He lost track of time, of place, of himself. All that existed for him was Sadie and her love.

Chapter Twenty-Eight

"Well, I delivered your gown and my job is done. I'm going down and join Mother and Father in the garden." Ellen gave her a hug and walked to the bedroom door, then turned and smiled. "Your gown is beautiful, Sadie."

"Thank you, Ellen." She brushed her hand over the wide band of smocking that emphasized her narrow waist and glanced down at the double rows of scalloped ruffles at the hem of the long, full skirt. "Your mother is a wonderful seamstress."

"And a *fast* one. It's been less than a month since you told us the news." Willa laughed and gave her a hug. "I still can't even *believe* you are marrying Cole, and Mrs. Hall has made your gown."

"*And* her headband. Hold your head up and stay still, Sadie, or I'll stick this pin right in your scalp!"

"Threats! And on my wedding day." She laughed and held her head perfectly still as Callie tugged the wide white ribbon adorned with silk roses a little tighter around the coil of hair at her crown and secured it with hairpins.

"There!" Callie gave her hair a pat and stepped around in front of her. "Oh my…" She swallowed and laughed and wiped at her eyes. "You are so *beautiful,* Sadie."

"And that from a woman who does not use the word frivolously." Willa drew a breath, wiped her own eyes and smiled. "Are you nervous, Sadie?"

"Yes." She smiled and looked out the window toward the wooded path, placed her fingertips below the narrow band of white lace at her throat and felt the strong, steady beat of her heart. There was no panicked, wildly skipping pulse for her today. "But I'm not afraid."

Willa swallowed hard, stepped close and gave her a fierce hug. "I'll go tell Daniel and Matthew you're ready."

"And I'll go down and join Ezra." Callie gave her a hug, stepped back and smiled. "It's natural to be nervous, Sadie. I was trembling like a leaf in a windstorm when I married Ezra, and I love him with my whole heart. I pray you and Cole will be as happy together as we are." She blinked, wiped her eyes and followed Willa from the room.

She was alone.

Ye shall know the truth, and the truth shall make you free.

The Scripture settled in her heart as it had that other time when she had been so upset and confused by her love for Cole. "Thank You, Lord, for Your truth."

She blinked her vision clear and walked from her bedroom. When she returned, it would be as Cole's bride. They would make their home here, where they could care for Poppa and Nanna. Cole had already started to build a new shop for making the rolling chairs. What a wonderful, generous and loving man would share her life.

She blinked her eyes again, took a deep breath to steady her emotions and started down the stairs.

"Hey, Quick Stuff. I hear you're getting married." Daniel looked up and gave her a mock scowl. "Looks like I've lost you, too." The scowl turned to a warm smile. "And right when you turned so beautiful."

She laughed, took his offered arm and walked with him to the dining room door, went on tiptoes and kissed his cheek. "You'll always have a special place in my heart, Daniel." She gave him a teasing grin. "And there's still Ellen."

Something raw and pained flashed in his eyes. She caught her breath. "Daniel—"

He shook his head, grinned and pulled open the door. "Let's get you married, Quick Stuff. I've things to do."

He escorted her across the porch, down the steps and onto the garden path. She smiled at Ellen and her parents, Callie and Ezra and Sophia Sheffield, Willa and Mr. and Mrs. Dibble all gathered in a group around her grandparents.

She leaned down and kissed her poppa.

"He's a…good man…Sa…die."

"He's a *wonderful* man, Poppa. I'm so glad you didn't listen to me." She smiled at his soft chuckle then turned and kissed her nanna's cheek. Her grandmother's small hands grasped hers and tugged her close.

"I told you he was in love with you, sweeting."

The joyful whisper brought tears to her eyes. "And you were right, Nanna. You are a very wise woman." She smiled and blinked away the tears. *Thank You, Lord, that Nanna is having a good day.*

She took a breath and straightened, and Cole was there, holding his hand out to her.

"Be happy, Quick Stuff." Daniel kissed her cheek and stepped back.

She put her hand in Cole's, felt the rush of love and safety his touch always brought her and smiled.

His grip tightened; his eyes warmed. Her heart raced. She would see that special only-for-her look in his eyes for the rest of their lives.

A male throat cleared. "If you are ready, Cole?"

"Now and always. I love you, Sadie Spencer." He whispered the words into her ear, tucked her hand in his arm and together they turned to face Matthew Calvert, who was waiting to join their hearts and lives forever.

* * * * *

Dear Reader,

I'm so pleased you decided to join me on this third visit to Pinewood Village. I've become so at home in Pinewood, I feel as if I should go to Cargrave's and ask Mr. Hubble for my mail. I hope you feel the same.

This third book in the Pinewood Weddings series about lifelong friends began as Sadie's story—as an exploration of her trauma from Payne Aylward's heinous attack. But I quickly realized that Cole also suffered deeply from his brother's actions. I found my emotions deeply engaged while writing about these two young people brought together by the traumatic situation thrust upon them by another—Sadie, facing down her fears out of love for her grandparents, and Cole, standing strong in his effort to atone as best he was able for his brother's cruel deed, became true heroes to me. The Bible says, "There is no fear in love; but perfect love casteth out fear: because fear hath torment." It was my delight to use this truth to deliver both Sadie and Cole from their fears so they were free to love one another.

I am reluctant to leave Pinewood without telling Ellen's story, but she has thus far resisted my efforts to coax her home. Her hurts go deep and she prefers to focus on the social whirl she enjoys in Buffalo.

I do enjoy hearing from my readers. If you would care to share your thoughts about Sadie and Cole's story, or about Pinewood village and its residents with me, I may be contacted at dorothyjclark@hotmail.com or www.dorothyjclark.com.

Until I can convince Ellen to come home to Pinewood,

Dorothy Clark

Questions for Discussion

1. Sadie Spencer is forced to return to Pinewood. What compels her to return?

2. Sadie has suffered a terrible trauma in Payne Aylward's attack on her. Do you find her resulting fears believable? Have you or anyone you know suffered such fears from a traumatic experience?

3. Cole Aylward suffers his own fears. What are they? Do you find them believable? Why or why not?

4. What are Cole's motivations for helping Manning Townsend? Do you find them admirable?

5. When they first meet, Sadie cannot bear the sight of Cole. Do you think her attitude is realistic? How would you have felt and acted in Sadie's circumstances?

6. Cole is drawn to Sadie immediately, but he has reservations about her. How does Sadie represent a threat to Cole?

7. Sadie's experience leaves her with several symptoms of post-traumatic stress disorder. What are they?

8. Do you know any alcoholics? Do they say or do things when they are drinking they would not do or say when they are sober?

9. Do you know any children of alcoholics? Are they like Payne or Cole? Do they follow in their parents' footsteps, or do they go the other way?

10. Cole was willing to give up all he had worked to achieve in Pinewood. Why? What were his achievements?

11. The story is set in a rural village in 1841. Would Sadie's circumstances be improved or worsened if the story took place in the present? Give the reasons for your opinion.

12. Sadie's love for Cole proves stronger than her fear. What event in the story proves this? How does it convince Cole of her love?

13. What drove Cole to become the man he is?

14. How did Cole's past dictate his treatment of Mrs. Townsend?

15. Have you or someone you know ever suffered a traumatic event that affected your faith? Was the effect positive or negative? What makes the difference in the outcome?

REQUEST YOUR FREE BOOKS!

2 FREE INSPIRATIONAL NOVELS
PLUS 2
FREE
MYSTERY GIFTS

Love Inspired.
HISTORICAL
INSPIRATIONAL HISTORICAL ROMANCE

YES! Please send me 2 FREE Love Inspired® Historical novels and my 2 FREE mystery gifts (gifts are worth about $10). After receiving them, if I don't wish to receive any more books, I can return the shipping statement marked "cancel." If I don't cancel, I will receive 4 brand-new novels every month and be billed just $4.74 per book in the U.S. or $5.24 per book in Canada. That's a saving of at least 21% off the cover price. It's quite a bargain! Shipping and handling is just 50¢ per book in the U.S. and 75¢ per book in Canada.* I understand that accepting the 2 free books and gifts places me under no obligation to buy anything. I can always return a shipment and cancel at any time. Even if I never buy another book, the two free books and gifts are mine to keep forever.

102/302 IDN F5CN

Name _____ (PLEASE PRINT) _____

Address _____ Apt. #_____

City _____ State/Prov. _____ Zip/Postal Code_____

Signature (if under 18, a parent or guardian must sign)

Mail to the Harlequin® Reader Service:
IN U.S.A.: P.O. Box 1867, Buffalo, NY 14240-1867
IN CANADA: P.O. Box 609, Fort Erie, Ontario L2A 5X3

Want to try two free books from another series?
Call 1-800-873-8635 or visit www.ReaderService.com.

* Terms and prices subject to change without notice. Prices do not include applicable taxes. Sales tax applicable in N.Y. Canadian residents will be charged applicable taxes. Offer not valid in Quebec. This offer is limited to one order per household. Not valid for current subscribers to Love Inspired Historical books. All orders subject to credit approval. Credit or debit balances in a customer's account(s) may be offset by any other outstanding balance owed by or to the customer. Please allow 4 to 6 weeks for delivery. Offer available while quantities last.

Your Privacy—The Harlequin® Reader Service is committed to protecting your privacy. Our Privacy Policy is available online at www.ReaderService.com or upon request from the Harlequin Reader Service.

We make a portion of our mailing list available to reputable third parties that offer products we believe may interest you. If you prefer that we not exchange your name with third parties, or if you wish to clarify or modify your communication preferences, please visit us at www.ReaderService.com/consumerschoice or write to us at Harlequin Reader Service Preference Service, P.O. Box 9062, Buffalo, NY 14269. Include your complete name and address.

LIH13R

SPECIAL EXCERPT FROM

He was her high school crush, and now he's a single father of twins. Allison True just got a second chance at love.

Read on for a sneak preview of
STORYBOOK ROMANCE by Lissa Manley,
the exciting fifth book in
THE HEART OF MAIN STREET *series,*
available October 2013.

Something clunked from the back of the bookstore, drawing Allison True's ever-vigilant attention. Her ears perking up, she rounded the end of the front counter. Another clunk sounded, and then another. Allison decided the noise was coming from the Kids' Korner, so she picked up the pace and veered toward the back right part of the store, creasing her brow.

She arrived in the area set up for kids. Her gaze zeroed in on a dark-haired toddler dressed in jeans and a red shirt, slowly yet methodically yanking books off a shelf, one after the other. Each book fell to the floor with a heavy clunk, and in between each sound, the little guy laughed, clearly enjoying the sound of his relatively harmless yet messy play.

Allison rushed over, noting there was no adult in sight. "Hey, there, bud," she said. "Whatcha doing?"

He turned big brown eyes fringed with long, dark eyelashes toward her. He looked vaguely familiar even though she was certain she'd never met this little boy.

"Fun!" A chubby hand sent another book crashing to the floor. He giggled and stomped his feet on the floor in a little happy dance. "See?"

Carefully she reached out and stilled his marauding hands. "Whoa, there, little guy." She gently pulled him away. "The books are supposed to stay on the shelf." Holding on to him, she cast her gaze about the enclosed area set aside for kids, but her view was limited by the tall bookshelves lined up from the edge of the Kids' Korner to the front of the store. "Are you here with your mommy or daddy?"

The boy tugged. "Daddy!" he squealed.

"Nicky!" a deep masculine voice replied behind her. "Oh, man. Looks like you've been making a mess."

A nebulous sense of familiarity swept through her at the sound of that voice. Not breathing, still holding the boy's hand, Allison slowly turned around. Her whole body froze and her heart gave a little spasm then fell to her toes as she looked into deep brown eyes that matched Nicky's.

Sam Franklin. The only man Allison had ever loved.

Pick up STORYBOOK ROMANCE
in October 2013 wherever Love Inspired® Books are sold.

LIEXP0913

Eve Pickering knows what it's like to be judged because of your past. So she's not about to leave the orphaned boy she's befriended alone and unprotected in this unfamiliar Texas town. And if Chance Dawson's offer of shelter is the only way she can look after Leo, Eve will turn it into a warm, welcoming home for the holidays. No matter how temporary it may be—or how much she's really longing to stay for good….

Chance came all the way from the big city to make it on his own in spite of his secret…and his overbearing rich family. But Eve's bravery and caring is giving him a confidence he never expected—and a new direction for his dream. And with a little Christmas luck, he'll dare to win her heart as well as her trust—and make their family one for a lifetime.

Texas Grooms

A Family for Christmas

by

WINNIE GRIGGS

Available October 2013 wherever
Love Inspired Historical books are sold.

LIH82983

SUSPENSE

RIVETING INSPIRATIONAL ROMANCE

FALL FROM GRACE by MARTA PERRY

Teacher Sara Esch helps widower Caleb King comfort his daughter who witnessed a crime. But then Sara gets too close to the truth and Caleb must risk it all for the woman who's taught him to love again.

DANGEROUS HOMECOMING by DIANE BURKE

Katie Lapp needs her childhood friend Joshua Miller more than ever when someone threatens her late husband's farm. Katie wants it settled the Amish way...but not everyone can be trusted. Can Joshua protect her...even if it endangers his heart?

RETURN TO WILLOW TRACE by KIT WILKINSON

Lydia Stoltz wants to avoid the man who courted her years ago. But a series of accidents startles their Plain community...and leads her straight to Joseph Yoder. At every turn, it seems their shared past holds the key to their future.

DANGER IN AMISH COUNTRY,

a 3-in-1 anthology including novellas by
MARTA PERRY, DIANE BURKE **and**
KIT WILKINSON

*Available October 2013 wherever
Love Inspired Suspense books are sold.*

Find us on Facebook at
www.Facebook.com/LoveInspiredBooks

LIS44558R